beneath these
SCARS

MEGHAN MARCH

UNAPOLOGETICALLY SEXY ROMANCE

about this book

I'm the guy you love to hate.

In every story in my life, I seem to end up playing the villain—and I've got the scars to prove it.
That role works fine for me, because I'm sure as hell not anyone's hero. I run my life and my empire with an iron fist—until she knocks my tightly controlled world off its axis.

She's nobody's damsel in distress, but I can't help but want to save her anyway.

I guess we're about to find out if there's a hero buried beneath these scars.

Beneath These Scars is the fourth book in the Beneath series, but may be read as a standalone. However, if you prefer, it may be best enjoyed after reading *Beneath This Mask* (Beneath #1), *Beneath This Ink* (Beneath #2), and *Beneath These Chains* (Beneath #3).

acknowledgments

With every book, it takes a village to bring it from a spark of an idea to what you're reading today, and I'm incredibly fortunate to have an awesome village. Special thanks goes out to:

Angela Smith, the best PA and friend an author could be blessed to have, for being with me every step of the way on this crazy journey.

Rachel Brookes, my amazing critique partner and friend, you have no idea how much I value the gift of your insight and time.

Angela Marshall Smith and Pam Berehulke, editors extraordinaire, for helping to wrestle this story into submission (not that Lucas would ever submit) and polishing it until it shone.

Chasity Jenkins-Patrick, kick-ass publicist, for talking me off more than one ledge and always pushing me in the right direction.

Sara Eirew for shooting a fab cover pic, and Sarah Hansen for creating yet another gorgeous cover.

My mom, for being the most supportive parent a daughter with crazy dreams could ask for. I love you.

The Meghan March Runaway Readers Facebook group, for being the most fabulous collection of ladies I've had the pleasure of (virtually) meeting. Hope to hug you all at events soon!

All the book bloggers who take the time to read and review this and any of my other books. Your time and dedication is truly appreciated.

My readers—you're the reason Lucas's story is laid out on these pages. Thank you for loving this series, and I hope you enjoy what's coming next.

Lucas

SWEAT DRIPPED INTO MY EYES AS I BOUNCED ON THE balls of my feet. Someone had to be calling out how much time was left in this round soon. My pride was on the line, and there was no way I would hand it over to Con Leahy. He'd already gotten the girl, and I wasn't about to let him humiliate me in the ring in this piece-of-shit New Orleans gym too.

My muscles burned, but that was nothing compared to the heat of victory—or the sting of defeat. What had started out as a boxing lesson had quickly transformed into an all-out brawl for dominance and respect.

Only you would pay a million dollars to get your ass kicked, Titan. The voice in my head mocked me as I bobbed and weaved. But I hadn't paid a million to get my ass kicked. I'd done it because that night at the charity auction I'd been drunk, pissed off, and determined to prove a point—he might've gotten the girl, but I was still the one

1

with the power. I got a sick sense of satisfaction that every time Con bought something for his gym and these kids, he had to think of me.

I swung with another right hook. The blow connected with Con's jaw and snapped his head to the side.

Yeah. That's right. But my mental cheer came a moment too soon, and pain exploded in my left side.

Shit, that's going to hurt tomorrow.

I stumbled back but threw myself forward again, shooting out my fist with an uppercut that knocked Con back a step. This was how it had gone for the last several minutes—trading punches and circling each other.

There was no love lost in this ring, that was for damn sure, and I was ready for this to be over. I would walk out of here with every bit of the respect I was owed. Fuck anyone who thought otherwise.

Con moved toward me and the circling started again. The cheers and chants from the crowd surrounding the ring in the old warehouse gym seemed to grow every time I glanced beyond the ropes. A flash of blond hair caught my eye as I stepped left and Con shifted to the right.

Vanessa.

She threw her head back and laughed at something said by her redheaded friend, Elle. I turned my attention back to the man in front of me, but my focus wandered again when a huskier, sexier laugh echoed through the room.

My eyes strayed from Con for a second too long as I tried to track down the source of the laughter. Pain burst through my jaw, catching me by surprise, and I stumbled back into the ropes. Using their momentum, I shoved off to the side, my pride stinging from my momentary lapse in concentration. Embarrassed and now thoroughly pissed off, I surged forward and attacked.

One punch. That was all I landed before the bell rang, signaling the end of the round and my very expensive "lesson."

I pushed off Con, and my knee might have slipped as I stepped back . . . and caught him directly in the balls. It was probably an accident. I huffed out a chuckle, but Con didn't share my humor.

"Goddamn it!" he roared. "Are you fucking serious?"

It was like stabbing a bull with a matador's sword, but I was ready for him. I jumped out of the way as Con charged, and shifted into a defensive stance when he swung.

"Should've expected a cheap shot from you, motherfucker." Unrestrained anger flashed over his face as every shred of coaching mentality fled, along with that smug superiority he'd been giving me.

Good. You aren't better than me, Leahy. I could buy and sell you a hundred times over.

He might've gotten the girl, but I wasn't going to let him get away with her clean. I wanted blood.

"Should've expected you to strut around this ring like a fucking cock of the walk," I shot back.

Con feinted and swung again, but I'd been studying his movements. I bobbed and weaved, and got the hell out of the way.

I threw my own punch as soon as I had a clean shot. It landed just below Con's left eye, splitting the skin over his cheekbone and sending blood spattering everywhere.

The taste of victory was sweet. "First blood," I said under my breath.

Apparently my words weren't quiet enough because Con's head snapped up and he glared at me with disgust, as if I needed to be put down like a rabid animal. "This ain't a fuckin' duel, you piece of shit."

"It sure isn't a friendly competition either."

"Paid a million to get that cheap shot in, didn't you?"

My lips twisted into a mocking smile. "I sure didn't pay a million to have you show me up."

Con dropped his hands and shook his head. "Just when I thought you weren't a complete fucking asshole."

"You were wrong," I replied, turning for the ropes.

Con's fists lifted and before I could react, one connected with my cheekbone. The instantaneous gush of blood told me I'd have a scar to match his, but it didn't matter. One more scar wouldn't hurt my banged-up face.

I roared as I charged, but I didn't get the chance to retaliate. Shouts filled the room, and beefy arms wrapped around my body, holding me back.

"You're not half bad when you're not being a shady rich prick," Lord's voice said in my ear.

I lunged toward Con, but Lord's grip only tightened. "Get your goddamn hands off me," I growled at him.

Leaning closer to my ear, he lowered his voice. "When you calm the hell down and realize you're making an ass of yourself in front of a bunch of kids and women."

I glanced out to the crowd and read disgust on so many faces, including Vanessa's. Like it mattered what a single goddamn person in this gym thought of me. I could buy and sell them all.

Lord was still holding me back when Con came toward us. He yanked his gloves off and wiped at the blood still dripping from the gash on his face.

"You're also not half bad when you're paying attention—and when you're not throwing a knee into my nuts. But I think you've overstayed your welcome."

I jerked at the arms trapping me. "Call off your dog, and I'm gone."

"You ever want another round, it's gonna cost you two million next time," Con said.

"For another chance to make you bleed? I'd pay even more."

Con nodded to his brother, and Lord let me go. The crowd had already started to disperse. The only person in the building who probably didn't want to run me down in the parking lot was my COO, and arguably my friend, Ryder Colson. And he was nowhere to be seen.

Instead of Colson, I saw a group of women moving toward the door—Vanessa Frost in her white cotton dress, Elle Snyder in her yellow retro number, and two others I didn't know. One looked familiar with tanned skin the color of honey, her hair in dark waves, and a curvy body displayed by a funky teal dress with hot-pink polka dots. She hooked her hands on her hips, and that husky laugh echoed through the room again. Apparently she was the one who had distracted me in the ring. My eyes didn't move from her to take in the fourth woman.

Colson came up beside me. "Who knew there'd be so many hot pieces of ass in this shit warehouse?"

I turned toward him. "Give any of them a shot, and you'll probably find yourself bleeding on the floor."

Ryder shrugged off my comment. "Go get your shit. I'll wait."

He was gone before I could tell him he didn't need to wait around for me. But then again, he was my only ally in a building full of people who undoubtedly would have preferred to see me KO'd on the floor of the ring. Just one more place I'd never be welcome.

Good thing I didn't give a fuck.

I'd showed up, gone toe-to-toe with Con, and had taken back a piece of my pride. That was enough.

For today.

I was already thinking of hiring a trainer as I went for my bag.

"Not interested. Save your breath."

"Come on, baby. You have a better offer tonight?"

"Do I look like a whore to you? And a desperate one at that? Because I'm not."

I followed the voices as I strode across the black-and-white checkered floor that started at the door to the gym and led down the hallway to the building exit. The conversation was coming from a doorway on the right, a giant commercial kitchen with a huge prep table and stainless steel appliances.

The woman in teal and pink was standing in front of a cupboard, stretching as one hand reached high inside. Ryder Colson stood nearby, leaning against the prep table in front of the fridge.

"Sweetheart, you don't look like a whore to me, but—"

"Colson." My friend's name came out sharp on my tongue, and I didn't take any time to assess why that might be—or why irritation and possessiveness spread through my veins. I'd just watched Vanessa fuss over Con's bloody face, and it was another reminder that I'd missed my shot with her.

Both Colson and the woman turned their attention to me.

"You ready to go?" I asked him, and he shrugged.

"Ms. Santos and I were getting acquainted."

"Is that what we were doing?" the woman snapped. "Because I thought you were being a dick who didn't understand I'm *not interested*."

Her name jogged my memory. Yve Santos. I remembered her from the charity auction. She'd modeled a piece of jewelry; a necklace, I think. But I hadn't even looked at it, too caught up in the way her red dress had clung to every curve of her killer body. I'd wanted to fuck her then, even though my eyes had spent ninety-nine percent of the night on Vanessa.

Not surprisingly, Yve still looked as gorgeous as she had that night.

"You can leave, Colson," I said, giving him a pointed look.

His expression darkened before his cheeks reddened with embarrassment. He'd have to get over it. If she were going to spend tonight in anyone's bed, it would be mine.

He scowled in Yve's direction before pushing past me and stalking through the doorway. "I'll see you tomorrow, Titan," he called over his shoulder.

My eyes found Yve again. "He bother you?"

"I can take care of myself."

"Did he bother you?" I repeated.

7

"*You're* bothering me."

I studied the flush coloring her dusky cheeks, and the subtle rise and fall of her chest. "I think you like it."

"And I think you should follow your friend right out that door," she shot back. "I'm not interested in what either of you have to offer." And with that she was gone, heading for the same door that Colson had exited a moment before.

Women didn't walk away from me. It was completely unacceptable.

I stalked after her.

"I'll walk you out." It wasn't an offer. I was simply doing whatever the hell I wanted, just like I always did.

That laugh with its husky, sexy tone rang through the hallway. "I can take care of myself, Titan. Don't need a rich man to do it for me." The door swung open at her touch and slammed behind her.

I paused as the realization hit me. *She knows who I am.* Good.

She was going to know a lot more of me.

2

"**M**OTHER EFFING CHRIST." I BANGED MY hands on my steering wheel. "Don't do this to me now, you piece of—" I cut off my words, as if not insulting my car would somehow help the engine sputter back to life. I turned the key again. Nothing.

I popped the hood latch and got out of the car, slinging my purse over my shoulder. In this neighborhood, it might have seemed like a dumb move to get out of the car and bring my purse, but I wasn't helpless. I was locked and loaded with my .38 Special. Ever since Elle had dragged me to the shooting range with her one night, I'd been hooked on the idea of being able to protect myself. The only question I couldn't answer was: why hadn't I done it sooner?

Although if I had, I'd probably be in prison right now.

After propping the hood open like I knew what I was doing, I stared down at the steam rising off the radiator—at least I thought that was where it was coming from. I didn't know jack about cars. Nope, I was more likely to find vintage Chanel at a roadside antique shop than to figure out what had gone wrong with my semi-reliable Jetta. But my Blue Beast was getting old; she was going on seventeen.

Shaking my head when looking under the hood gave me no answers, I dug into my purse and pulled out my cell phone. I scrolled through the contacts, teeth gritted. I hated asking for help, hated having to admit that I couldn't take care of my problems myself. But sometimes a girl didn't have a choice. Cousin Stevie's Happy Hookers would be a lot cheaper than—

My thoughts were cut off as a sleek dark gray sports car slowed to a stop beside the Blue Beast and me. What I knew about cars could fill a shoebox, but even I recognized *expensive* when I saw it. The darkened passenger side window lowered as I reached back into my purse, wanting the comfort of my Smith & Wesson in my grip. Just in case.

I relaxed a fraction when green eyes set beneath dark brows pierced me.

"Trouble, Ms. Santos?"

Lucas Titan. The same asshole who'd landed a cheap shot in Con's balls, and whose friend thought I looked like an easy pickup tonight.

"I've got it handled."

One dark eyebrow lifted and he pulled away, but he didn't go far. No, he pulled up and parked in front of the Blue Beast, and his driver's side door opened.

Great. Just what I need, some rich prick thinking he knows how to handle my business better than I do. Titan gave off that *master of all I survey* vibe that rubbed me the wrong way on every level. Old habits die hard, and all that.

I looked back down at my cell and found Cousin Stevie's contact info. Before I could hit the Call button, Titan stood beside me, looking pissed off.

"Why the hell did you get out of your car? It's not safe. If you break down, you sit your sweet little ass inside, call a wrecker, and wait."

Oh. Hell. No. If he was expecting me to nod my head like a pretty little doll and follow orders, he was in for a shock. I'd come a long way from the days when I fell in line just because a man told me to.

I spun to face him. "I don't live my life according to the laws of Lucas Titan, so you can feel free to get back in your car and go on about your night."

I wasn't sure what I expected from him, but it wasn't a deep, rumbling laugh.

"Everyone lives according to the laws of Lucas Titan. You just don't know it yet." He leaned in closer until the green of his eyes reflected the interior light of my car, and I could clearly make out the five o'clock shadow shading his jaw. "Don't worry, sweetheart, you'll enjoy the hell out of it."

The combination of the sexy laugh and innuendo-filled words sent shivers through me. I didn't give a damn about Titan or his cocky attitude. I just needed to get my car on Stevie's tow truck so he could take it to the shop.

I shrugged off my unwanted reaction, getting back to what was important. My car. "Whatever. Now that you know I'm fine, you can go on about your evening."

He flashed a wolfish smile. "And lose my one chance to play the white knight? Why would I do a thing like that?"

When he lifted a hand as if he intended to touch me, my entire body tensed in anticipation. "Because I'm no damsel in distress. And white knight? I think that's a hell of a stretch for you, Titan."

His hand curled into a fist, and he dropped it to his side. My eyes snapped up to meet his now cold stare, and disappointment slid through me. *What the hell, Yve?*

"Good to know you've got no misplaced assumptions about me being one of the good guys. Apparently you've got a better sense of self-preservation than your actions imply. Now get your stuff and get in my car. I'm giving you a ride home."

"Wh-what?" I sputtered. "I have a cousin with a tow truck. He'll figure it out."

"I said get your stuff," he repeated. "I'll have my guy come get it and bring it back to his shop."

I didn't handle decrees well. And by that, I meant *not at all.* "Not necessary. I've got it covered."

"I didn't ask if it was necessary. Now get your stuff."

Each of the last four words were bitten out in a harsh tone that pushed all my buttons. Simultaneously. My hands hit my hips, and I squared off with him to give him a piece of my mind.

"Now listen here, Titan. I'm not about to let you roll up and start ordering me—"

Gunshots echoed in the distance, halting my tirade mid-breath.

Titan flew into action, slamming the hood shut and turning to face me. "Get your shit. We're going."

I wanted to argue, but a second round of shots and the shriek of squealing tires nearby made my decision to shut up and comply a little easier. "Fine."

I strode to my car and leaned in to pull my keys from

the ignition, then slammed the door and locked it. I didn't wait for an invitation, just marched around to the passenger side of his still-idling car and reached for the handle.

Titan beat me to it. I jerked back, jumpy at having him sneak up behind me so quietly. He was a big man; he shouldn't be able to move that soundlessly. But those old, fearful reactions—the ones I'd fought to overcome—were shoved aside by an altogether different kind of awareness. Heat zipped down my spine where his body was only an inch from mine.

No. That's impossible. Lucas Titan is the last *man who should pull that kind of reaction from me.* My body couldn't be trusted. I steeled myself against the growing urge to press back against him as he opened the door, and I slipped inside the car.

I knew from the outside that it was expensive, but the interior proved it, especially when I read the embroidery on the floor mat. *Aston Martin.* There were several things I knew to be true, and one of them was that my ass did not belong in a seat this pricey. But I didn't have time to think about that because Titan was already in the driver's seat, throwing the car into gear and pulling away.

"You're stubborn, you know that?"

"And you're bossy," I replied.

His gaze cut to me before shifting back to the windshield. "You want to get caught in a drive-by? Is that on your agenda for this evening? Jesus, woman. You should have a better sense of self-preservation."

Words. So. Many. Words. And they all bubbled up inside me to spew at him. To tell him exactly where he could shove his judgments of me. But I didn't. I held them back because he didn't need to know my sad little story, or how I had dragged myself out of a relationship that could have made me the guest of honor at a funeral parade.

"Where do you live?" he asked, slowing at the next light.

"Tremé. Take a left at the third light."

An awkward silence filled the car, making me wish he'd hit the gas a little harder, because God knew this fancy car could move quicker. The interior wasn't small, but Titan's presence was overwhelming. And Jesus Christ, why did a man who was such a dick have to smell so damn good? Clean with a hint of some exotic, expensive spice. On any other man, I would have leaned closer to inhale the intoxicating scent.

But not him. No way. I'd done rich man before. I knew how that story ended.

When we neared the major cross streets closest to my apartment, I decided we'd gone far enough. "You can drop me here," I said as he slowed at a stop sign.

Titan's dark green eyes pinned me to my seat. "Here. At the corner." His words weren't a question; they were a wry statement.

"Yes. Here. At the corner," I parroted back at him.

"You have a problem with someone seeing you to your door?" His tone dripped with condescension.

Lord, but I'd never disliked someone quite so quickly in my life. "Maybe I don't trust you to know where I live."

"And I don't let women out on random street corners in neighborhoods that aren't safe after dark."

"There are a lot of things that aren't safe about this neighborhood, and I know them all. You're the wild card here, Titan."

I reached for the handle and tugged. It didn't move. I ran my hand along the panel, looking for the lock. Stupid expensive cars, everything had to be sleek and hidden. I found it and popped the door open.

"Are you always this stubborn?" he asked as I climbed out.

I thought of the time in my life when I'd let a man walk all over me. "I am now," I replied.

"Good, then you'll recognize stubborn when I follow you to your door and make sure you get inside without getting shot or stabbed."

I slammed the door, and he pulled into an empty spot along the road.

Screw that. It might have been undignified and downright ridiculous, but I ran across the street and ducked between two houses. Darting down the narrow space, I headed for the alley that skirted along the back of the house where my apartment sat on the second floor.

"Goddamn it," I heard him grunt. "You're fucking kidding me."

A small grin tugged at my lips, and I jogged down the alley to let myself into the side gate. Apparently not everyone lived under the law of Lucas Titan. It should be a good lesson for him.

It wasn't until I reached my door that I realized I'd left my car keys in the Aston Martin.

Shit. I sat down on the steps of the porch, listening for the sound of the Aston Martin to come purring up the road, but the low rumble never came. With a sigh of relief, I pulled out my phone to call my landlord to let me in.

That was one way to distract myself from these unwanted thoughts of Lucas Titan.

Yve

MY HANDS SHOOK AS I READ THE LETTER. IT WAS just a piece of paper, and yet it had enough weight behind it to rock the foundation of my world—and my world was centered around this store. I didn't need to lift my eyes from the letter in order to visualize the bright blue walls of Dirty Dog and the shiny black trim. Or the vintage dress forms I used instead of mannequins, and the shabby chic armoires I'd chosen and refinished myself. This shop was my life.

But I only managed it. Harriet owned it. And now she was selling it.

The letter from a business broker, already creased from my sweaty palms, thanked Harriet for engaging them and said they were looking forward to finding the right buyers for her entire portfolio of businesses. I lowered it to the display case and eyed the envelope as if it might contain anthrax. It had been addressed to Harriet, but like all the other mail, I'd automatically opened it anyway.

I sucked in a breath but my lungs were malfunctioning; I couldn't get enough air. Pain shot through my chest, and my stomach churned in big, swamping waves. My eyes burned with tears I'd never let fall.

I can't lose this place.

The door chime jangled, snapping me out of my downward spiral. I hauled in a full breath and pasted on my customer-friendly smile.

"Hey, lady! How's it goin'?"

Elle's cheery voice filled the shop, and my lip wobbled until my smile fell away. If it had been anyone else walking through the door, I wouldn't have revealed a chink in my armor. But this was Elle, one of the few people I trusted. The woman who'd held my hand and poured me tequila when I'd first heard my ex was up for parole. The woman who hadn't called me crazy when I'd sat on her apartment floor and stitched a voodoo doll of him to take out my frustration, disgust, and bone-chilling fear. I could count on one hand the number of people I'd let see me in that state, and Elle happened to be at the top of that short list.

Elle's forehead crinkled and her brows drew into auburn slashes as she took in my expression. "Whose ass do I need to kick? Is it him? Did he do something?"

The *him* she was referring to was obviously my ex. And—knock on wood—he was the one thing I wasn't worrying about at this very moment. As far as I knew, he was still in prison, pending release.

"No. Nothing like that. It's . . ." I didn't even want to say the words out loud, because then what was written in the letter would be real.

Picking up on my mood immediately, Elle came to the counter and leaned her elbows on the glass. "Seriously, hon. What's going on?"

I pushed the letter toward her. "Looks like it's the end of an era."

Her brow creased, and she picked up the paper. I watched her face as she scanned it, expecting commiseration, platitudes meant to placate me. But when she'd finished, instead I got a pointed look and her no-bullshit attitude.

"Why don't you buy it then?" she asked as she handed the letter back to me.

It was such a simple concept, but my brain struggled to wrap around the idea. "B-buy it? I can't—" I sputtered.

"Why not? You've run this place without Harriet's supervision for years. There's no one who would be a better owner. Actually, I'm surprised she didn't come to you first. It would've made the most sense."

That thought hadn't even made it through my thick brain. Why *hadn't* Harriet asked me first?

Because you're nothing but a shop girl—not owner material, a voice inside me taunted.

My hands curled into fists. I'd been fighting that voice for years—the one that told me how worthless I was at every opportunity. And still I couldn't shut it up. It was a remnant of *him*.

Who else could possibly love you? he'd told me. *You're lucky I even put up with your ass. Don't you know how much better I could do? I picked* you *because I knew you needed me to love you.*

I gritted my teeth as an unwelcome burst of his negativity flooded my brain.

Fuck. Him.

I *could* own this shop. Hell, I *should* own Dirty Dog. No one was more qualified to run it. Who else knew where to get the best inventory? Who else could keep the quirky reputation intact? This store was *mine*.

"You're right," I said as I lifted my head and squared my shoulders. "I should buy it."

Elle's lips curled into a wide smile. "Atta girl. That's the sassy Yve I know and love."

Seconds later, practicality battered my newfound determination. How could I ever pay for it? My savings account was okay, but not anywhere near flush enough to buy a business in the French Quarter.

Elle's brain bounced right along the same track as mine. "You need a backer? Silent partner? Because I know a girl . . ."

The offer should have been tempting, but I would walk away before I accepted a handout.

Strings. Money always came with strings.

"Uh. No. I mean, I've got some ideas. You know what they say about taking money from friends, anyway. I'd never want to lose you, and certainly not because of that."

The crease in Elle's brow deepened. "You think I'd—"

"No. I'm just saying . . . I appreciate your offer, but I'm going to have to decline."

"Do you really have other ideas? Or are you feeding me a line of crap?"

My brain shuffled through all the possibilities. The bank? The SBA? Maybe one of those organizations that support young entrepreneurs? I'd figure out something.

I met her frustrated stare. "I've got some ideas. I swear. No bullshit."

"If you're sure . . ."

"I'm sure." My tone rang with finality, which Elle didn't miss.

"Okay. Dropping it. Now let's talk about this dress you've got for me. Hand it over."

I turned and unzipped the garment bag hanging on the funky iron hook behind me. Parting the sides, I revealed emerald-green satin perfection. Elle was going to look amazing. And I happened to know that her man, Lord, had a thing about his redhead in green.

"Oh!" Elle clapped her hands. "It's so much better than I even thought. I'm gettin' lucky when I wear this."

She dug her credit card out of her purse and handed it over. "You are the best. See—*this* is just one more example of why you were born to own this place. It would never be Dirty Dog without you. It would be just another touristy shop. *You* are the lifeblood of this store. Harriet has to know that."

Her words unleashed a shimmer of pride inside me. I *was* the driving force behind the success of this store. It wouldn't be the same without me. I needed to find a way to make it mine permanently, and I needed to meet Harriet as an equal—as a businesswoman with a plan. Shoulders squared again, I charged Elle for the dress as my mind spun with what I needed to do next.

This determined Yve—the one I'd forged out of broken pieces—never backed down from a fight.

Lucas

I F I HADN'T SCHOOLED MYSELF IN KEEPING MY expression completely blank, I would have given away the rage coursing through me. I was a man with simple expectations: do what I ask, the way I ask you to do it, and do it right the first fucking time. I held myself to a ridiculously high standard. No one could keep up with the demands I placed on myself, but I expected people to live up to the lower expectations I had of them. How fucking hard was it to be a goddamn lobbyist? I paid them to get shit done.

And yet shit wasn't done.

"So, what you're telling me is since the last time we met—over a month ago—you've gotten absolutely no support for this bill?"

Cartwright, the principal of the most prestigious lobbyist firm in the state of Louisiana, seemed to shrink a little in his starched French collar shirt. "I'm sorry, Mr. Titan. I thought one of my associates was handling the matter, and it appears he was more fixated on handling a young legislative aide. He's been terminated."

Wonderful. A guy led by his dick—and in a way that totally fucked my chances of getting this bill passed.

"Then what's your plan, Cartwright?" The man better have a plan. I didn't take well to people who brought me only problems and not even a hint of a solution. People needed to show a little goddamn initiative.

"Well, Mr. Titan, I hadn't really thought beyond solving the immediate problem. I'll go back to my office and brainstorm some ideas."

I said nothing for a few moments, just let the silence of the room wrap uncomfortably around him. Finally, I nodded. "Go. I expect an answer by midnight."

His eyes bugged wide. It was already after five.

"Or you're fired," I added. "And I know damn well Titan Industries is over a third of ygour business."

Nodding his head in a jerky movement, the man backed away until he hit the door with his heels. Then he turned and shuffled through it, and the room was silent once more. Until Colson spoke.

"You should've fired him on the spot."

Anyone else questioning my judgment would have caught the sharp side of my tongue, but Colson was an exception to the rule.

"Giving him a few extra hours is easier than bringing on a new lobbyist at this point. I'm doing it for me, not as a favor to him."

"Still, he doesn't deserve it. Besides, if he'd been thinking on his feet, he would've offered up the obvious solution."

And this was why Colson was my COO. Because he was smarter than ninety-nine percent of the people I came in contact with.

We first met at Stanford in business school. He'd been universally hated for screwing the curve in our strategic management class by acing the final, and I'd been the only person who didn't care, because I'd only been one point behind him and wrecked the curve in the other three classes I was taking that semester. To find someone more disliked than myself was a novel feeling. Both his brain and his absolute disregard for what anyone else thought were the primary reasons I'd brought him on after I acquired my first few companies.

I leaned back in my chair, curious as to where he was going with this. "And what's the obvious solution?"

"Johnson Haines. Old Southern powerhouse politician. He's got enough pull to rally his own party, plus persuade the others across the aisle to vote our way."

It sounded too easy. He was only one man, someone whose name I knew but hadn't considered. Why hadn't I considered him? Normally I was all over this shit. I'd made meeting the who's who of New Orleans society a top priority, and yet I hadn't met him.

Oh yeah, that's right—because my arrangement with Vanessa Frost had gone sideways when Con Leahy had gotten involved. Or rather when *they* had gotten involved. Either way, my introduction into the upper echelons had been halted temporarily. Not because I'd accepted defeat, but because I'd thrown myself back into what was important— my business, preparing to dominate the market, and make a fuck ton of money.

Dad, you're about to be proven wrong, I thought before returning to the conversation at hand.

"And you think he'll be on our side because . . . ?"

Colson shrugged. "Haines is a typical politician. You scratch his back, he'll scratch yours. He's supported a lot more unlikely causes than any other senior legislator, but only when there's something in it for him. You dangle the right incentive, and we can take advantage of his talent for building bipartisan coalitions."

It was a solid suggestion. Which was a damn good thing, because there was nothing I wouldn't do to see this project through.

I gave Colson a nod. "Set something up."

"I'll get something on the calendar tomorrow."

"Good. I'll be available by e-mail tonight. Let me know what you figure out."

"Will do." Colson turned for the door but paused before reaching it. "You get the name of that woman Friday night? At the gym? She was one hot piece of ass. I'm thinking about tracking her down and giving it another shot."

Yve Santos. When I realized who he was talking about, something unfamiliar and unwanted surged inside me. The woman was nothing to me, a momentary fascination that had ended with her running from me. *She was smart to run.*

"She didn't seem too receptive last night," I said, my tone bored.

Colson smirked. "I was off my game. Won't happen again."

It wasn't until the door shut behind him that I uncurled my hands from the fists they'd clenched into.

"HOW DID A STRAIGHT GUY LEARN TO FOLD clothes so perfectly?" I asked my newest— and only—full-time employee. I'd hired him shortly after Elle had left me to work at Chains about six weeks ago.

Levi looked up from straightening a stack of Seven For All Mankind jeans, which were some of our only non-vintage items, and one of my weaknesses. "Does a guy have to be gay to know how to fold properly?"

I cringed at the stereotype. That was pretty shitty of me to say, so I backpedaled. "I'm just not used to guys being as neat and organized as you."

Levi's smile told me he wasn't offended by my jerky comment. "Military school."

"What? You?" I couldn't picture the skinny dark-haired kid who fell firmly into the hipster category attending military school.

"Yeah. I was a little shit growing up. Apparently it was the best solution to straighten me out. It was a good experience, but one I'll leave firmly in the past."

His comment about leaving things in the past coincided with the chime jangling at the front door, and a piece of *my* past walking through it.

"You want to start steaming those dresses the UPS guy dropped off? In the back?" I asked Levi.

He glanced at the regal silver-haired woman who'd walked in—not the type you'd normally expect to see in the shop—then looked back to me and nodded. "Sure thing, boss. Yell if you need anything."

I smiled at him, but it felt as fake as it probably looked.

As soon as he slipped through the door to the stock room and shut it firmly behind him, Geneviève came toward me, and I smiled.

Her bearing screamed proud matriarch, and that was exactly what she was. Tasteful diamonds decorated her ears and throat, accenting her Chanel skirt suit. I was guessing her destination was either a NOLA Garden Club meeting, or perhaps a Junior League luncheon.

I came around the counter and stopped before her.

"Yve, my dear. It's been much too long." She leaned forward, squeezed my shoulders, and air kissed both my cheeks.

Warmth spread through me. Her approval was something I still valued, even to this day. She was the only person from *that* part of my past I hadn't desperately tried to block out.

"It's a pleasure. I've missed you."

She reached down and gripped my hand. "And I've

27

missed you. You need to come visit an old lady more often," she said, chiding me gently. "You never know when she'll breathe her last."

I laughed. "You're going to outlive us all, Ginny."

Anyone else would have gotten a sharp reprimand for calling the dignified woman by such an informal nickname, but I occupied a unique space in her life. I was the girl she'd taken under her wing when the rest of my life was falling apart, and I'd had nowhere to go. I'd been bruised, beaten, and alone. Geneviève had broken ranks with her family—in secret—to shelter and help me.

"You know I'll try, dear." She patted my arm. "But that's not what I came here to talk about."

The pleasant surprise of seeing her in the shop faded away when the purpose of her visit became clear.

"I know."

"He's going to be out soon, Yve. We need to talk about what happens next."

The *he* in question was my ex-husband and Ginny's grandson. The one who'd spent the last ten years in the closest thing there was to a cushy prison for rape. Not my rape—oh no, because his father had made certain any allegations that had come from me were discounted to the point that they were laughable. No, Jay had made the big mistake of targeting a woman whose father was a judge. Someone who would not allow his daughter or her accusations to be ignored.

Because money made the world go 'round.

"When exactly is he getting out?"

Ginny's gaze dropped. "My son hasn't seen fit to share that information with me, but soon." She paused. "Are you sure you want to be here when he gets out? There's no telling how he's going to react to being on the outside again. His father and I can only do so much to keep him on a short leash. You know how he is."

And I did know how he was. But I hadn't let him—or his father—run me out of town before, and I wouldn't let him now. Leave my friends? Dirty Dog?

The instant leaving Dirty Dog popped into my head, I cringed. I might be doing that anyway, whether I liked it or not. I was still trying to shove the thought out of my head as Geneviève kept talking.

"What if I helped you set up a shop just like this one, anywhere you wanted? You pick the city, and I'll help you make it happen. It would be a fresh start, Yve."

I snapped my attention back to the conversation. "What are you talking about? You want me to leave town, and you want to pay me to do it?"

Ginny's expression softened. "You know I don't want you to leave, but Jay's release will stir up all the old gossip, and it's going to get uncomfortable here. Not only for the family, but for you. I know you didn't want to leave before, but you also haven't moved on, Yve. Have you dated? Had a relationship? Is being in this city part of what's keeping you from moving forward with your life and living it?"

Her words shot pangs through my heart, because she was right in some respects. It was quite possible I hadn't moved on, hadn't had a relationship beyond a fling that lasted a few nights, or a few weeks at most.

But I completely disagreed as to the reason why. It had nothing to do with this city and everything to do with the fact that I wasn't willing to trust anyone the way I'd naively trusted Jay before he became a monster. Never again would I make myself such an easy target. Vulnerability was an invitation to be walked all over.

"I'm not leaving. This is my home."

"I just think that you might be more comfortable if you—"

"No," I said, my tone resolute. "I'm not leaving."

Ginny's expression fell. "I just want what's best for you, dear. If you change your mind, you know I'm here whenever you need me."

I leaned forward and pressed a heartfelt kiss to her cheek. "Thank you. You know I never would've made it this far without you. I promise I'll be fine. This town is just going to have to be big enough for both of us."

Which was ironic, because he was going to have to stay away from me at all times. My restraining order would be active when he was released from prison. But that flimsy piece of paper wouldn't keep me safe if Jay decided he wanted to get to me.

Geneviève squeezed my hand once more before turning to leave. Unease filtered through me, along with a sense of loss. The loss was my delicate feeling of safety shredding to pieces. Thoughts of vigilantly watching my back at every moment of the day hammered me. Would I ever feel safe again once he was out?

The door chime jangled again, and Levi poked his head out of the back room. "Everything okay out here?"

"Everything's great," I said, forcing cheer into my voice. "Everything's perfect."

But it was all a big, fat lie. And the lie started to crumble when my cell phone rang a few hours later.

"He's out." It was Valentina—Jay's other victim, the judge's daughter—and her usually confident and calm voice shook.

"What?" My voice trembled to match hers.

"He's out, Yve. They let that animal out of his cage, and they didn't even give me the warning I was supposed to get first. I just got a call from the victim's rep, and he was oh-so-apologetic that they were calling late."

My phone slid from my grip and thudded to the counter. Geneviève had been wrong—Jay wasn't getting out soon. He was *already* out.

I snatched it up again. "Holy shit." My response wasn't eloquent, but any other words escaped me.

"My daddy's PI has been on the trail since about five minutes after I got the call, but he's coming up with nothing. It's like Jay got picked up at the gates and just disappeared. We're still trying to get the security footage. How that asshole got out of going to a halfway house . . . Well, I'm sure we can both figure that out. Money talks."

Those feelings of safety I was hanging on to? Sliced to pieces by her words. But my determination to stand my ground? Multiplied exponentially.

"Watch your back, and I'll watch mine," I said.

"I'll be watching mine with a loaded weapon," Valentina vowed. "He comes near me, he dies. Dead men make excellent witnesses. Be safe, Yve. I'll call if I hear anything at all."

"You be safe too."

When we hung up, I considered my options. I would

not let Jay control my future; I'd already let him have too much of my past.

I picked up my phone and dialed another number. "Hello, this is Yve Santos. I'd like to make an appointment to speak with one of your small business loan officers."

Dirty Dog was going to be mine. Jay would never control my life again. I wouldn't hide from him, and I wouldn't let him run me out of this town.

And I definitely wouldn't let him win.

Lucas

I SLAMMED THE DOOR OF MY ASTON. IT WAS THE ONLY
exhibition of frustration I allowed myself. Then I dialed
Colson to fill him in on my meeting with Johnson
Haines.

"How'd it go?" Colson didn't bother with a greeting.
We didn't do meaningless small talk.

"He wants too much." I'd expected big demands because all politicians operated on a *quid pro quo* system, but
Haines's request wasn't something I could agree to lightly.

"Like what?"

"An open-ended favor. Anything he needs, whenever
he needs it. And a hefty donation to his re-election campaign."

"We expected the donation."

"No shit, but I'm not going to be at the beck and call of
some pompous politician."

Haines had been the caricature of a Southern politician, his big gut testing the limits of his suspenders in his navy pin-striped suit and red power tie. All he'd been missing was a big fat cigar.

"He's a power junkie. Having you on his list of favors would give him a boner. Can't say I'm surprised."

Colson was right. Haines was the kind of man who liked having others under his thumb, and I could see the power light his expression when he'd explained that in exchange for my marker, he'd have to call in several others. But he was confident he could swing the tide in favor of the bill.

When I didn't respond, Colson asked, "What'd you say?"

"That I'd think about it." The money wasn't the problem; it was being beholden to someone. I didn't put myself in a position of anything but power, and owing a favor like this jeopardized that. I fucking hated politics, and this was exactly the reason why.

"He give you a deadline?"

"No one gives me goddamn deadlines, Colson. I make the deadlines."

"Fair enough. When are you going to decide?"

"Do your job. Find another way. Get creative. I don't care what it takes, as long as it's not this."

"How creative?"

I knew what he was asking. "Feel free to color outside the lines on this one."

"Done."

Nothing more needed to be said, so I hung up. All I wanted tonight was a glass of Macallan—and a big fat Cuban cigar, in honor of the state senator. Giant asshole.

No one, and I do mean *no one*, pushed me into doing anything I didn't want to do. I controlled my empire and the world around me to a merciless degree. Handing even a slice of control over to someone else wasn't in my nature, and to a politician, it would have to be a last resort. But *fuck*, I needed this to happen.

My father had said it would never work, said it was a waste of time. But he was wrong. This project would make me more money than I could spend in several lifetimes. Without the political catalyst, it would be an uphill battle. With it, I'd practically be printing money. It might sound like a shady way to do business, but the ends justified the means, in my book.

I just needed to get my ass back into the office to finish up a few things, and then to Lakefront Airport and a jet to Europe—with my cigar and Scotch. It was time to get back to making money.

It was one of the two things I excelled at.

"YOU SURE YOU'RE GOOD WITH GIVING ME A ride?" I asked Levi as I locked the shop's back door. "What time is your flight again?"

"I've got plenty of time. You know I don't mind."

We climbed into his Karmann Ghia and it started up more smoothly than my Jetta, which was ironic considering his Volkswagen was about forty years older than my car. I rattled off directions to my house, which was actually within walking distance to work and no big deal, but the box of accessories the UPS man had delivered needed to be sorted, assessed, and priced tonight, and carrying it home would be awkward as hell.

Getting a ride from Levi reminded me of the one I'd gotten from Titan. And the note that had arrived three days ago. Dark, slashing script on paper that even felt expensive, as did everything when it came to that man. It was arrogant and to the point—just like him.

Your car is being repaired at Uptown.
You can thank me later.
—Titan

Lucas Fucking Titan. Fucking should really be added to his name as an official title. It was appropriate. I held in a giggle at the thought.

Surprisingly, it was the same shop I would've had Cousin Stevie tow it to, so I wasn't cringing too horribly at the cost. Not yet, anyway. Titan having it taken there was surprisingly not assholish, which, given what I knew about the man, seemed out of character. The note, however, seemed perfectly in character.

When we pulled into a parking spot behind my building, Levi shut off the VW and hopped out.

"What are you doing?" I asked.

"Carrying the box up for you. Can't say I'm not a gentleman."

Smiling, I led the way up the walk to my exterior stairs. "You're a good kid, you know that? Apparently military school was the right choice for you."

At my door, I reached for my keys and slid one in the lock . . . but the knob turned freely before I twisted the key. It was already unlocked.

What the hell?

Levi bumped into me from behind. "Whoa. Sorry."

My hand hovered over the door handle as I hesitated to push it open, fear gripping me as my mind spun with thoughts of what could be waiting inside. Did I forget to lock it?

Valentina's call haunted me. Jay was out on parole. The

fact that I'd moved three times while he'd been in prison meant nothing; money had a way of making it easy to track people down. Jay could find me, could get to me. It wouldn't be a problem for him.

"Yve? You unlocking the door?"

I shoved my hand in my purse and wrapped my palm around the grip of my Smith & Wesson. "The door's unlocked," I whispered.

"Did you lock it this morning?" Levi asked, caution coloring his words.

I racked my brain, trying to remember. "I think so. I always lock my door. This is Tremé, for God's sake."

"Then, do you think we should call the cops? Maybe you had a break-in?"

Fuck the police. They'd done nothing for me last time, and right now I only had an unlocked door freaking me out.

"I guess I'll find out when I get inside."

Levi lowered the box to the small bistro table on my little deck. "Let me go first."

"Baby boy, I'm armed. I'll go first," I replied.

I didn't wait for him to protest, just pushed the door open and kept my grip on the gun. My apartment was still and quiet. I scanned the room, and Levi stepped in front of me.

"Jeez, kid."

"Like I could let you do this yourself. Or let you go first. I was raised better than that."

"I've been taking care of myself a long time," I said with a snort that was more than a little bravado.

He grunted, and together we moved from room to

room. Everything was in its place, right down to the blouse and skirt I'd tried on this morning before work and then tossed on my bed.

I circled the kitchen again, and that was when I saw it. The glass I always kept next to the sink was upside down in the drying rack.

A memory crashed into me. The burst of pain as the back of Jay's hand slammed into my cheekbone, and he murmured words in the quiet, menacing tone that never failed to make my stomach drop. "I told you I didn't want to see that glass sitting out again. Put the goddamn thing in the dishwasher when you're done, Yvie. How many times do I have to tell you before it gets through your head? Next time, I'll break every fucking glass in this house and you can drink out of the goddamn dog bowl."

Jay. He was back. He'd been here.

My skin crawled as if I'd just rolled in fire ants, and ice water filled my veins. Rational thought stopped and instinct kicked in.

Fight or flight.

"I can't stay here tonight," I blurted and headed for the door. "I can't. I have to leave."

Levi might have said something, but the blood rushed too loudly in my ears for me to hear anything. I was already outside and down the stairs, falling onto the tiny garden bench in the back, before Levi closed the door to my apartment and made his way to me.

"Yve, what the hell? You're freaking me out. What's going on?"

Razor-sharp shards of helplessness twined around me, tearing through my courage and determination as if it were nothing but tissue paper, and shredding my illusion of safety. I was powerless again. Terrified. Waiting for the other shoe to drop.

All the horrible feelings I'd spent years eradicating came flooding back. I wrapped my arms tightly around my middle when I whispered, "I can't stay here. I have to go. He was here."

Levi dropped to the bench beside me, and I couldn't stop the instinctive flinch. He scooted away and gave me some space.

"Then we'll go. Let me get the box. You get in the car."

I did as I was told while Levi returned the box to the car. When he climbed in and we pulled away, I was already feeling ridiculous. Two blocks away, I wondered if I was imagining things. Could my mind be playing tricks on me? Did I wash the glass?

No. I knew I hadn't. Someone had been there.

So much for not running. Apparently I was just as weak as I'd always been, but running wasn't the answer.

"You can take me back. I'm good now. I just . . . freaked," I told Levi. Embarrassment seeped through me at my overreaction.

"Um, I don't think that's a good idea. You didn't freak, you flipped the fuck out. I've never seen you like that. And if your first instinct was to get out of your place, then I'm going to make sure you stay out—at least for tonight."

"No, I'm fine. We can go back." My skin prickled and my heart hammered even as I said the words. I didn't want to go back to my apartment; I needed time to toughen up my armor before I went to slay that dragon. It was a momentary weakness. I could allow myself that, right? But *only* momentary.

I turned to Levi. "Just drop me at a hotel by the airport. That way you can catch your flight. I don't want to make you miss it."

But Levi turned in the opposite direction and headed for the Garden District. "I have a better idea."

"Um, what?"

"Stay at my place. It'll be empty, so it's perfect."

It sounded like a great idea. Until I saw his place.

I turned to Levi. "Who the hell are you?"

8

THIS WASN'T THE KIND OF PLACE I SHOULD BE staying as a guest. A woman like me had more business cleaning this house than curling up between sheets that probably cost more than my car. Hell, even cleaning this house would require a background check. It felt all sorts of wrong to be wandering around it by myself.

When I'd asked Levi who the hell he was, he'd just smiled and said his brother was loaded and had left the country today on a business trip. I'd stowed the urge to ask more questions, not wanting Levi to miss his flight.

Please, God, don't let Levi's brother be a drug kingpin. That would just be too much for me to handle right now. But then again, if he were some kind of cartel badass, then I guess I was in about the safest place possible. The panel of the security system mounted on the wall by the front door had taken a fourteen-digit code to enter, and I still couldn't believe *I* had it.

This mansion was even bigger than the house my mama's man lived in. The one she wasn't ever allowed to go in because she was the *mistress*. I came from classy roots, no doubt about it. The blood of owned women ran in my veins going back almost a hundred years. It was the family tradition, a dynasty of whores, if you would. And I'd thought I'd been flouting tradition by marrying the man who wanted me. Turned out that marriage to a man like that was an even worse sort of slavery.

A shudder racked my body. I needed to find something to do before thoughts of Jay had me freaking out again. So I wandered the first floor, avoiding the rooms with closed doors until I smelled chlorine.

Seriously? An indoor pool?

As if I needed more evidence Levi's brother was loaded. I stared longingly through the glass walls at the blue water surrounded by a gorgeous tile mosaic floor in shades of cream, aqua, and gold.

The house was empty . . .

Could I indulge a little? I weighed the decision. How often did a girl from Tremé get to use a private indoor pool with one of those lap lanes that let you swim against the current and keep going forever?

The answer was simple. *Almost never.*

And if I were swimming, maybe I could finally shut off my brain before I drove myself crazy. There was just one little problem—I didn't bring a bathing suit. I pushed through the door to the pool room anyway, breathing in a deep lungful of the chlorine-scented air.

Again my mind went to the fact that the house was

empty. Just little old me rattling around inside. Levi had said his brother wouldn't be home for a week. I'd be gone tomorrow, so tonight . . . *screw it.* I kicked off my sandals next to a lounge chair and tugged my shirt up and over my head. My bra followed, and then my skirt and underwear. *In for a penny, in for a pound*, I thought.

I strode to the side, curling my toes over the tile edge, and dove in.

My body relaxed and I breathed a sigh of relief as I broke the surface and swam a few yards underwater. It was the perfect temperature, and the thrill of naughty, decadent freedom built with every pull of my arms and kick of my legs.

I made my way down the length of the pool, diving under the surface and pushing off the bottom to pop my head up again. Reaching the lap lane, I swam to the side and wondered where the control was that would activate the current. Locating a small panel at the end, I tested the buttons one by one until the current surged to life.

Win.

I let it push me backward before lowering my head and paddling against it with what felt like long, smooth strokes. I swam until my arms, shoulders, and thighs burned with fatigue. Finally ready to get out, I let the current sweep me back again until it lessened, and I dropped my feet to the tile bottom and got my footing.

A low, deep voice came from behind me, and I froze.

"How the hell did you get in here? And more importantly, how can I have you strip on command if you're already naked?"

Lucas

I T HAD BEEN A LONG FUCKING DAY.

I was supposed to be on my way to Dusseldorf right now, but the week of meetings I'd been scheduled to attend had fallen apart three hours ago when the CEO of the supplier had been hospitalized with a heart attack. A quadruple bypass had a way of changing plans. Inconvenient as hell, and yet not a damn thing I could do about it.

So now I had a rare evening free of plans or commitments. Which meant I'd worked until everyone had left for the day plus another hour before finally heading home.

I'd planned to do nothing but relax with my cigar and Scotch until I walked past the glass walls of the pool room that stretched along the back quarter of the house. And that was when I saw the intruder.

What the hell?

I shoved open the glass door, and my eyes zeroed in on the bare, heart-shaped ass and toned legs that flashed in the water as a woman swam in my lap lane.

How? I had no idea. Who? Also no fucking clue. But I wasn't going to interrupt this show for anything. My night had just gotten a whole hell of a lot better.

She swam for another few minutes before floating out of the current and standing with her back to me. Time to solve the mystery.

"How the hell did you get in here? And more importantly, how can I have you strip on command if you're already naked?"

She spun to face me, all wet, naked curves. Immediately my eyes dropped to her round tits tipped with nipples just a shade darker and pinker than her skin.

Her mouth dropped open and she screamed. The shrill sound echoed off the glass walls of the room, and she ducked underwater just as she remembered to cover herself.

A shame, really. My eyes moved up to her face.

What the hell? Was that—? No way.

Yve?

My dick, already hard from watching her swim, pulsed against my zipper. My dress pants would do little to hide my hard-on, but I didn't give a damn. This was my house, and she was the one trespassing—naked.

Her expression flashed from confusion to realization, and then morphed into indignation. "What the fuck are *you* doing here?" she demanded, her words rife with disbelief.

"What am *I* doing here? It's *my house.*"

Her brows wrinkled together into a deep V, as if she was working out some complex scenario. "You're Levi's brother," she finally said. "No way. No goddamn way. His name isn't Titan."

Levi. She was fucking my brother? The punk was on his way to New Zealand. Why the hell did he have his girlfriend in my house? *And why didn't I know the woman I haven't stopped thinking about is fucking my brother?* Frustration and anger boiled through me hot and fast.

"It was before he decided to legally drop it and just go with Levi. Like the kid is Prince or something."

It had been a rebellious move as soon as he'd graduated from military school and told me he was going to pursue his career in music. One year living in LA waiting tables had cured him of that, but the legal name change had already been done. Now he was finally back in college, and on an extended mid-semester break. And what did my little brother do? Use his quarterly trust fund distribution to buy a plane ticket to New Zealand to visit a sheep farm or some shit like that.

Yve couldn't be involved with Levi. But then, how the hell would she know him if she wasn't dating him? Levi didn't exactly have many friends. But if they were together, wouldn't he have told her who he was? No. He wouldn't have. That was my brother. Deny the money to the very end, *except* when he got the bright idea to spend a couple of weeks in New Zealand.

I still didn't believe it. She had to be almost ten years older than him. Not that there was anything wrong with that, but wouldn't I have known? It didn't make sense.

"How do you know my brother, and why are you here if he's on his way to New Zealand?"

Yve's gaze on me was hard as she wrapped her arms

around her body more tightly, almost as tightly as her lips were pressed together. "He works for me at Dirty Dog. He said no one would be home."

His boss? Then she was fair game. Satisfaction pulsed within me.

"That doesn't answer my question about why you're naked in my pool. Not that I don't appreciate the view."

Her cheeks flushed a deeper pink, and the color reminded me of her nipples. My dick once again jerked against my suit pants in response. Now that I'd seen those tits, I'd never get them out of my head. I needed to see them again. Now.

"Look, I didn't know," she said. "I never would've come here if I'd known this was your house. He said it'd be empty, and I needed a place to crash for the night." She lifted her arm, unable to suppress the natural urge to gesture, and the movement revealed a flash of nipple.

Come on, gorgeous. Throw yourself at me like the rest of them. I'll fucking catch you.

Flushing deeper when she realized what she'd done, Yve slapped her arm back down to cover any other accidental peeks, and sank further beneath the surface.

Some of the most beautiful women I'd ever seen had performed intricately planned stripteases, and that little flash of nipple from Yve Santos was having more of an effect on my cock. Apparently my dick had declared its preference for honey-tanned skin, dark brown waves, and eyes the color of amber.

I wasn't going to argue with it, because I wanted her. So I would have her. That was how life worked when you were Lucas Titan.

"I think you've overstayed your welcome in my pool," I drawled.

"Then how about you hand me a towel?" she shot back.

"I think you're capable of getting it yourself, woman."

Her eyes widened in shock. Was she expecting a gentleman? I wasn't in the mood. No, I wanted to see Yve dripping wet and naked. I wondered if she'd turn this into a battle of wills. The thought turned me on even more.

What was it about this woman?

She straightened her shoulders even as she hugged herself again. "You're a dick, you know that?"

"I'm aware. It's also my house, my pool, and my rules."

Mulish. That was the only word I could use to describe her expression. Would she do it?

Her eyes narrowed on me with that strange and haunting golden-amber color. "Fine. If you insist." She dropped her arms, stood tall, and walked toward me, every bare, naked inch of skin slick with water.

Fuuuck.

She made her way to the stairs, and my eyes were riveted on her as she climbed out.

Jesus. Fucking. Christ.

I swallowed hard, but fought to maintain my trademark smug smile. Yve's body could stop a rampaging mob in its tracks. My resolve to have her under me shot up to *needs to happen right the fuck now.*

She stared me down, which surprised me. Most women didn't have the guts to do it. I could think of only one who'd gone toe to toe with me, and sadly, she now belonged to another man.

Yve was in a class all her own, though. Round, high

tits, a narrow waist, and a smooth, gently curved stomach flowed into the sinfully perfect flare of her hips. Naked, proud, and sexy as fuck, she strode toward me. I expected her to go right for the stack of towels, but she didn't.

My cock, already hard, surged against my zipper, testing its strength. She stopped in front of me.

"As big of a dick as you are, I hope you've got the equipment to match." Her hand shot out, and before I could guess her intent, her fist wrapped around my cock.

"Jesus fuck, woman—" I grunted.

"Don't you ever try to humiliate me again, you rich prick." She squeezed my dick in warning, and Christ almighty if it didn't get even harder.

But I wouldn't back down from anyone, even now. So I repaid her in kind, reaching out a hand to cup her lush, full breast. Good God, did I want to fuck those tits.

She swallowed and jerked, but not before I rolled her nipple between my thumb and finger and squeezed. Her pupils dilated. She wanted this. Wanted me.

A rush of power laced my pumping blood. She was wild—and unpredictable if my dick in her hand was any indication. But I would bend her to my will. And we'd both fucking love it.

Her grip on my cock tightened again.

"You getting a good feel for it, Yve? Getting wet thinking about how I'd stretch your tight little cunt and fill you up?"

She sucked in a sharp breath. "You have no shame, do you?"

I shook my head slowly. She might have had me nearly by the balls, but I was still the only predator in this room.

"None at all. In fact, I'd give a whole hell of a lot to watch you sink to your knees right now so I could fuck that sassy mouth of yours."

She swallowed, and once again, moved faster than I anticipated. Before I knew it, she released her grip as her other palm cracked against my cheek.

I caught her wrist midair as she pulled it back for another run at me. "You get one. That's it."

"Let. Go. Of. Me." Yve spat the words from between gritted teeth.

"For now." I released her wrist and she spun, stalking stiffly to the towels.

My dick, missing her grip already, throbbed at the sight of her perfectly heart-shaped ass, and I bit back a groan. *Mmm. That ass.*

She wrapped a towel around her, covering all that smooth, sleek skin—skin that I could spend hours tasting—and turned as she jammed a corner of the towel between her breasts.

Her eyes flashed with anger. "You're an asshole."

"That's not news," I replied. "What is news, however, is that you've got the most perfect tits and ass I've ever seen."

The dusky hue of her nipples once again stained her sharp cheekbones. "An asshole and a pig."

"And you've got a lot of explaining to do. Dry off, and I'll meet you in the conservatory. I have a feeling this is going to require Scotch." I stepped toward the door of the pool room, and paused. "In case you haven't familiarized yourself with the house beyond the pool, the conservatory is in the east wing. Next door after you pass the library."

As I pushed open the door, I was pretty certain I heard

her whisper, "What the fuck is a conservatory, and why the hell does he need one?"

A smile curled along my lips at that little gem.

"HOLY SHIT," I MUTTERED AS I GRABBED another towel and dried my hair. "Lucas Goddamn Titan. No fucking way."

And what the hell did I just do? I'd grabbed the man's dick.

Granted, he'd forced me to. Well, he hadn't exactly taken my hand and wrapped it around the biggest cock I'd ever encountered—based on the sheer feel of it—but he'd taunted me. Challenged me.

I wasn't the kind of woman who would back down from a challenge anymore. And certainly not from a rich asshole like Titan. No, men like him understood one thing and one thing only—power and sheer defiance of it.

I still couldn't believe I hadn't put it together. How could Titan be Levi's brother? They didn't share a last name—because as Titan had said, Levi didn't *have* one. I'd thought he was crazy when he'd handed me his ID for his employment paperwork, but I didn't ask questions because . . . well, this was New Orleans, and he wouldn't be my first employee to be in a unique situation. Now that I was looking for it, I could see the resemblance between them. Even though Levi didn't have the height or the solid build quite yet, he had the same black hair, albeit shaggy, and green eyes.

I tried to wrap my mind around this entire thing while I squeezed the water out of my hair. I really needed a shower first, but I wasn't about to risk taking that kind of time. The *master* of the house might notice and find me naked and wet. Again.

Good Lord. That man . . .

I should have wanted to claw his hand off when he touched me, but . . . I hadn't. Clearly, I was traumatized from earlier or something, because my reaction defied explanation. When his dark green eyes had speared me, I'd almost arched into his touch like a cat in heat.

It was a mistake. A crazy reaction. I didn't want him.

He was rich. Arrogant. Entitled. Most likely to try to crush me into a pliable shadow of myself. Screw that. But in a corner of my mind, I knew the truth. I wanted to screw him.

No, Yve. You know better.

Self-loathing was a horrible thing, so I shoved the thoughts aside. I didn't want him. Wouldn't want him. I *hated* him and everything he stood for. I'd stare him down again, and this time, I would do it with my pride intact.

I spotted several fluffy white hotel robes hanging from hooks on the wall, which would have been really nice to notice before. *Damn it.* I grabbed one and slipped it on before sliding into my flip-flops and heading for the door. I was leaving what had happened a few minutes ago in that room and I would never think about it again. I'd also strike the dick-grabbing move from my list of knee-jerk reactions to being challenged.

As I reached for the door handle, I looked down at the palm of my hand like it was going to explain to me why it jumped out and grabbed Lucas Titan's junk.

Shake. It. Off. Yve. Squaring my shoulders, I headed in the direction of the library. At least I knew where it was. I'd drooled over it almost immediately upon entering the house. It was something out of *Beauty and the Beast,* and now that I knew who owned the house, that comparison seemed a lot more fitting.

I paused near the stairs. Meeting Lucas Titan in a bathrobe was not a good idea. I hated that I'd be at a disadvantage. This kind of conversation would be easier to have in my sassiest red dress and tallest fuck-me heels—an outfit that packed a double shot of confidence to face down his arrogant self.

Not like when I ran from him at the corner instead of letting him see me to my house.

But even after I'd done that, he'd still arranged for my car to be repaired.

Titan was a damn puzzle. And I didn't have time to solve the path through his twisty brain these days.

Instead, I squared my shoulders and followed a hallway in the direction I assumed was east. Soon I passed the library and another set of glass doors that led into what would definitely be another of my favorite rooms of the house. With all glass walls and a vaulted glass roof, it held a couple of comfortable-looking sofas and a long, narrow table with several fancy bottles filled with amber liquid. As I approached, Titan stood pouring what I assumed was some kind of expensive booze into two glasses.

"You drink Scotch?" he asked without looking up.

"Apparently I do now," I replied.

That answer got his attention.

His sharp gaze landed on my face before dropping to my feet and climbing up my body. Once again, I felt him everywhere his stare touched. Beneath the robe, my nipples tightened against my will and better judgment.

"Yes, you do."

"So says the king." I laughed, but I didn't move closer to him. My flip-flops seemed rooted to the slate floor.

"Indeed." He held the glass out, studying my face intently. "You look like you're about to make a run for it."

"I didn't expect to find *you* here. I never would've come."

A smirk tugged at the corners of his mouth and slowly curled into a smug smile. "I can't say the surprise was unwelcome. In fact, coming home to see a naked woman swimming laps in my pool is something I could easily get used to."

"Nice," I said with a snort. It wasn't an attractive sound, but I wasn't worried about impressing this man. "And why don't I believe this is the first time you've walked in on someone naked in your pool? You've got money. You aren't exactly ugly. Women should be dropping their panties at your feet."

His eyebrow lifted, the arrogant prick. "Who says they aren't?"

"Well, Vanessa Frost sure didn't." I lifted an eyebrow

back at him, now glad that I'd paid attention when Elle had filled me in on all of the dirty details from Titan's pursuit of Vanessa.

Titan's smile died. "Touché." He held out a tumbler, but the mood in the room had shifted.

Was his pride still stinging over that? *Huh. Go figure.* Men and their fragile little egos. Maybe Titan was human after all.

I took the glass and crossed to the window, ignoring the eyes that followed me. Outside was a garden arch covered in pale whitish-blue lights. It seemed an odd touch considering two men lived here.

Titan came up behind me, his reflection setting my nerves on edge once more.

"What are you doing in my house?" he asked.

I held his reflected stare, even though my instinct was to drop it. I would not let this man see a single hint of weakness from me. I knew he was the type to exploit any he might detect.

"I told you I wouldn't have come if I'd known it was your house."

"That doesn't answer my question." He lifted the tumbler to his lips and sipped.

I wasn't too proud to admit to myself that I watched his Adam's apple move as he swallowed. The man was nothing less than striking with his black hair, perfectly cut and styled in a way that clearly said *I don't have to try to look gorgeous*, along with dark green eyes, tanned skin that stretched over sharp cheekbones, and a strong jaw. He would have been nearly perfect if not for the scar slashing through his eyebrow into his hairline. I wondered at the story behind it.

Because God knew, all scars seemed to come with a story.

And of course, I couldn't forget the huge cock. My cheeks—and other parts of my body—heated against my will. *Leave it in the pool room, Yve. Forget that you know how big his dick is.*

Titan raised an eyebrow, the unscarred one. My assessment of him hadn't gone unnoticed—or my dirty thoughts, it seemed.

"I had a problem at my place." I looked away as I said it, flipping a hand as if it weren't worthy of concern.

His eyebrow dropped and lines creased his forehead. "What kind of problem?"

Like I was going to tell Lucas Fucking Titan about the glass in my dish rack that made me flip out. He'd think I was crazy, and maybe I was. All I knew was that something in my gut had told me to *get the hell out* of that house.

I listened to my gut, which was probably the only reason I'd ended up in the hospital rather than in a casket the night my ex had come home with a different sort of crazy burning in his eyes. After he'd finished with me, I'd awoken with every inch of my body screaming with pain, and found the house quiet. Something had told me if I were still there when he came back, I wouldn't live through the night.

So I'd called Ginny, and she'd called the ambulance. If I hadn't, the doctors told me my internal injuries would have finished me off before he could. *Intuition for the win,* I thought.

I gave myself a mental shake and focused on the present, finally admitting, "I thought maybe someone had broken in."

The lines deepened as he scowled. "What did the police

say?"

It was an obvious question, but I felt like a tool giving him the truth. "I didn't call the police."

"Why not?" he demanded.

"Because I didn't think there was anything missing."

"Then how would you know someone broke in? Was the lock picked? The door broken down?"

I shook my head and brought my tumbler to my lips, coughing a little when the Scotch hit my tongue.

"That's fifty-year-old Scotch; it should be smooth as silk going down." The words were just as smooth in Titan's deep voice.

I swallowed, nodding as the fiery liquor slid down my throat. "It's not bad. Just not what I expected it to taste like." I hoped the subject change would stick, but it didn't.

"Why didn't you call the police?"

I decided to be as honest as I could. "The door was un-locked, and it looked like something had been moved, but there was nothing else to report."

I expected him to tell me I probably forgot to lock it, or that I was imagining things, but he didn't. He turned and I watched his reflection stalk to the side table. I swiveled away from the window to face him as he lifted his phone and tapped on the screen.

"What are you doing?" I asked.

"Calling Hennessy, a detective at NOPD."

"What? No. Don't do that. It's fine. I—"

He must have found the contact he was looking for because he raised the phone to his ear. I strode across the room, not even thinking before I snatched it from him and disconnected the call.

Titan's hand shot out and wrapped around my wrist. He plucked the phone from my fingers with his other hand. The quick movement—and his hand getting so damn close to my face—had me flinching away and lifting my arm to shield myself. It was another instinct of mine, and it was a telling one.

Titan immediately dropped his hold on me and stepped back, his eyes wide and his lips parted. "What the hell, Yve? Did you think I was going to hit you? Jesus, I might be a total dick sometimes, but the only time I'd ever hit a woman is when I've got her bent over, ass out, and pussy dripping." His wounded expression made him seem more human than anything he could have done.

Mortification rushed over me in hot waves. I backed away, the tumbler sliding through my sweaty palm until I set it down with a *clunk* on an end table. I flew out of the room and raced down the halls of the huge house, intent on getting the hell out of there. But I didn't know where to go.

I should've walked out as soon as I knew whose house this was.

"Yve, wait."

Titan's voice came from behind me. Something in his tone made me freeze in mid-stride. I didn't turn, but my shoulders hunched forward as if my instincts were screaming at me to protect myself.

I wasn't a victim. Not anymore. I was a survivor. And I never wanted to see anyone look at me with pity again. Shoulders back and spine straight, I whirled around to face Titan.

Concern creased his features, an emotion that looked completely wrong on his arrogant face. I hated it, and the urge to lash out clawed through me.

"I don't feel the need to be interrogated by you or some cop. If you don't want me in your house, I'll be on my way."

"Not until you tell me who hit you."

His nostrils flared and his hands were curled into fists, but surprisingly, my fight-or-flight response faded. I didn't feel threatened anymore. He wasn't pissed *at* me, but *for* me. That was new and different. Still, it didn't mean I was about to share my pathetic story. Who wanted to admit they'd been beaten and let it keep happening? Or worse, that at the time I'd believed my husband when he'd told me it was my fault.

"It doesn't matter anymore."

Except it did matter if my intuition was right and Jay had been in my apartment. Then it would matter very, very much. The day I'd testified in open court, at the trial that had sent him to prison, he'd sworn he'd never let me go. But then his grandmother had pushed the divorce through as soon as the court would grant it.

Even I appreciated the irony of the situation, that someone in *his* family had been the one to set me free from that nightmare forever. I thought about Ginny's visit to Dirty Dog. The woman who'd helped me then was trying to help me again now, but this time she was trying to help me straight out of town. Did she know something I didn't? Had she really told me the truth when she'd said she didn't know when Jay was getting out?

I'd gotten so caught up in my thoughts that I completely checked out for a few moments. Titan was staring at me, studying me, and as soon as I was conscious of it, I felt the weight of his inspection all the way to my bones.

"I'd say it matters a whole hell of a lot," he said finally.

"And I don't know why you'd care."

"Because something scared you bad enough to run, and I don't think you scare easily. I may not be a good guy, but I'd fuck up any man who hurt a woman."

I snorted. *Right.* Lucas Titan, billionaire, asshole of the first order, was probably a man who wouldn't even fetch his own newspaper, let alone go after someone who hurt a woman.

"You don't believe me? Do you want me to prove it to you?"

I outright laughed at this. "Quit, Titan. You don't need to go ghetto and throw down. I'm fine, and nothing needs proving."

He opened his mouth to protest but my stomach growled. Loudly. I expected him to ignore it, but the man continued to surprise me.

"When did you eat last?"

I thought back to earlier and all the craziness of the day. "I don't know. Breakfast, I guess."

"Come on. Follow me." And he walked off down the hall, not even slowing to see if I was coming.

I guessed in Titan's world, when the king said "follow me," he didn't have to wonder if his orders would be obeyed. My stomach growled again, and that was the only reason I hurried down the hall after him.

Lucas

I RARELY WONDERED IF SOMEONE WOULD DO WHAT I asked. But with Yve, I was learning quickly that she was more likely to do the exact opposite. In a way, she reminded me of Levi when he was a kid. He was just eight years old when I became his guardian, and the years that followed had been . . . difficult.

I pushed open the door to the kitchen and flipped on the light. For as little time as I spent in the room, it was surprisingly one of my favorites. Kitchens had always been my refuge as a kid when my father would lose his shit—he'd never set foot in one, as far as I knew—so I could always escape his wrath there.

Seeing it empty of Jerome, my majordomo, chef, and keeper of all things, was not surprising given it was his night for poker. He'd joined my father's household when I was sixteen, when my father had first been sent to France as an engineer for a multinational corporation. Jerome had followed us from France to Germany two years later when my father founded his own company. Without Jerome, I wouldn't have been able to keep Levi from going to a secondary guardian after my father's death. My mother had passed away before we'd left the United States, taken too fast by an aggressive form of breast cancer.

Every time I thought about my mother, sadness followed. But every time I thought about my father, I shut down all thought and emotion. I would not think about that day, the one that had ended with him in a body bag and me in the hospital.

No.

Jaw set, I crossed to the fridge and yanked it open. Grabbing a container of hummus, I turned and slid it across the counter.

"Why are you doing this?" she asked.

"Offering to feed a guest in my home?"

"An unwanted and unwelcome guest in your home," Yve clarified.

"A guest who greets me naked is rarely unwanted and unwelcome."

"You know what I mean," she said, her cheeks coloring.

Fuck. With that blush staining her cheeks, I couldn't stare at her without recalling how gorgeous she'd looked naked or the feel of her nipple between my fingers. She might not spell her name like the first woman to tempt a man, but that didn't make her any less of a temptation.

I wanted her naked again. The robe wasn't the obstacle, though; it was Yve herself. But she didn't have to like me to fuck me; she just had to want me more than she hated me.

Yve kicked this little game into overdrive when she'd

wrapped her hand around my cock. I'd watched her pupils dilate. Her nipples had been practically diamond tipped. She wanted me.

The question was—how badly?

I crossed to the pantry and pulled out a carton of flat-bread. Returning to the kitchen island, I set it next to the hummus. "Eat."

Her eyes lifted to mine once more. "Why?"

"Because you need energy if I'm going to bend you over and fuck you on the counter."

Her mouth dropped open and her pupils dilated before rage bloomed in her eyes. "You mother—"

"Tell me you don't want it," I taunted her.

"Fuck—"

I cut her off before she could curse me out. "Tell me you're not thinking about how hard my dick was when it was pressed against your palm, and how much you want it filling you. Tell me, Yve. I dare you."

"You—"

"Have Yve Santos pegged completely."

Her golden eyes blazed. "I hate you."

I smiled. "But you want me."

"Fuck you, Titan."

"No, Yve. I'm going to fuck you. And you're going to love it."

I stepped forward and reached for the tie to the robe. The woman was completely unpredictable, because once again she reached for me. But not my dick this time, my belt. She had it unbuckled as the robe slid off her shoulders.

"Don't think this means I like you," she bit out.

"Trust me, I know you don't," I said before I lowered

my mouth to hers and took her lips.

Yve tore her mouth away from mine. "No. Don't kiss me. You want to fuck, then we keep this impersonal. That's *my* rule, Titan. You break it, and this is over."

"Fine." I groaned as she unzipped my slacks and palmed my cock, bare skin to bare skin.

Fuuuck.

I reached out and cupped her breast—the other one this time—and squeezed her nipple.

"These tits . . . I don't know how you expected me to keep my hands off you once I'd seen them. Fucking perfect."

Yve's blush spread from her cheeks down her chest, but she said nothing while she pumped my dick. Christ, just the clasp of her hand was better than some pussy I'd fucked.

I dropped my mouth and followed the trailing color to Yve's other nipple. Taking it between my lips and teeth, I sucked and tugged until her grip tightened and her hips shifted closer to mine.

Lowering my hand from her breast, I skimmed it down the curve of her stomach, along the flare of her hip, and cupped her ass. Jesus. That ass. Reaching between her thighs, I slid two fingers into the wet heat slicking her pussy lips.

I lifted my head from her nipple for a beat. "Jesus, woman. You do want this. You're soaked."

"Shut up and fuck me," she ordered, her gaze burning into mine.

A triumphant grin stretched my mouth, and I plunged two fingers inside her.

"Oh God—"

"No. Say my name, Yve. That's what I want from you.

I'll make you come harder than you've ever come in your life, but you have to scream my name so there's no doubt who's fucking you."

"Shut up. You're ruining this—"

I withdrew my fingers and spun her around before she could protest, pressing her forward over the countertop. My dick missed her touch instantly and I gripped it, focused on how good it would feel when I buried it inside her tight pussy.

Fuck. Condom.

I leaned over her and spoke into her ear. "Don't you dare move. I want this ass out and waiting for me, or I swear I'll make you beg for an hour before I let you come."

"What?" The single word came out on a moan.

"Don't move. I'm getting a condom."

She didn't reply, but I took her stillness for assent. I pulled my pants up over my cock and headed for the stairs. If she moved, then I'd jack off and pretend it was her sweet hand wrapped around my dick. If she didn't move . . . then I guess I'd have my answer as to whether she wanted me more than she hated me.

Condom in hand from my bathroom, I strode back to the kitchen. A smile stretched my lips when I saw Yve bent over in the exact position I'd left her.

"Good girl. I'm going to make you come so fucking hard, and I'm not even going to make you beg."

"Stop talking. Just fuck me."

By the time her words were out, I'd already rolled on the condom and positioned myself behind her. I pressed the head of my cock to her entrance, and the tight, wet heat taunted me. In that moment, I had something to prove.

She'd remember this moment for the rest of her damn life, and she'd be feeling me tomorrow.

"If this isn't the best sex you've ever had, I'll hand over the keys to my Aston."

Yve's husky laugh echoed through the kitchen. "Cocky bastard. I'll enjoy—"

I drove inside her before she could finish the sentence.

"Holy shit," I said on a breath, coming to a halt almost instantly. "You're so damn tight."

"I'm not screaming your name yet, Titan." Her hips bucked back into me, taunting me and daring me to take her. Knowing she was as desperate for this as I was ratcheted up my determination another notch.

Challenge. Accepted.

I pulled almost all of the way out and plunged back inside as I slid my hand around her hip to tease her clit. Setting a powerful, even rhythm, I fucked her until her moans turned to broken cries.

"Give it to me," I demanded.

"Shut up."

"Do you want me to stop?"

"Don't you goddamn dare—"

"Then you better tell me who's fucking you."

"Such an arrogant—"

I slowed, and her insult died.

"Just fuck me, Titan. God damn you."

Hearing my name on her lips, edged with the raggedness of her need, spurred me on harder and faster. Within minutes, Yve's inner walls fluttered around my cock. She was close. Holding off my own orgasm was testing the limits of my control.

"Give it to me, Yve. Let me hear you."

"Oh my God."

I pressed down harder on her clit.

"Titan!" Yve screamed as her muscles spasmed around me and she shuddered beneath me, her fingers gripping the far edge of the countertop.

"That works for me," I said, and then I let go. My own roar of triumph bounced off the high ceiling. My hips continued to pump of their own volition. She'd stolen my control, ripped an orgasm straight from my balls.

As soon as I finished, Yve shifted beneath me. I stepped back, sliding from her body and promising myself it wouldn't be long before I was back inside her.

This woman pushed all my buttons, taunted me, challenged me, mocked me. And the perverse son of a bitch that I was, I wanted more.

Yve slipped out from between me and the countertop, grabbed the robe off the floor, and shoved her shaking arms into the sleeves. Watching her, I rid myself of the condom, zipped my pants, and noted her heaving chest, wondering what she'd say next. I didn't have to wait long.

"I . . . I have to go."

"You need to eat," I reminded her.

She turned to the door, and my first instinct was to reach out and grab her hand to stop her, but her reaction from earlier in the conservatory surfaced vividly. Someone had hit her—that much was clear. I was determined to hear the whole story where that was concerned. I might be a prick, but I would rip a man's hands off if he raised them against a woman.

"Yve, stop."

I FROZE AT THE COMMANDING TONE OF HIS VOICE.
What the hell had I just done? I mean, beyond letting
Lucas Titan bend me over and bang me like a cheap
screen door on his kitchen counter.

Classy.

That's exactly what I was.

My inner muscles clenched in protest; apparently they
didn't give a crap about whether I was classy or not. My
body wanted more. That it was a problem of epic propor-
tions wouldn't be the understatement of the century.

Still motionless, I debated whether I should turn and
face him, but decided instead that I'd wait to see what he
said next.

Thirty seconds of awkward silence ticked by. I knew,
because I counted. Finally he spoke.

"Sit. Eat. I'll leave you alone."

My stomach growled again, the traitor, and I squeezed

my eyes shut. For the record, the awkwardness after hate-fucking on a kitchen countertop hugely outweighed the awkwardness after a drunken one-night stand. There was nothing to do but brazen it out.

Chin lifted, I spun, hoping I looked remotely composed. "You don't have to leave. After all, it's your house."

Avoiding his intense eyes, I grimaced at the unappetizing hummus. *No thank you, Mr. Titan.* But at least the flatbread would be decent. I reached for it, bypassing the round container. From the corner of my eye, I could see Titan's gaze tracking my movements.

"Not a fan of hummus?"

I shook my head, opting not to speak with my mouth full. *Mama would be so proud.* The mocking, throwaway thought skidded to a halt in my brain.

I was sitting in a billionaire's kitchen. I'd just let him— no, *begged* him—to screw me.

No, Mama wouldn't be proud; she'd wonder why I'd done it for free. Shame coursed through me at the realization that I was fucking another rich man. I'd made that mistake before, and look how that had ended. Would I never learn?

Every bit of moisture leached from my mouth, and I struggled to swallow the cracker as I stood. "You know what? I'm not really hungry. Thanks."

Titan's expression shuttered. I had no idea what he'd say. The man was as unpredictable as lightning strikes, and probably just as destructive.

"Did Levi show you a guest room?"

Good. I supposed that meant this awkwardness was coming to an end sooner rather than later.

71

"No. He just gave me the code and told me to make myself at home."

Titan barked out a harsh laugh. "Not surprising."

My curiosity got the better of me, and instead of running for the door, I asked, "Why does your brother work in my store?"

The word "my" struck me in the gut as soon as it was out of my mouth. Because it wasn't *my* store, and it might never be. I guess I'd see after my appointment at the bank with the loan officer.

Titan crossed his arms.

Jesus, the man was sexy. And an arrogant asshole. Wouldn't forget that part.

And he fucked like a god. *Couldn't* forget that part.

I snapped my mind out of the gutter as Titan responded, "Because he's still going through the rebellious teenager phase, even though he's no longer a teenager."

"And working at Dirty Dog is a rebellion?"

"When he could have a highly sought-after spot in the Titan Industries intern program? Yes."

"But he wants to be an artist, not work in corporate America."

The muscle in Titan's jaw ticked. "You think I don't know what my brother wants to do? Shockingly enough, I'm the one who pays his tuition. And he can want to be an artist all day, but eventually he's going to have to choose a career that will allow him to pay his own bills. He doesn't get access to the majority of his trust fund from our parents until he's thirty-five, and he needs to figure out how to support himself before then."

"And if he chooses to be a starving artist?" I asked.

"Then he'll starve. Or he'll hit it big and appreciate the hell out of his success because it required sacrifice."

"So, when does the gravy train end for Levi?"

"He's got three years of college left. I told him I'd cover him until then. If he decides to take longer, he's going to be on his own dime."

"You sound like his father, not his brother."

The muscle ticked more visibly. "Because I've been both for over a decade."

"What happened to your parents?"

"That's not up for discussion. If you're done here, I'll show you a room." He strode out of the kitchen. And that was apparently how Titan ended a conversation.

I tightened the belt on my robe and followed him. I wasn't sure where I expected him to take me, but it wasn't up the curving staircase and into a room that was sage green, gold, and white. It was altogether too fine for the likes of me.

I opened my mouth to protest, but Titan gestured to an open door. "There's an en suite bathroom. It should be stocked with anything you need. Did you leave your bag downstairs? In the pool room?"

I shook my head. "No bag. Wait, no. I left my purse on a chair in the foyer."

Titan's attention held on me. "You didn't even pack a bag? So, whatever chased you out of that house scared the hell out of you, didn't it?"

I stilled in my survey of the room. It wasn't any of his business, and I wouldn't share. But my skin prickled again at the thought of the glass in the dish rack. "I . . . I just wanted to get out. I don't need much anyway. I'll be fine. I'll change at work when I get there."

"And what makes you think you're going to feel safe at your place tomorrow when you go back there and no one has checked it out?"

He had a point, one I hadn't considered yet because I'd been too busy running, then swimming, then . . . Heat edged out fear at the memory of my cheek pressed to the cool granite countertop as Titan—

I shook it off. Not happening again. Besides, I had more important things to worry about than Lucas Titan.

"I'll have someone meet me there tomorrow to check it out."

"Fine," he said, nodding. "I'll get your purse."

He turned on his heel, leaving me in the delicately feminine bedroom, uncomfortably aware that I didn't belong here, despite the delicious soreness settling between my legs.

Lesson learned from Mama: *You could fuck a rich man, but that didn't mean you'd ever be welcome in the big house. Better never to set foot inside the door.*

But I wasn't a goddamn mistress. I'd never take that path.

Turning away from the door, I studied the bedroom. White lace hung from the windows, and a sleigh bed carved with roses and lilies dominated much of this side of the room. What looked like an antique divan, side chairs, and table made up a small sitting area near the wide bay window. An armoire matching the sleigh bed sat alongside a vanity table.

The room was incredibly ladylike, and it seemed completely at odds with Titan's overly masculine nature. It must have been like this when he moved in. I couldn't imagine him choosing any of this. Or maybe it was the work of an interior decorator?

I had very little time to explore before he reentered the room, my purse in hand. The big teal number looked ridiculous in his grip, and I might have imagined it, but he looked slightly amused as he handed it over.

"Thank you." I set my bag on the bed and had just shoved my hand inside it when he stepped up behind me.

He bent low, speaking into my ear. "You need anything else, I'm right next door."

I stilled as he leaned against me, the already growing bulge in his pants pressing against the crack of my ass.

Ignore, Yve. Ignore.

My eyes shot to the closed door on the far wall of the room as something dawned on me. This was the suite designed for the mistress of the house, back when husbands and wives slept in separate rooms and the husband visited the wife at night for his marital relations.

He should have put me in the servants' quarters.

Titan must have followed my glance to the door, because he added, "It's locked. From your side. Feel free to join me anytime. I'll be hard as fuck, thinking about taking you in the kitchen."

His raw words held no subtlety, and neither did the hand that gripped my waist and slid around to the front of the robe.

I could have jerked away, but when his palm slipped inside and covered my breast, I wasn't sure I even remembered how to breathe. I should hate his touch, but slickness gathered between my legs and would have made me a liar.

"Are you wet for me again, Yve? Are you thinking about how good it felt to have my dick stretching your tight little pussy?"

"I hate you," I murmured, pressing my ass into his erection and my breast into his palm.

His hand slid lower, fingers splaying out over me. "Fuck. You're so wet."

I swallowed back my moan, but couldn't fight the urge to rock against his hand. My clit was already sensitive, and rubbing against his palm put me right back on the edge within moments. But before I could come, he pulled his hand away and jerked back.

Shameless, I spun around, robe hanging most of the way open. "What the hell, Titan?"

"You want more, Yve? You come to me."

He strode to the threshold and shut the door behind him. The click barely echoed, but his words repeated through my brain over and over, along with my conclusion from earlier. *Lucas Titan is dangerous.*

I needed to put what had happened out of my head. Never to be repeated. Ever.

But when I slid naked between the ridiculously soft sheets of the bed, I could think of nothing but Titan. So was it any surprise that I dreamed of him?

No, the surprise was that I wished my dreams had been only of him, rather than peppered with flashes of the man who still haunted me.

Lucas

"So you decided to fend for yourself, but couldn't manage to put it away when you were finished," Jerome observed as he tossed the hummus in the trash. No matter how old I was, Jerome could always make me feel like I was sixteen again and had tracked muddy footprints all over a clean floor.

I had no excuse to give the old man; I'd been too caught up in Yve to remember to put the food back in the fridge.

"Actually, it wasn't for me. It was for someone else," I replied absently, wondering whether the woman in question would venture out this morning.

Why was I so fascinated with her? Apparently a sexy-as-hell body plus a disrespectfully sassy mouth were all it took to get my attention lately. I smiled to myself at the thought of her telling me to shut up and fuck her.

The smile instantly turned to a frown when my dick flexed in my pants, and Jerome's faded blue gaze snapped to

77

mine. Not the time or place for that thought.

He lifted one shaggy gray brow. "Care to elaborate?"

"An unexpected houseguest arrived last night."

"And why do I assume you're not talking about the snake I found in the laundry room this morning?"

"Because I rarely offer food to snakes."

We both heard the creaking in the ceiling that signaled someone moving around upstairs. In an old house, even though the walls and ceilings were thick, it was almost impossible not to step on something that would creak and give away your location. Levi had learned that the hard way when he was home on breaks from boarding school, and after he'd been kicked out of enough of those, military school.

"It seems your houseguest is still here." When the front door opened and shut, he amended wryly, "Or was here."

What the hell? Yve was just going to sneak out? I checked my watch. It was only just after seven. Perhaps she thought her exit wouldn't be noticed? She didn't realize that normally I was at the office by now, and I was altering my routine to figure out what to do with her.

"I'll be back."

Jerome's chuckle followed me out of the kitchen. "Finally, one who runs away from you, instead of throwing herself at you."

Funny.

Except Jerome didn't realize this wasn't the first time she'd run from me, and it was a habit that was starting to piss me off.

I yanked open the door and walked down the front path to the driveway. Yve was tugging on the gate and feeling around for the latch.

"You have somewhere pressing to be this morning, Yve?"

She turned and squared her shoulders, a pose that seemed to be her go-to when facing me. "Didn't want to overstay my welcome."

"Or say hello or maybe ask for a ride?"

"I don't need a ride. I can walk."

"And you wouldn't need to walk if you'd just asked."

Her chin went up. It was a gesture I was beginning to know well.

"What was I going to do? Knock on the door to your bedroom this morning? I don't think so." Her stance softened when she added, "I do appreciate the hospitality, though. I'm just . . . I need to be on my way."

I studied her flushed cheeks. "How many times did you think about that door last night and begging me for round two?"

Her eyes widened and her spine straightened again. "I didn't. At all."

I stepped forward and lifted my hand—slowly—to grasp a lock of her hair between my thumb and index finger. "Little liar."

"You wish."

"You're right—I do. Because if you'd come to me like I'd wanted, it would've been your lips wrapped around my cock instead of my hand. I will fuck you again. It was too damn good to let you walk away." I slid my hand into her hair and cupped the back of her head. "I spent all night wondering if you taste as good as I think you will."

Yve's mouth dropped open into a little O, and once

again color stained her cheeks. She blushed so easily, and it pushed me to shock her further. It also cemented my earlier decision.

I would have her again, and I always got what I wanted. I just wondered how hard she'd make me chase.

Yve's mouth snapped shut and her eyes narrowed. "Not gonna happen, Titan. Never." She enunciated both syllables of *never*, and I couldn't help but grin.

"Ahh, Yve." I released my grip and lowered my hand to skim down her body to her hip. She immediately took a step back, but was trapped by the fence.

That's right, sweetheart, nowhere to run now.

"You're telling me no, but every ounce of your body language is screaming at me to pin you to this gate and fuck you right here. It just makes me more dead set on having you again."

"Never," she whispered again.

I leaned down, bringing my face close to hers. "Lie to me all you want. I felt how hard you came in the kitchen and how fast I brought you to the edge in the bedroom. You can't make me believe you aren't dying to let go like that again."

"You don't know a damn thing about me, including what I want."

"Lying to yourself is pointless, Yve."

I squeezed her hip before sliding my hand down her thigh until I hit bare skin. She didn't stop me—didn't do anything but pin me with that challenging stare—as I slipped underneath her skirt and retraced my path until I hit . . . more bare skin.

I bit back a groan as I cupped her naked ass. "You're so

goddamn sexy, and if I were inclined to let another man see you, I'd take you right here up against this fence."

Yve's nostrils flared, and her throat bobbed as she swallowed. She said nothing, but her actions spoke louder. She pressed her ass into my hand.

I stared into her tawny eyes as I released my grip and skimmed my palm around to her front and covered her pussy. "You're so fucking wet for me. Again."

"I can't help it that my body wants you. Doesn't mean I'm gonna give in."

I smiled, feeling like a class-A predator. "You won't be able to resist, so why fight it?"

"Because you're a prick."

I laughed. "I've never been so entertained to be insulted by someone." I shifted my fingers so one covered her clit and pressed. When Yve sucked in a harsh breath, I slid one finger inside her. "And I still want to make you come, even after that. Are you going to let me? Or are you going to keep lying to us both?"

Yve's hands shot out and shoved hard against my shoulders. I released my hold on her instantly and stepped away, hands raised.

"Fine. Fight it. But you know where I'll be when you decide you want more."

"I won't."

"That's one of us then." I brought my hand to my face and sucked my fingers into my mouth. Sweet, tangy Yve. Fucking perfection. "And for the record, you taste amazing."

Her mouth dropped open, and I turned toward the house. "If you want breakfast before I give you a ride to get

81

your car, you can come back inside."

"Wait, my car's done?"

I knew that little nugget of information would get her attention. "It is. I'll take you to get it after breakfast."

"Just like that. You expect me to sit down and eat with you just like that? After you . . . you . . ."

I glanced behind me as I pulled the front door open, pleased to see that Yve was right on my heels. "After I copped a feel, figured out you weren't wearing panties, fingered you, and tasted your pussy? Yes."

Yve slowed and pinched the bridge of her nose. "You're a freak show. That's all I've got."

"I'm not the one going commando under a skirt."

"Shut up. I didn't have any clean underwear."

"I'm not complaining. Now, I believe you know your way to the kitchen."

Yve strutted ahead of me, her head held high while I hung back, watching her go.

She'd be back for more. I was confident of that.

Yve

WHEN I WALKED BACK INTO THE KITCHEN, I didn't expect to see a tall, thin man with a shiny bald head standing in front of the stove. He turned when I walked through the door, a big smile on his face.

"And here's the mysterious lady who had Lucas digging through my kitchen last night." He stepped away from the stove to hold out a hand. "I'm Jerome. I'm the master of all you survey, including Mr. Titan."

My eyebrows shot up. "Does he know that?"

I felt Titan's presence behind me without him touching me. And surprisingly—even after everything that had just happened—it didn't make me jumpy.

"He knows," Titan said. "He just lets Jerome continue his delusions. Or maybe I'm the one who's delusional," he added, his lips altogether too close to my ear for comfort. I had a feeling the man saw me as a challenge, and I needed to put that out of his head.

Jerome's faded blue eyes lit with a spark. "As they say, we're all mad here."

"Then I guess I fit in better than I thought." *Because I've got crazy down to a science*, I added to myself. That was the only explanation I had for not elbowing Titan in the gut right now.

Jerome's gaze scanned my attire. "I think you'll fit in just fine, Miss . . ."

"Santos. Yvonne Santos."

"It's a pleasure. Now, I'm making omelets for breakfast, if that suits your fancy. If not, I also make a mean crepe or a Belgian waffle."

"An omelet sounds lovely. Thank you."

While Jerome confirmed my preferences, I stepped to the side, needing to get the heat of Lucas Titan away from my back. I wouldn't give in. I needed to get back on solid ground. It didn't help that I glanced down at his flat stomach covered by a crisp white dress shirt.

"How do you not have an enormous gut having someone cook for you all the time?"

His tanned hand dropped to span across what I could picture as being a rigid six-pack. *What the hell, imagination? Seriously? Stop. You're not helping.*

"I swim. And run. And now I punch people."

Jerome's head swung around. "You mean you punch *pads*, Lucas. We don't punch people in this house."

Hearing Titan being taken to task like he was a five-year-old was enough to make me think that Jerome was right; they were all mad here.

The moment was broken by the buzz of technology. Titan dropped his hand from his shirt to reach into the pocket of his suit pants and withdraw a phone. He looked at the screen.

"Excuse me. I have to take this." His eyes lingered on mine for a moment. "Don't leave."

"Since you're apparently my ride, I don't think I have a choice."

"Good."

And then he was gone. My gaze dropped to his ass as he walked away. *Hot. Damn.*

Stop it, Yve.

"So, Ms. Santos, tell me about yourself."

I turned to Jerome to find a smile playing around the corners of his mouth, as he'd clearly been following the direction of my gaze. *This is embarrassing.*

"Not much to tell," I replied, hoping my cheeks weren't stained with my overactive blush. It was a trait I wished I could eliminate.

"Why do I think that's complete and utter bull?"

Well, now. We had a straight shooter on our hands.

"What do you want to know?" I asked.

"How'd you find yourself sleeping in this house last night?"

I glanced at the kitchen counter. *That* hadn't been sleeping. That had been . . .

I shook off the memory because here it was—the protective, *stay away from him because he's class and you're trash* speech. Not a first for me. It had just been a while.

"Levi offered me a place to stay when I had some trouble at my apartment." I held back the rest of the words that wanted to bubble forward. The ones that would assure him

I had no designs on Titan, or his ridiculous number of dollars.

"He's a good boy. Good heart." Jerome's gaze narrowed further, and I could swear his thoughts were being projected into the air in front of his head. Something along the lines of *You aren't going to get the money that way either, girl.*

"Levi works for me. At Dirty Dog."

Jerome's skeptical expression morphed into confusion and then something altogether unexpected. Surprise and warmth radiated from him as he said, "You're *Yve.*"

"Yeah, that's me."

"I didn't put it together. Young Levi has talked about you since he started at the store. You're the one with the keen eye for fashion and a bargain. And you were also the one who sold him a pair of impossible-to-find Chanel enamel earrings that matched the ones my sister lost thirty years ago. According to Levi, you were going to keep them for yourself and he begged just enough for you to concede and sell them. Thank you for that."

I knew exactly what he was talking about. They'd been mint green, enamel flowers with the little Chanel logo on one petal. Cute as hell. I'd gotten them for a steal, and was just about to put them on when Levi had started gushing about a woman he knew who'd lost the pair her husband had given her after the Korean War. The husband was dead, and she'd worn the earrings in their engagement photos.

Jerome gave me huge smile. "You made me the best brother on the face of the planet with those earrings. She cried rivers when I gave them to her."

"I'm glad she enjoyed them."

Obviously they were much more sentimental to her than to me, so I didn't mind giving them up. I was a sucker for a story like that; God knew I didn't have enough of them in my family. Our stories mostly went along the lines of *I didn't really have skills to get a job other than fucking a man, so I did that instead. Now he buys me pretty things.*

If Jerome only knew the illustrious line of mistresses I'd come from, he'd probably toss me right back out that door because he'd think for sure I was trying to get my hooks into Titan.

He'd be dead wrong. I wasn't sinking my hooks into any man. Except maybe that banker I planned to meet with. Him I would corner and cajole until I got the loan I needed. Because Yve Santos wasn't going to earn her dreams on her back. No. She'd earn them on the heels of stilettos while dressed in a power suit.

Which were in my apartment. That someone had been inside. And maybe that someone had been Jay. *Shit.*

I needed to woman up and go home and call a locksmith. And that was exactly what I'd do. After work. And maybe I'd work late. Because . . . that's what a good manager did.

"Ms. Santos, your omelet." Jerome slid a steaming plate in front of me.

Yum. An excellent way to take my mind off the things I couldn't control.

Speaking of which. "Should I wait for . . . uh . . . Mr. Titan?"

Jerome's kind smile seemed perfectly at home on his face. "You can call him Lucas, my dear. And there's no need. Who knows how long he'll be?"

Before I lifted the first bite to my mouth, I stopped. "Aren't you going to join me?"

He looked marginally surprised, but smiled. "Thank you, but I've had my steel-cut oats and coffee already."

It was awkward to dig in while he stood and watched, and I hesitated. As if he felt my discomfort, he turned, poured two cups of coffee, and joined me at the kitchen island.

"So, tell me more about this Dirty Dog of yours."

Lucas

I DROVE AWAY FROM THE REPAIR SHOP AND TOLD myself not to look in the rearview mirror at the woman I couldn't think about without getting hard. Yve was sexy, headstrong, and had a body that could stop traffic.

Sure, I'd been attracted in an academic sense to Vanessa Frost, even though it made me sound like a dick to admit it. She'd been the perfect Southern belle, all blond and curvy with a perfect pedigree.

The upper crust of New Orleans society was a closed group I hadn't been able to break into on my own. I'd needed a leg up, and blackmailing Vanessa to get me into events that would help me solidify my contacts had been an effective but assholish move. A few more events and maybe I would have been prepared for the open-ended favor that Johnson Haines wanted. As it was, his request pissed me off. I wasn't the kind of man who would ever willingly let someone else have the upper hand.

I needed to narrow down my list of pedigreed former debutantes to continue my push to the heart of NOLA's moneyed and influential families. There was one who had floated to the top, Valentina Noble, daughter of Judge Harold Noble. But I couldn't find the necessary enthusiasm to make the approach. Valentina was the kind of woman you courted and married, and I had absolutely no desire to go down that path.

And now my dick was on a hair trigger for Yve Santos. Her last name must have come from the Spanish influence around New Orleans, because she was clearly of Creole descent.

What the hell was it that made Yve so intriguing? I'd figure it out the next time I had her under me. But for now, I needed to get my head back into business.

I needed a new plan, and one had already started to form. The lobbyist had left his list of targeted senators, so I had other names to consider. I'd build my own coalition of support for my bill. After all, if you wanted something done right, you had to do it yourself.

Plan firmly in place, I headed to the office, determined to forget about Yve for now . . . and how I'd never be able to look at my kitchen island without picturing her bent over, taking my cock.

I would have her again. No other alternative was acceptable.

Yve

GIVEN THAT LEVI WOULD BE GONE FOR TWO WEEKS, I'd had to resort to a temp agency to send me some help for Dirty Dog. When I arrived at the shop, I automatically assumed the petite woman waiting out front was my temporary employee.

I smiled in greeting. "Hi, I'm Yve. Are you Jennifer?"

Her brow furrowed and her head jerked back. "How did you know my name?"

Oh Lord, they better not have sent me an idiot. "The temp agency gave it to me."

Her frown deepened. "What temp agency?"

Okay, this is getting strange. "The one sending me someone to help out for the next two weeks."

She shook her head. "I'm Jennifer, but I'm not *that* Jennifer."

I pressed my fingers to my temples. Today was going to be a long, rough day. I just had a feeling.

"I'm sorry for the confusion. The shop isn't quite open yet. If you'll give me half an hour, I'll be ready for you."

I needed a few moments to compose myself, along with some time to change into fresh clothes. The royal blue-and-black striped A-line dress I had in mind needed a quick steam before it would be wearable. The black platforms I was wearing would go just fine, and I could borrow jewelry from the display.

The woman, Jennifer, nodded and said, "I guess that's fine," and she walked away.

I unlocked the door, muttering to myself, "*I guess that's fine.*" Yeah, honey, it would be fine because that was when the damn store opened.

I slipped inside and flipped the lock behind me. Forgetting about her, I switched on the lights and made my way to start on the dress. The monotonous process of steaming allowed my mind to wander back to last night.

Lucas Titan had seen me naked. We'd had sex on his kitchen counter. He'd left me hanging on the edge of orgasm in the bedroom. And then this morning he'd fingered me in his front yard.

What the hell had I been thinking? Oh, that's right, I hadn't been thinking at all, I'd just been reacting. To his orders. His commands. His arrogance.

None of those things should turn me on. In fact, given my history, I should have been cringing away and retreating into myself, but—except for the one move that took me by surprise—I'd responded to his advances like a cat in heat.

There was clearly something wrong with me. I hated that he could get to me like that, make me *want* like that.

Stop, Yve. I resolved not to think about him anymore.

I had a shop to run, one I needed to figure out how to buy. That was my only priority.

Finally dressed and ready to kick off the day, I unlocked the door and propped it open invitingly. The woman from earlier was nowhere to be seen, but she'd seemed strangely determined—if showing up a half hour before we opened was any indication—so I expected that she'd be back.

And within a half hour she was.

The morning was slow, and having at least one customer poking around kept my mind off *him*.

Mostly.

"So, where do you find all of this stuff?" Jennifer asked from the front corner of the store.

She was practically drooling over the vintage Dior cocktail dress on the dress form, and easily the most expensive piece of clothing in the place. It was ice-blue satin with a ruched bodice and a sweetheart neckline. The crystals studding the dress matched the Swarovski crystal belt wrapped around the waist.

Secretly, I thought of it as the Cinderella dress, and every time someone approached it, I got a sick feeling in the pit of my stomach, worrying they might buy it. That was the problem with being a shopkeeper in such a kick-ass store—I wanted to save so many things for myself, and Lord knew, I did that already. Too much. But it just so happened that the Cinderella dress was in my size. It would undoubtedly make the woman who wore it feel like a princess.

Then I remembered that Jennifer—who that dress was *way* too big for—had asked a question.

"Oh, I have a network of people who keep an eye out for me. I also hit estate sales, keep up on eBay and a few vintage wholesale stores online. It's basically a never-ending cycle of hunting down awesome stuff."

"Wow. That sounds like a lot of work."

I shrugged. It *was* a lot of work, but I loved my job. Harriet had entrusted the shop to me for this long, and I'd made it my own. She'd never once had to worry about not having it fully stocked with unique inventory. I had several regulars who came in weekly because they knew I was constantly finding new stuff. For a few special customers, I took requests and kept an eye out for the particular pieces they wanted.

Jennifer stepped away from the Cinderella dress, and I silently breathed a small sigh of relief. She moved to the stacks of Seven jeans and dug through for her size, messing up all of Levi's perfect folding. It was a never-ending cycle. They messed; we straightened. She also pulled a skirt and a cherry-red dress out of the armoire and looked around the store.

"Fitting room?"

"Of course. Right this way." I led her toward the back and pulled the black-and-silver striped curtain open for her. "Let me know if you need any help with the zipper on that dress."

She smiled and shut the curtain. I crossed to the jeans table and began refolding and straightening. The task made me miss Levi, and also wonder where the hell Jennifer-the-temp was.

"So, how long have you worked here?" she asked from behind the curtain.

"Several years."

"Did the store carry all of the same kind of stuff before

you started working here and tracking it down, or did you do that?"

It was a more personal question than I'd expected, but I was proud of what I'd done here.

"It was more kitschy and commercial before I started. It took a decent amount of time to replace everything with stock that I'd handpicked."

"Wow, so this place wouldn't be the same without you, would it?"

Exactly. Which was why I was so determined to make Dirty Dog mine.

"I'd like to think I bring something special to the table," I replied, keeping my tone casual.

Jennifer shoved the curtain open and turned so her back was toward me. "Could you do up this zipper?"

"Of course. I'm happy to."

I was pulling the zipper tab up when she said, "I guess when I own this place, maybe I'll have to convince you to keep working here."

I froze, and my hands faltered on the hook and eye. I forced myself to finish and stepped away. "There. All set."

She didn't even look at me, didn't acknowledge the bomb she'd just dropped. She just took two steps toward the three-way mirror and twisted this way and that to view the dress.

Objectively, it looked lovely on her, the red against her fair complexion and blond hair. I wanted to rip it off her and tell her to get the hell out of *my* store.

Jesus, Harriet was moving fast. My appointment with the bank wasn't even until tomorrow, and she already had a potential buyer lined up?

I needed to talk to her. Tomorrow. After I had my ducks in a row. Determination steeled my spine and was the only thing that kept the tears burning in my eyes from falling.

Then the punches just kept coming.

"Do you think I could try on that blue dress up front?" she asked. "I think it could be altered to fit me."

Years of training myself to hold a serene expression even when I was getting the hell knocked out of me helped me fake a smile. I swallowed back the words I wanted to scream, and instead said, "I'll get it. Would you like me to unhook you from this one?"

She said yes, and I reversed the process I'd just completed, all the while keeping that vapid smile on my face. I'd taken three steps out of the dressing room when a phone started ringing, and it wasn't mine.

"Hey, baby," Jennifer cooed to whoever was calling her. "Oh, of course. I'll be right there. I can't wait either."

She hung up the call, and I heard the rustle of clothes. "I'll have to come back to try on the other one. I've got to go." She stepped out of the dressing room. "I'll take the red one if you can wrap it up real quick."

"Of course." My movements were wooden as I ran her credit card, wrapped the dress in tissue, then put it into one of Dirty Dog's signature bags and tied it shut. I handed it over the counter.

She winked. *She fucking winked.* "I'm sure I'll be seeing you soon. It was so nice chatting, Yve."

And then she was gone. As soon as the door chimed, I sank onto the stool behind the counter and dropped my head into my hands. "No way. I can't. I just can't."

"You can't what?"

I jumped off the stool as the deep voice scared the ever-loving shit out of me. Titan stood in front of me. The door hadn't chimed again, had it? I was losing my mind.

"Jumpy?"

I pressed a hand to my pounding heart and sucked in a breath as I ignored his question. "If you're here for round two, you might as well turn around and walk your ass right back out the door."

I had no idea where *those* particular words came from, and immediately wanted to snatch them back. I was supposed to be pretending last night had never happened.

His green eyes lit with something, and I absolutely did *not* want it to be a challenge. *No. Hell no.*

"I dare you to lock that door and flip the sign to closed. I'll take you right here." He nodded to where I stood at the counter behind the register, and his voice lowered to a husky growl. "I'll bend you over just like I did in my kitchen."

The words sent ripples of heat through me, and my nipples hardened against the thin cups of my bra. He was going to see them; he wouldn't be able to miss them.

I held his stare, not wanting him to see how easily my body responded to him. "Never gonna happen."

"For every time you tell me *never*, I'm going to make you beg longer to come the next time I have you."

"Go to hell," I spat out, hating that my inner muscles clenched, the ones I could still feel him pounding into. I'd been so right; the man was dangerous.

His eyes dropped for a beat as his smile darkened. "I've been there, and it's not pleasant. I think I'd prefer to stay here and see how much harder I can make those pouty little nipples of yours."

So much for him not noticing. I needed to put a stop to this conversation right now.

"What do you want, Titan? I've got a shop to run."

As if he'd flipped a switch on his entire demeanor, he stiffened and the heat drained from his eyes. "The garage called me. They forgot to clear the codes on your car, so I'm guessing your service lights are on."

What? "Um, I didn't notice. Maybe?"

This time his smile was very male and very patronizing. Before he could say anything further—and I could tell him to shove his patronizing smile up his ass—the door opened and a group of five women entered the store.

Shit. Tourists. A necessary evil.

Instantly they started crowing over finds, their grabby hands messing up my displays. I should have been thrilled about their excitement, but today I just wasn't in the mood, not when I was manning the place all alone.

"I have to help them."

Titan nodded as if dismissing me. *The dick.* "Do what you need to do."

I slipped out from behind the counter and sidestepped him, not willing to get any closer than absolutely necessary because my body couldn't be trusted around the man. With that in mind, I decided the tourists were not a necessary evil, but rather a sign of divine intervention.

They fired questions at me and I scurried around, answering them and hauling clothes to the fitting room. Ten minutes later, Titan was still leaning against the counter.

"Why are you still here?" I hissed at him. "Don't you have something better to be doing? Like making another million or something?"

He eyed me. "Levi's gone, so you're running this place alone?"

I shrugged. "I need to call the temp agency and bitch them out because the girl who was supposed to come help was a no-show."

Titan nodded. "Give me your keys. I'll take your car over to the garage and bring it back."

I couldn't stop the belly laugh that hit me. "You're my errand boy now? Did I trip into an alternate universe? You gonna leave me the keys to your Aston too?"

His eyes hardened. "I don't leave anything undone. And considering I took this task on, I'll finish it."

Whoa. I'd pricked some kind of nerve there.

"Could you help me with this zipper," one woman called out from the dressing room.

"I'll be right there."

Sighing, I reached under the checkout counter and dug my keys out of my purse. I looked up at Titan, completely unsure of what to make of this man and his seemingly multiple personalities.

I took the simplest route, wanting this strange interaction to be over. "Thank you."

He took the keys and walked out without another word.

It wasn't until I was ringing up the purchases of the group of tourists that I noticed the Aston's keys just behind the register.

No. Way.

The next hour was pure craziness. Tourists had apparently

all decided that today was the day to shop at Dirty Dog. It seemed that my signature bags were being carried around the Quarter, and word of mouth was responsible for the abnormal foot traffic. It was good for business and kept me running my ass off, which in turn kept me from thinking about Titan.

When the door chimed again, I fought the urge to sigh. I needed a break. I was hungry and I was tired, because Lord knew I didn't sleep last night for a multitude of reasons. So combine those two things together, and I was getting downright *hangry*. Hungry-angry. Not a good thing for the proprietor of a store to be. I plastered a smile on my face to welcome the newest guest. My brow furrowed when I saw it was Jerome, Titan's man-of-all-things.

My brain finally kicked back into gear. *He must be returning my car and retrieving the Aston's keys.* Apparently the master only had so much time to assist peasants. *Fine by me.* I didn't think I could handle another encounter with Titan today.

Why didn't he send Jerome in the first place?

I studied the old man and my eyes halted on the bag in his hand. Normally people left here with bags; they didn't enter with a paper sack giving off some of the most tempting aromas I'd smelled all day.

The last browsing couple called a quick thank-you as they pushed open the door and left, leaving me alone with Jerome.

He set the bag on the counter. "I heard you were short-handed, so I've brought lunch and have come to offer up my services."

What in the world? "Titan sent you to . . . help?"

"He actually told me to locate a temp agency to find someone with suitable qualifications, but I decided that after all the chattering Levi has done about this place, it was my turn to play shopkeeper. If you'll have me, that is."

My smile was wide and genuine this time. "I'd love to have you. Thank you so much. I'm . . . stunned."

He grinned. "I was also instructed to return your car and retrieve the keys to Mr. Titan's vehicle."

Which was as I figured, but I still rolled my eyes. "He tell you to check for scratches too?"

Jerome shook his head. "Not at all. He did mention that you need a new vehicle, however. Apparently the indignity of driving a Jetta not from this decade nearly unmanned him."

I laughed at the visual of Titan driving around in my Blue Beast. "I'm sure."

"Now that I'm temporarily hired, you are taking a break to eat."

I looked at the bag. "Lunch?"

"Yes. Mr. Titan was very concerned that you might not have had time to feed yourself properly, and I was instructed to make sure you ate."

What the hell? I didn't like this guy meddling in my life. I was a grown woman, completely capable of taking care of myself. I didn't need someone else trying to do it for me.

I didn't realize I'd mumbled the words aloud until Jerome replied quietly, "He can't help but meddle. He's a fixer, my dear."

My eyes jerked up to Jerome's blue ones. "I shouldn't have said that."

"It's fine. I know he doesn't come off as the most kind

and thoughtful man, but there's a lot you don't know about Mr. Titan."

Uh-oh. We were treading into dangerous territory here. "I think I'm probably better off not knowing. Except for you helping me out today while I straighten out the temp situation and his brother working here when he gets back from his trip, I don't think I'll ever have another encounter with *Mr.* Titan."

I emphasized the "mister" and I had no idea why. To raise some kind of mental barrier? Whatever.

I pushed the thoughts away and rubbed my hands together. "So, what did you bring?"

Jerome unloaded a prime rib sandwich dripping with juice, along with hand-cut potato wedges and a green salad.

My eyes widened. "Dang, I should be paying you instead of putting you to work."

"Nonsense. I quite enjoy feeding people. It's my nature. Now eat, while I familiarize myself with the merchandise."

I began to eat, tucking away the sandwich first—it was heavenly—and then digging into the wedges and salad. Jerome made a silent circuit around the shop and on his second pass, he began shooting questions at me. Mostly how old were several pieces of the jewelry, and what was their provenance.

When he reached the Cinderella dress, he stopped and sighed. "This would look lovely on you, my dear. You'd be quite the belle of the ball in this dress."

I laughed. "Considering I'm not going to any balls, I think it's better on that display."

He turned to look at me. "But what if someone else buys it? That would be tragic."

My smile died. "I can't keep them all, Jerome. Otherwise I'd be living in the back room instead of my apartment."

"Understandable, but surely . . . This one, it's exquisite."

"They're all exquisite, trust me. I need to have some willpower."

"Speaking of your apartment, you had some sort of trouble there? Have you sorted that out yet?"

The lunch I'd just eaten rolled in my stomach, and I forced a smile. "It'll be fine. I'll handle it today after I get out of work. I just got spooked, is all. You'd think that a girl who'd grown up in Tremé wouldn't be capable of being spooked."

Jerome turned and crossed the shop to stand in front of the counter. "I think we're all capable of being spooked. Do you want to tell me about it?"

"It's fine. Not an issue."

Surprisingly, I did feel the urge to spill and tell him everything. Was it his kind blue eyes, or the way he seemed to be so even-tempered? It had taken me a lot of years to trust my gut again when it came to people, but my instincts told me that Jerome was a good person—and a good ally.

But his close connection to Titan stopped me from sharing my entire life story. It was a sad one anyway—married at eighteen, broken ribs by my husband at nineteen, and still I stayed with him for another two years, perfecting my makeup skills covering bruises. No, I wouldn't share that. I didn't want to see those kind eyes shadowed by pity.

Jerome raised a gray eyebrow. "If you change your mind, the offer does not have an expiration date, my dear."

I was saved from having to reply by the chime of the

door and four new customers.

Oh Lord, these girls already had beads and their hands were wrapped around plastic hurricane glasses. This would be interesting.

Lucas

YVE'S CAR WAS A PIECE OF SHIT. I HAD THE mechanic doctor the bill to show that it only cost $300 to get it fixed, when in reality the thing was barely fit to be on the road. I had a strong suspicion that Yve would insist on paying me back, and there was no way in hell I would let her give me the five grand it had actually cost to make the Jetta safe enough to drive.

Idly, I wondered if she'd noticed the keys to the Aston. Even more, I was curious if she'd actually take it for a spin. Knowing her, she would never even think about leaving the shop while it was open, but it amused me all the same to leave the keys as an answer to her taunt.

I was not a good man. I didn't have a heart of gold; I had a heart that knew how to make gold. Midas was the comparison I received most often. But it seemed the project in front of me was going to turn to shit rather than gold.

Knowing that Yve was in good hands with Jerome, I

105

forced my thoughts away from her. He was former British Special Forces, and even at the ripe old age of seventy, he could still kill a man with his bare hands. He could also make even the most stubborn woman unbend a rigidly stiff spine.

Shit. I was thinking about her again. This wasn't acceptable.

The door to my office opened and Colson entered. Finally, a welcome distraction.

"Have you contacted the senators on my list?" I asked, not wasting a breath on greetings or small talk. That wasn't how Colson and I worked.

"Yes. Hendricks and Shuman are willing to meet for dinner to discuss it. They of course picked the priciest place in town, and you know it's on your dime."

"Like I care."

"I know you don't, but I never cease to be amused by the greed of some of these politicians."

"Good. What else?"

Colson said nothing but his gaze darted to the windows, telling me there was something he didn't want to share.

"What?" I asked.

"Have you thought about just agreeing to Haines's request? It's one favor. Your marker. It's really not that big of an ask, Lucas, and it would get us over the finish line without having to deal with all these other politicians and environmental groups."

The question was a fair one, but that didn't mean it didn't grate on me. "I don't pay you to question my judgment. I'm not going there unless we have no other alterna-

106

tive."

Colson shrugged. "Your choice."

And it was. This was my empire, and no one but me would decide how it moved forward.

But it seemed Colson wasn't done. "I know how much this means to you—"

"*Don't*. Do not fucking psychoanalyze me. This is business."

Colson crossed his arms and stared me down. "Anyone else might believe you, but I know the truth. You won't be able to rest until you've proven your father wrong—and made billions doing it."

I slammed my palms down on my desk. "Leave it alone."

"You wanna lie to yourself, go for it."

I'd said something very similar to Yve earlier, and I hated having my own words thrown back at me.

"Get out. Go do your damn job."

Colson nodded. "Fine. Be a stubborn bastard."

A S I FLIPPED THE OPEN SIGN TO CLOSED, I COULD
feel Jerome's eyes on me even as I heard him
shuffling around the interior of the store. He'd been
an amazing help today. We'd been inundated with people,
and while I could have survived without him, I would've
had a lot more unhappy customers because they would
have been waiting much longer while I helped others.

Wondering if my unease at going home was actually
visible, I frowned. The shrewd old man seemed to read me
too easily. His next words answered that question.

"I'm more than happy to follow you to your apartment
and lend my assistance in any way I can."

"That's very sweet of you, really," I said with what I
hoped looked like an unconcerned shrug. "But I'm fine.
Besides, you probably have the master's dinner to prepare."

I'd gotten used to Jerome's easy chuckle during the afternoon we'd spent working together. It rippled across the

store again.

"The master rarely dines at home in the evenings."

I bet he doesn't. Probably wining and dining half the town, especially the female half.

Whether I wanted to admit it or not, Lucas Titan was one of the sexiest men I'd ever seen. He made tall, dark, and handsome his bitch. The man had to be at least six foot three, and had thick, black hair that always seemed perfectly styled without trying. Add his dark green eyes, wide shoulders, and narrow hips to the mix, and there weren't many women who wouldn't pause to watch him walk by. The diagonal scar slashing upward through his left eyebrow into his hairline added an undeniable hint of danger.

My body lit up at thoughts of him, and I tamped the reaction down. Not going there. Again. It didn't matter how hot the sex had been; it wasn't worth my pride.

I pulled my purse from beneath the counter. "Thank you again for your help today." I was stalling on this last part and couldn't believe I was actually going to say the words, but I needed to give thanks where it was due. "And thank Mr. Titan as well. Sending you was very thoughtful of him."

Jerome inclined his chin. "Your thanks is accepted and will be passed on to Mr. Titan." He walked toward me. "Now, would you at least make an old man feel somewhat useful by taking my phone number in case you run across something troubling at your apartment again?"

"Sure," I replied. Didn't mean I'd ever call it, but it was a sweet offer.

"Good," he said before rattling off the digits, and I punched them into my phone.

We both left the shop, and I locked up behind us. My Jetta was parked at the curb and Jerome climbed into the Aston, which honestly didn't look that unusual parked on the streets of the Quarter. This area was prime real estate, which translated to *big money*. Which was why I was going to need a hell of a lot of cash to buy Dirty Dog from Harriet.

I waved good-bye as he drove off, and I got into my own car. A piece of paper sat on the seat. Picking it up, I saw the bold handwriting across the bottom. *Paid in full*. It was the invoice for my car repair.

When I saw the total, I breathed a sigh of relief. Three hundred bucks. *That* I could handle. And I'd make sure Titan got a check from me ASAP. I wouldn't let the man buy me a damn thing.

As I drove home, I debated whether to mail it to his office or his house, and still hadn't made up my mind when I pulled into the back alley parking spot for my apartment. After turning off the engine, I eyed the exterior stairs for a good five minutes, but didn't exit the car.

I decided to make a call before I got out. Quickly scrolling through my phone's contacts, I found her number.

"Hey, it's Yve," I said when Valentina picked up.

"Hey, I know."

"You hear anything from your daddy's PI? About Jay? Where he might be?"

"Not yet. Daddy has him giving us daily updates, and this morning's was a joke. Jay has disappeared. Daddy is pissed, and he actually hired me a bodyguard until they find him. The cops have increased patrols in my neighborhood too. I bet if you called in a concern, they'd do it for you too."

Right. Because the cops would run extra patrols in Tremé because one scared nobody of a woman had no proof of anything. Unlikely. I thought of the detective Titan had offered to call. I bet he could have made it happen, but then again, what couldn't he make happen?

Stop it, Yve, you're sounding complimentary about the man.

"Well, stay safe, honey. I'll be fine," I said.

"I will, Yve. Watch your back. I don't trust that bastard."

Before she could hang up, I asked, "Have you seen anything weird? Like signs that Jay might've been around you? In your house?"

Valentina actually laughed. "This place is locked down tighter than Fort Knox. No way in hell he could get in here. My dad made me move home the second we lost our bid to have his parole denied again."

So maybe I was the only crazy one here.

"Good. Take care, Valentina."

"You too, Yve."

After I hung up, I took what I hoped was a deep, courageous breath and climbed out of my car. I tucked my hand into my purse and wrapped my palm around the grip of my revolver. I would never be defenseless again.

I climbed the stairs, unlocked the door, and pushed it open. As soon as I was inside, I withdrew the gun from my bag and held it tightly in both hands in front of me as I walked through every room of my place. I studied every surface, every item, looking for anything that might have been moved. I found nothing.

Saving my bedroom for last, I stepped inside. Everything looked exactly the same, right down to the rumpled sheets on my unmade bed, something that had driven Jay absolutely insane and had earned me that first cracked rib. The drawers to my dresser were all still halfway open, a bad habit that during my marriage had earned me a broken finger, courtesy of being slammed in the drawer as he shut it to prove his point.

The joints and bones in question twinged in horrific memory. But there was nothing else out of place that I could identify. I turned to walk out of the room, but froze three steps from the door.

The mirrored tray where I put my night creams and perfume had an empty space. Chanel No. 5 was gone.

It had been Jay's favorite scent, and when I'd first gotten away from him, I'd refused to wear it for that very reason. But it was also my favorite perfume, so I'd decided I wouldn't let him steal that small piece of me. I'd bought a new bottle and wore the perfume whenever the hell I felt like it, but it was gone.

I went to check the bathroom on the off chance *I'd* moved it. It wasn't there, and I couldn't remember moving it.

Someone has been in my apartment.

The same gut-twisting panic from yesterday stole over me, but this time I shoved it down. I wasn't going to let that man run me out of my own house. I *would not.* This was my home, and if I left again, I'd be letting him win.

Instead, I picked up my phone and Googled the number of a twenty-four-hour locksmith and a security company. Both agreed to be here within the hour.

I would feel safe in my own home, goddamn it.

I would *not* let him win.

THE NEXT DAY, I WALKED OUT OF THE BANKER'S office and into the lobby with the knowledge that it didn't matter whether I wore a designer power suit and kick-ass pumps, or ratty old jeans and a T-shirt. I was wearing the former, and the business loan officer had still told me in no uncertain terms that there was no way in hell they'd lend me what I needed to buy Dirty Dog.

I doubted they'd loan me even ten dollars, and what I'd asked for was exponentially more. All my neatly calculated numbers and projections, and proof of past successful management and profit—none of it meant a damn thing because I wasn't what the bank considered a "safe bet."

I shouldn't have been surprised, and yet the decision hit me with the force of one of Jay's blows to the gut. I was barely conscious of my surroundings when an uncomfortably familiar deep voice called out my name.

"Yve?"

I looked up. The man seemed to show up everywhere lately. Was it some kind of cosmic joke?

I nodded at Titan and continued toward the door, but he crossed the marble floor of the bank quickly, his big strides eating up the space between us.

His hand on my arm stopped me. "What are you doing here?"

I was still hovering embarrassingly on the edge of tears at the banker's no-nonsense words informing me that neither this bank nor any other bank in the state of Louisiana would be willing to take a chance on me. The last thing I wanted to do was look Titan in the eye and have him see my despair.

I squeezed my eyes shut and hastily pulled myself together before raising my chin to meet his green gaze. "Am I not allowed in a bank?" I asked, my tone sharp.

His eyes narrowed. "What happened?"

Could he really read me so easily? Didn't matter; I wasn't going to lay it all out. Especially not in the lobby of a bank when I was feeling like ghetto trash.

"Mr. Titan, it's a pleasure to see you," the loan officer said from behind me. "We're so happy you could join us for the board meeting."

Titan ignored him, his eyes never leaving mine.

Irritation flooded me that the same loan officer who'd basically tossed me out of his office kowtowed to Titan. But then again, everyone did.

"Looking for a loan?" Titan asked me.

"None of your business. Now, I need to get to work."

Titan's hand tightened the slightest fraction around my arm, enough to make me want to tug it away and run, but

I didn't.

"Mr. Titan, I didn't realize you were . . . uh . . . acquaint- ed with Ms. Santos," the banker said as he came closer.

Titan released my arm and I started to step away, but found myself pulled flush against his side. "Yes, Yve is a friend of the family."

I'm a friend of the family? Since when?

"I hope you were able to assist her with whatever she came in for."

The loan officer's face paled a shade. "Well, you see . . . we weren't able to . . . Ms. Santos isn't exactly . . ."

My eyes snapped to the banker's. "Wow, and here I thought whatever we discussed in your office was confi- dential. I think I'll be going now." I tugged away from Titan again, but he held me fast.

"That's very disappointing to hear. As is the fact that you'd discuss her business with me." The reprimand in Ti- tan's tone was sharp and cutting.

"Um, I'm . . . I'm so sorry, sir. I—"

"Don't worry, I'm sure your boss will be happy to send you through another round of confidentiality training, just to make sure you truly understand the concept."

"Yes, sir. Of course. I will notify him myself."

"You do that."

If I hadn't been absolutely humiliated and livid, I might have found some humor in the conversation, but as it was, I just wanted to get the hell out of this godforsaken bank.

I jerked out of Titan's grip. "I have to get to work."

I didn't wait for a response as I rushed to the door. But before my hand could land on the wide metal bar to push it open, a larger hand beat me to it.

I shook my head. *Whatever.* Apparently Titan decided now was the appropriate time to employ manners. I couldn't care less; I just wanted to be gone. I needed to lick my wounds in private and begin working on Plan B.

He pushed open the second door for me, and I stepped out into the parking lot, heading for my car.

"Yve, stop."

"Told you, I'm late. My temp is actually supposed to show up today. I don't want to take the chance that I'm not there and she just leaves."

"Give me two goddamn seconds, and I'll let you go."

The nerve of the man. "You don't get to *let* me do anything, Titan."

I didn't slow until I reached my car. I fumbled in my purse for my keys, and once I had them in hand, I jammed one into the keyhole in the door.

"Your remote works now."

My head jerked toward Titan of its own accord. He stood, arms crossed, not even five feet away from me.

"What?"

"The remote, I had them fix it."

I hadn't even tried it. I pushed the button and, sure enough, the lights flashed and the locks clicked open.

"Getting the remote fixed on top of everything else would've put that repair bill over $300," I said. Realization dawned, and I glared at him. "You had them change the bill, didn't you?"

He shrugged. "I admit nothing."

I spun on my heel and took the two steps necessary to close the distance between us. As I shoved a hand against his chest, I tried not to notice how rock hard it was.

He didn't budge, but he did slap a palm over my hand to hold it in place. "That wasn't nice, Yve."

"Fuck you, Titan. I'm not nice."

"Neither am I," he growled. "Which is why I'm not going to apologize for doing this."

Before I could move—or even breathe—he ducked his head and his lips landed on mine. His hand wrapped around my hip and dragged me against him. I opened my mouth to protest, but he used the move to his advantage, and his tongue delved inside.

Jesus, Mary, and Joseph, the man could *kiss*. Suddenly I wasn't shoving him away. Instead, my hand wrinkled his starched shirt as I grasped it to hold him close. A deep vibration emanated from his chest, and I felt it all the way to the marrow of my bones.

I kissed him back, taking from him just as much as he took from me. It was a struggle for power, for dominance, and I was clueless as to who was winning. Somewhere in the back of my mind, a hazy voice screamed, *Stop! No kissing!* But I ignored it. I hadn't been really kissed in so damn long. And it was safe to say I'd never been kissed like this.

One moment his lips were pressed to mine, his tongue taunting me, and the next I was standing a full two feet away from him, watching the rapid rise and fall of his chest.

"Why the hell did you do that?" I demanded, unapologetically wiping the back of my hand over my lips as if to clean the taste of him from me.

Fat chance of that happening. I'd never forget what Titan tasted like. Spice and dominant man. Who knew *sexy as hell* had a flavor? Dairy Queen could make a killing.

Damn it. Focus, Yve.

"Because I wanted to." His green eyes blazed with heat and anger, and I wasn't even sure what else.

What the hell did he have to be angry about? He was the one who kissed *me*. *I* should be the angry one here. And I was. It had been my boundary—and he'd crashed right through it.

"Don't do it again. Not unless you want my palm print on your face."

A smug smile tugged at the corners of his lips. "For a woman who didn't want to be kissed, your participation was enthusiastic."

"Go to hell," I snapped. Turning on my heel, I stomped back to my car, yanked open the door, and practically threw myself inside. When I tore out of the parking lot, Titan was still watching my every move.

He was a dick.

But a dick who could kiss.

Lucas

WELL, THAT WAS A FIRST.

What was it about Yve Santos that made me absolutely insane? The challenge? Her sassy mouth? The way she practically vibrated with disdain for me?

God, I must have been some serious kind of twisted because whatever it was, I wanted more of it.

I waited outside a few minutes, to let my body calm the hell down, before I went back into the bank for the board meeting. James Richards, the loan officer I'd taken to task in front of Yve, scurried up to me.

"Mr. Titan, I'm so sorry. I didn't realize that Ms. Santos was a friend of yours."

"What was she here for?" I asked.

His eyes widened with shock. "But, sir, you said that I shouldn't—"

"Answer the damn question if you want to keep your

119

job," I ordered.

"Well, she wanted a loan to buy the business she currently manages. I believe it's called Dirty . . . something."

"Dirty Dog."

"Yes, that's it."

"And you turned her down." It wasn't a surprise. The bank turned down a high percentage of applications, especially for risky small businesses.

"Yes, sir."

"How much?"

His eyebrows shot up. "I shouldn't—"

"How much?" I repeated.

He rattled off a number, and I nodded. "Now, go learn how to keep your clients' information confidential."

"But, sir?"

I walked away.

So Yve wanted to buy Dirty Dog. Interesting. From everything Levi had rambled on and on about his boss, she ran the business independently for an absentee owner, and by his estimation, it was a profitable business. Levi actually knew more about business than one would think, given that he'd soaked it up hanging around me. I rarely talked of anything else, despite his constant protest when he was a kid.

Now I had to wonder—what would Yve do next? How determined was she?

With anyone else, I would have taken the information and filed it away to be employed at a useful time, but with Yve, my curiosity was piqued to a ridiculous degree. Also, with anyone else, I would have relayed my orders to Colson to find out what was going on, but I still remembered the way he'd looked at her in the kitchen of the gym. He wanted her.

Possessive instincts flooded me once more. She wasn't for him. Which meant I'd handle this matter personally.

And the thought of the gym gave me my next source of information. I was due to pay Con a visit to see how he was spending the cool mil I'd dropped on that boxing lesson. I'd decided to consider myself a patron of the place, which would piss him off to no end. But if he was willing to bargain, I'd be willing to pay for more information about Yve.

Might seem shady to some, but I was a man who got what I wanted, and damn the means.

Decision made, I flipped open my board packet and settled in to listen to the meeting.

Two hours later I was pulling into the parking lot of the gym. It was probably a crapshoot as to whether my car would still be here when I came out, but considering Con's Harley and Lord's 'Cuda were parked there and unharmed, I took the chance.

But then again, people in this neighborhood actually *liked* them. I was *persona non grata*, even before the boxing lesson. But what Con didn't know was that he no longer had to worry about me trying to steal his woman; my interests had moved firmly elsewhere.

I knocked on the heavy steel door and pressed the buzzer. A solid two minutes later, the center plate in the door slid open and Reggie's dark brown eyes peered out.

"Whatcha want?"

"To talk to your other coaches."

"They're busy."

"I'll wait."

He slammed the metal plate home, and I wondered if I'd be waiting in my car. But Reggie apparently decided that I passed muster because the door swung open.

"You can help Vanessa and Elle in the kitchen while the boys finish up. Don't need no flashy distractions. Or cheap shots."

I looked down at my three-piece Armani suit. Was the old man insane? *No, I'm the crazy one because I'm here looking for answers.* But my need to know kept growing. I'd get what I came for and get the hell out.

I started toward the kitchen, but Reggie stopped me with a hand on my arm. "You try anything with Ms. Vanessa, and Con'll rip your dick off."

"Duly noted."

"Better be."

He continued down the hall, and I turned into the kitchen doorway. Vanessa Frost and Elle Snyder stood near a prep table covered with paper sacks, loaves of bread, peanut butter, jelly, apples, pudding cups, granola bars, and a mess of other stuff.

"Ladies."

Both their heads shot up at my greeting.

"What the hell are you doing here?" Elle demanded without preamble.

"Came to see how Con was spending my donation."

Vanessa's hands propped on her hips. "After your move? You're lucky Reggie let you in the door. Just when I think you aren't a total asshole, you always surprise me, Lucas."

She nodded to the table. "You want to see what your money is doing? Well, here's part of it. We've expanded our sack supper program a little and we're hoping to do even more. In the gym you'll see some new equipment, and a bunch of new pads and headgear for the kids as well."

"Good to know it's going to good use."

"Did you think it would go to bad use?" Elle asked, her tone wry.

"Not at all."

"You back to get your ass kicked? I'm sure Lord would be happy to take you on." This also came from Elle.

I looked down at my clothes. "Not interested."

Elle shrugged. "I'm sure the guys have extra clothes. And they'd probably love to throw some punches at you. I don't think that would ever get old. If you're lucky, you might be able to walk out under your own steam."

I laughed at the feisty little redhead. "Reggie has barred me from the gym until they're done training."

"And you're listening to orders these days?" Vanessa asked, a reluctant smile tugging up one corner of her mouth.

She'd been the most beautiful woman I'd ever seen—until very recently.

"When it suits my purpose," I replied, deciding I'd had enough small talk. "I seem to have made the acquaintance of a friend of yours, one who has run into some trouble lately."

"Friend? I doubt you travel in the same circles as *our* friends," Elle shot back.

"Yve Santos isn't someone you consider a friend?"

"How the hell do you know Yve?" Elle set down the

peanut butter knife and wiped her hands on a paper towel as she stepped toward me.

"It seems she employs my brother at Dirty Dog."

Elle's head tilted to one side for a beat. "The hipster kid who drives a Karmann Ghia?"

I nodded. "Yes, that's Levi."

"He's your brother? And here I thought you were hatched from the spawn of the devil."

"Elle," Vanessa said in a warning tone. "Be nice. If Lucas is here out of concern, we don't need to bust his balls too hard."

Hearing crass words from the regal blonde amazed me. "Leahy really has rubbed off on you."

"In the very best way possible," she replied with a grin. "But we were talking about Yve."

"Tell me about her," I prompted.

"How about you start with explaining your cryptic-as-shit statements about her being in trouble," Elle said.

"Has she mentioned anything to you about why she was afraid to stay in her apartment the night before last?"

Elle and Vanessa looked at each other. Both their heads swiveled back to me, and they looked confused. "No. Why?"

"Because she ended up at my house."

Elle's nostrils flared. "If you took advantage of her, I swear I will skin you alive and roast your balls over an open fire."

I stared down the little redhead. "I'll be sure to let Lord know that you're so interested in my balls."

"Dick."

I raised an eyebrow.

Elle's shoulders relaxed the slightest bit, and she lifted a hand to her mouth. "Shit. I wonder . . ."

"What?"

"Nothing. It's really none of your damn business, and if Yve wants you to know, she'll tell you."

Women. Stubborn as hell. Elle's defiant expression told me that demanding more answers would get me nowhere, so I tried a different tack.

"What about buying Dirty Dog? You know about that?"

Elle's eyes lit up. "She's really going to do it? Yay! I was so worried that she wouldn't dive in. That's so awesome."

Vanessa frowned. "I didn't even know it was for sale."

Elle filled her friend in, and the information proved to be exactly what I'd come here to learn—at least on that topic.

"Harriet is selling off all the businesses she owns. She's officially retiring from everything, except she didn't really tell Yve. Yve found out because Harriet got a letter from her business broker, and Yve opened it. Shit, Van. She was devastated. That shop is her life. It wouldn't be what it is without her." Elle's eyes shot to me. "But you didn't hear any of that from me. And if you tell Yve I told you, I'll deny it until they seal me into a crypt."

It wasn't everything I'd wanted to know, but I'd take it. I nodded. "As delightful as this has been, ladies, I'll be going."

"Oh no, you're not," Vanessa said. "You're going to get those billionaire hands dirty and make PB&J. It'll do you some good to do more than just write checks from your ivory tower."

I opened my mouth to tell her that would happen when hell froze over, but we were interrupted.

"You throwing my words around, princess?" Con said

from the doorway.

"Thought I'd drop by and see how you were spending that ivory-tower check," I said, turning to face him.

"Didn't come to check on my balls?"

If he expected an apology, he wouldn't get one.

"No."

"You're still a dick, Titan. So you want to keep tabs on your donation? Can't say I wouldn't do the same. I guess a mil should let you walk around, even if I want to toss your ass out. Come on. I don't want you alone with my woman. I still don't fucking trust you."

"Barbarian," Vanessa shot from across the room.

"Damn straight," Con replied. "Let's go, Titan."

I followed him out and into the gym.

Con didn't waste any time. "Why are you really here?"

I decided not to bullshit him. "Yve Santos. I want information."

Con stopped, and his features were branded with skepticism. "And you thought we'd give it to you?"

"Yes."

"You've always got an angle, Titan. So, what is it this time? You want to bang her?"

Now was not the time to tell him I already had, and would again. I stayed silent.

He snorted. "Don't want to tell me? That's interesting."

"Let's just say my intentions are . . . good enough."

"So that's how it is," he said and his eyes lit up. Con's shoulders shook as he took his time laughing at me. "If there's one woman I'm confident can take care of herself, it's Yve. She's liable to chew you up and spit you out. You deserve it."

My instincts sharpened. "You know her well."

"Better than you."

Possessiveness gripped me. That cheap shot in the balls? If I'd regretted it even remotely, that regret was now gone.

Before I could respond, Con said, "Here's a tip. If you try to buy that woman, you're gonna do nothin' but alienate her. I can promise you that."

My hands balled into fists at my sides. "I think I could have figured that out on my own. You gonna give me anything else?"

His mocking mood snapped to something infinitely more serious. "Yve's story ain't mine to tell, but you better step carefully around her. We will fuck you up if you hurt her."

I didn't acknowledge his warning; my thoughts were on Yve. The odds of Con or anyone else in this building telling me what had happened in her past were about as good as the odds as Yve telling me herself. Zero.

"You wanna get in the ring? I owe you a cheap shot."

"Maybe another day, Leahy. I've got better shit to do with my time," I said and turned to leave.

"Didn't peg you for a coward, Titan."

I spun back around. "You can't bait someone who doesn't give a fuck what you think about them. I'll see around, Leahy."

21

Yve

"HE DID WHAT?" I YELLED INTO MY PHONE.

"Ouch, girl. You're gonna blow my eardrum," Elle replied. "And yeah, Titan was here. Asking about you."

"I'm gonna kill him. Gonna hunt him down and—"

"Whoa, hold up, Yve. Don't tell me. That makes whatever you're going to do premeditated."

Of all the people I'd ever met, only Elle could make me laugh in any given situation. The woman was a total nut.

My chuckle came out more like a snort.

"That's better. I'm only telling you because it just seemed out of character for him. And if we were talking about anyone but Lucas Fucking Titan, I'd say he's into you. Like maybe for real."

Whoa. Now it was time for Elle to hold up.

"Excuse me?"

"He was concerned and stuff. Wanted to know about

128

the shop, and if we knew why you'd gotten spooked out of staying at your apartment." Her tone turned cautious, and maybe a little reprimanding. "By the way, what the hell was up with that? Why didn't you call me? Did it have anything to do with . . . *him*?" Meaning *he who shall not be named*, at least in Elle's book.

I appreciated her caution when bringing him up, but first things first. "What did you tell him?"

"Nothing really. Except maybe that you found out Harriet was selling the place and you were looking to buy it. I hope you don't care."

I would have preferred Titan not know any details about my personal life, but apparently that ship had sailed.

"It's fine. Just don't share anything else with him. Not that you probably need to—I'm assuming he has the resources to find out anything he wants to know." Although knowing how well my former father-in-law had covered things up with my ex-husband, it might even be a challenge for Titan to find. The proceedings were all kept closed, the records sealed. Money could buy you a lot of things in this town, including silence.

"So, are you going to tell me what the hell is going on? Did the voodoo doll you made not do the trick?"

Elle was referring to the voodoo doll I'd made of Jay the night Valentina had told me he'd been approved for parole. It had been one of those impulse things, something to make me feel better and take out my fear and frustration and anger on. It had helped, for that night at least. Elle had been her usual amazing self and hadn't wanted me to be alone. And now here I was, home, in an apartment that no longer felt safe.

"Not exactly," I said, finally responding to her question.

"Is there something you need to tell me about, Yve?"

I debated how much to say. I wanted to tell her everything, but I also wasn't looking to lay my problems on Elle's doorstep. I had to stand on my own two feet and deal with this myself, but I could share at least some of it.

"I think I'm just flipping out because I know he's out, but I don't know *where* he is."

"Oh shit. That's not cool."

"No. It isn't. And I think maybe I'm just jumping at shadows. I don't know."

"Look, babe. Trust your gut. If you think something isn't right, chances are it's not, okay? Don't write something off as crazy just because you're a little jumpy."

Her advice was certainly solid. And I would take it—by being extra careful.

"Okay."

"And promise you'll be careful."

"I promise."

"And you'll call me if anything freaks you out."

I hesitated for a fraction of a second. This was my problem. "I love you, Elle."

"Yve, don't think I'm missing the fact that you didn't promise."

"'Bye, babe."

"'Bye, hon."

I hung up, feeling marginally less crazy, but a hell of a lot more pissed off. I had a visit to pay to Mr. Titan.

I felt like I was storming the castle as I screeched to a halt in front of Titan's place.

Damn gate. He truly was a king behind his fancy wrought-iron fence, probably sitting up in his tower counting his billions and meddling in people's lives like they were pawns.

I climbed out of the Blue Beast, stalked up to the intercom buzzer, and pressed the button. A familiar voice answered.

"Ms. Santos, lovely to see you this evening."

Confused, I glanced around, looking for the camera.

"It's built into the intercom panel, my dear," Jerome replied, reading my movements accurately. "Please come right in."

The latch of the gate clicked and released, and I slipped inside. Striding up to the house, I tried to get my thoughts in order. What exactly was I going to say to him?

Stay the hell out of my life?

If you want to know something about me, then you damn well better ask me and not my friends?

Why are you invading my thoughts when I don't want you there?

Okay, that last one I'd keep to myself. But everything else was fair game.

Jerome was standing at the open front door when I reached it. "Don't you look lovely this evening, Yve. It's wonderful to see you again so soon."

I glanced down at my dress. It was a retro white number I'd picked up on eBay. It was after Labor Day, so my mama would have said I shouldn't have been wearing white. But guess what, I didn't care. *I'm a rebel like that.*

"Thank you, Jerome," I replied, trying to be polite, but I was a woman on a mission. "I don't mean to be rude, but where the hell is he?"

Jerome's lips quirked into a smile, and I could swear his eyes twinkled. "He's having a swim. Do you know where the pool room is located?"

The familiar heat of my blush rose in my cheeks. "Yes, I do. Thank you."

I'd taken only one step when Jerome offered a friendly, "Good luck, dear. He's in a mood tonight."

In a mood? I was the one *in a mood*.

The scent of chlorine grew as I neared the pool. Through the glass walls, I could make out the powerful muscles of Titan's back and arms as he cut through the water. Every flex and contraction conjured images of what he must have looked like pounding into me from behind.

You didn't come here to ogle the man's fine-as-hell, totally ripped body, and you're certainly not here for a repeat performance.

Taking a deep breath, I grabbed the handle and pulled the door open. I crossed to the edge of the pool and stood at the end of the lane Titan was swimming in.

Ignore the muscles, Yve.

Impossible.

I propped my hands on my hips and waited for about thirty seconds, and then my patience dried up. "Hey! I need to talk to you."

The words bounced off the walls of the room, and Titan's head jerked out of the water as he stood in the pool.

Oh hell . . . those pecs. Shit. The man did *not* look like he sat at a desk wearing a fancy suit all day. No paper pusher should be allowed to have abs like that.

I snapped my eyes to his face as he pulled the goggles off his head.

"Once again I find you uninvited in my pool room. You're wearing too many clothes this time."

I didn't acknowledge his comment before I launched into my tirade. "If you want to know something about me, you come to *me*. Don't go snooping around in my business or trying to get information out of my friends. If I want you to know something, I'll tell you. Otherwise, mind your own damn business. You get me?"

Titan moved to the edge of the pool, and I stepped back. It proved to be the right choice because he placed both palms on the tiled floor and lifted himself out of the pool.

Holy. Hell.

I had to avert my eyes. It was like looking at the sun, except he was all golden skin and lean, long muscles. And he was wearing tight enough swim shorts that his bulge was in no way concealed.

He'd felt huge when I wrapped my hand around him— and when he'd pushed inside me.

Focus, Yve. You don't like him.

But my body's reaction proved once more that I didn't have to like him to want him.

Lucas

I WONDERED IF YVE KNEW I COULD SEE STRAIGHT UP her dress before she stepped away from the edge of the pool. Unlikely, and I wasn't going to point out the fact. But still, it was a shame when she moved back. Unfortunately she'd chosen white lace today instead of going bare. I just wondered if it was a thong . . .

Already, I could feel my dick perking up in my swim shorts. Not surprising. The woman only had to breathe to get me hard.

I pushed out of the pool, letting the water cascade off me. Once I was on two feet, I stepped to the chair to grab my towel and began to dry off.

Yve stood silently. A glance in her direction showed her eyes glued to my body.

"Want me to drop the trunks so we're even? After all, I got to see all of you."

Her spine shot poker straight. "Not necessary. That's

not why I'm here."

I had no intention of letting her leave without getting another taste of her, but I could bide my time. For now.

I shrugged and tossed the towel aside. "Then why are you here?"

"Because you're meddling in my life."

I raised an eyebrow. "Meddling how? I haven't done a thing."

"You went to the gym trying to dig up information on me."

"I did." I wasn't about to hide it, but my confession didn't slow her down.

"You want to know something about me, then you come to *me*."

When she jabbed a finger at her own chest to make her point, I was reminded of her perfect tits and dusky-rose nipples. I needed to fuck her while we were both naked. Preferably in front of a mirror so I could see everything. But first, I wanted answers.

"Then you tell me. What the hell sent you running out of your apartment?"

"It's none of your goddamn business, Titan," she shot back.

"Guess what, Yve? I decide what's my business, and for some damn reason, I've decided you are."

She stepped toward me. "Well, undecide. I don't need you meddling in my life."

Stubborn woman. "Have you ever asked for help?"

"I don't need your help."

"That wasn't my question. My question was," I took another step closer, until the skirt of her dress pressed against my still wet thighs, "have you ever *asked* for help."

She refused to lower her eyes, but her chest rose and fell faster with each breath. "I don't see the point of asking for help. It always comes with strings attached."

She didn't step away, and I found that almost as fascinating as her answer.

"I knew you were a smart woman, because my help definitely has strings attached. I want you naked when I'm inside you next time."

Her golden eyes sparked and flashed, right before she pressed both hands against my chest and shoved.

I could have stopped the backward momentum, but instead I grabbed her waist as I stumbled backward over the edge of the pool—and took her with me.

"**Y**OU MOTHERFUCKER!" I SPUTTERED AS I broke the surface. Reaching out blindly, I shoved at anything I could reach, which happened to be hot, solid muscle. I yanked my hands back like I'd been burned and swiped the water out of my eyes. "You're such a dick."

Titan threw his head back and his laughter echoed through the room. I'd never seen a smile on his face like this one. Ever. In fact, I didn't think I'd really seen him smile. Smirk like an asshole? Sure. But smile? No.

Since when did I start keeping track of the man's facial expressions? Didn't matter.

"I've never pretended to be anything else," he said.

I fought the urge to scream. My dress was soaked—and it was white. I was wearing a very sheer white bra, and my nipples were now hard as pebbles and completely visible.

I moved to cover my chest with my arms, but Titan

backed me into the corner of the pool. My fight-or-flight instincts should have been waging an epic battle, but I was too pissed to be scared. He wasn't going to hurt me. I, however, might hurt *him*.

The skirt of my dress floated up in the pool around me, and I shoved it down.

"Fuck, you're gorgeous, Yve."

I jerked my head up to meet his eyes as Titan reached out to brush a wet curl away from my face.

I pressed both hands to his chest one more time, ready to push him away, but froze . . . because his head was lowering to mine.

"Wha—what are you doing?" I said breathlessly.

"Kissing you."

"I told you not to." His mouth was so close to mine, I was sure he felt the words on his lips.

"You didn't stop me last time. And I take what I want—which is you."

The burn of my anger morphed into flames of heat and need. My hands turned traitor and slid up to grip his shoulder and the back of his neck. Apparently my better judgment had left the building, along with my self-imposed rules.

For some reason only God himself knew, I wanted to kiss this man.

So I did.

Titan's firm lips landed on mine, and his tongue wasted no time delving inside. He pressed a palm to my face to tilt my head as he deepened the kiss. I had no idea why I let him lead; probably because he was so damn *good* at it.

It had been too long since I'd been kissed like I was the

air someone needed to breathe, and that was exactly how Titan kissed. It was all consuming.

I squeezed my thighs together as my mind immediately went to how all consuming he'd been when he'd taken me in the kitchen. I shouldn't want him this much, especially since he was a shining example of everything I despised. But I kissed him anyway.

Titan's other hand slid from my waist down to my bare thigh and then upward. My high-cut panties didn't provide any protection from his questing fingers as they gripped my ass. He lifted and pulled me against him. That rock-hard erection pressed exactly where I needed it. My clit came to life at the pressure and friction.

It didn't take long. *Hell.* I was going to come.

I should have been horrified that he could cause such a reaction from me, but all I did was rock against him harder and faster.

He lifted his mouth a fraction of an inch. "I want you to come for me. Right now. Can you get there?"

"Shut up. Kiss me," I mumbled against his lips.

His mouth crushed against mine again, and the hand previously guiding my face dropped to free my breast from the soaked fabric of my dress. My moans were lost in the kiss, but I could feel the orgasm rising in me. Just a few more—

I stiffened, letting it wash over me and vibrate out through my limbs. I rocked against him, not as hard this time, to keep the waves rolling through me.

Oh. My. God. I needed that.

I broke my mouth away from his as I drooped against him.

"Jesus Christ, that was hot."

It was his voice. Lucas Titan's voice. In my ear. After I'd just come. It should have ruined everything, but it just made me hotter.

I hated myself for liking it. I shoved away from him as self-loathing slid over me like the chlorinated water.

"Let go." I turned in the circle of his arms and tried to push out of the pool.

His hands wrapped around my waist and held me firmly, bringing me back against his chest. "Oh no. You're not going to run this time."

"Let go of me. Now." My tone meant business. Serious business.

Surprisingly, he listened, even backing up so I could scramble out of the pool. I lunged for the towel he'd used earlier and pulled it around my body.

I have to get out of here.

"Yve, wait."

I didn't know where my sandals were, probably somewhere at the bottom of the pool. *Fuck it.* I'd walked barefoot before. I dashed to the door and pulled it open.

I needed to get the hell away from Titan. He was dangerous.

140

Lucas

WELL, THAT ESCALATED QUICKLY.

Fuck. I dove under, grabbed Yve's sandals off the bottom of the pool, and climbed out. If she was going to run from me, I'd at least make sure she wasn't doing it barefoot.

I wasn't done with her yet. She could deny it all she wanted, but she craved this as much as I did.

I grabbed another towel off the stack on the table and dried off as I hustled out of the pool room. In the hallway, I could hear Jerome—God bless the man—talking to Yve.

"I'm fine," she was telling him. "I just need to go."

"But you're soaking wet, my dear."

"Well, that's what happens when an asshole pulls you into the pool."

"I think you're missing an important detail," I drawled, interrupting them. "Because you pushed me first."

Yve's head swiveled around, her cheeks deeply flushed

141

with what I wanted to believe was lust, but was more than likely embarrassment. I tied the towel around my waist, because my dick still hadn't calmed down, and I didn't need Jerome seeing that.

"Yve, we need to talk," I said.

Her eyes hardened. "I need to go. I have shit to do. And I also have nothing to say to you."

"Yve—"

Jerome interrupted. "My dear, how about I find you something dry to put on. You don't want to run off like that."

She looked at Jerome, then me. "You keep a lot of women's clothes in your house? You know, for occasions like this when you dunk them in the pool."

I held back what I really wanted to say, given our audience, and instead replied, "I'm sure Jerome could find you something. His nieces have been here."

"Yes," Jerome said in an even tone, "and I'm sure they've left something behind. If nothing else, Lucas will fetch you something of his."

"I think I'd rather stay wet."

My lips quirked into a smirk.

Holding the towel to her chest, she turned for the door. Hell, her dress really was transparent now that it was wet. Everywhere.

"Yve. Wait." She didn't, so I said a word I rarely uttered. "Please." When she froze, I continued. "Let us get you some dry clothes. It'll only take a minute."

My request hung in the air for long moments before she finally replied, "Fine. I'll wait."

"I'll return promptly," Jerome said before hurrying off

as fast as his old legs could carry him, leaving Yve and me alone.

She didn't turn to face me.

"So you come and then you go?" I asked.

Yve spun. "Fuck you, Titan. Don't you dare try to shame me—"

I closed the distance between us. "The only shameful thing here is that you're not naked and under me right now."

Her expression hardened. "This was a mistake. I shouldn't have—"

"Come from rubbing against my cock? I beg to differ. Although I'd prefer you wouldn't have stopped there."

"Jesus, you're crass."

"Just stating the facts."

She released one hand's grip on the towel, and it slid a little south. That hand went straight to her hip—propped and sassy. "I don't like you," she declared.

"I thought we'd established that you don't have to like someone to want to fuck them."

"Doesn't make it a good idea."

"Come on, Yve. Why not figure out an arrangement that'll work for us both—"

I wasn't prepared for the crack of her palm across my cheek, or the sting that followed.

"Fuck you and your arrangement."

She tossed the towel to the floor, yanked the door open, and stalked out.

A MISTRESS. THAT WAS ALL MEN THOUGHT THE women in my line were good for. Sex. That was it. Until I'd found the one who wanted to marry me.

God, I'd been so young and naive. I'd thought he loved me. Little did I know, he'd just wanted to own me. Some scars would never fade, and the ones Jay had left were equally as painful as the ones my mother had inflicted— except hers were invisible. Disguised as words of encouragement as I grew up, they still haunted me.

You're a pretty girl, Yve. You'll have no trouble finding a man to take care of you. You'll be just like your mama. Never have to work a day in your life, as long as you keep him happy.

An arrangement. That was exactly what a guy like him would want. I would never let a man *take care of me* in exchange for sex. Screw that. My determination to make Dirty Dog mine and prove myself as a competent businesswoman grew exponentially. I was not my mother. I had more to offer than my body. And screw anyone who believed differently. Especially Lucas Titan.

Yeah, I might have considered another round with the guy, but that was a far cry from a goddamn *arrangement*. Angry, I wrenched the steering wheel a little too hard as I turned down my street. The word set me off like nothing else. It was right up there with *understanding*.

In my book—which might be a messed-up one, but it was the only one that mattered—they were all euphemisms for the same damn thing . . . being a whore. Not a slut, not sleeping around—I was totally cool with that. What I wasn't cool with was someone offering to compensate me for the use of my pussy.

I slammed on the brakes after I pulled into my parking spot, and eyed the stairs to my apartment. The locksmith had installed all new locks, and the security people had installed an alarm system. Neither of which I'd run by my landlord, but he was going to have to get over it because all I cared about was my own damn safety.

I stomped to the stairs and climbed them. Despite the warm evening, I was shivering in my soaked clothes. As I jammed my key into the lock, the deep purr of an engine sounded from behind me.

If that was an Aston Martin . . .

I glanced over my shoulder. A strange pang hit my chest when I saw it wasn't an Aston Martin, a reaction I refused to believe was disappointment.

Get real, girl. Like Lucas Titan would ever chase after you like that. Not that I wanted him to.

I walked back down the stairs to meet Geneviève in the

middle of the small backyard at the cheap bench I'd put out there.

"Ginny. What brings you here?"

Ginny didn't do her hug-and-air-kiss routine. She didn't comment on my destroyed dress or my surely bedraggled appearance. No, she crossed toward me and grabbed my shoulders.

"He's out, Yve. He's already out."

"I heard."

Ginny's eyes widened. "How did you know? I didn't even know."

How could that be? That mystified me. She was the matriarch; she knew *everything* that happened in that family.

"A friend who was keeping tabs."

"Good. Good." She nodded with each word. "You need friends right now because I'm very concerned about his mental state. All those years in prison . . . he's not the same person anymore, Yve. I . . . I don't know what he might do."

Then why did you let him get out? I wanted to scream. But I didn't. Something about being around the usually unflappable Ginny helped me gather my composure. I thought about the glass and the missing perfume. It was harmless stuff, which was why I hadn't gone to the police. If he'd left a dead cat on my doorstep, then I would have had something to point to and tell anyone who would listen that they needed to throw his crazy ass back in prison.

"Do you know where he is?"

She shook her head. "My son won't tell me anything. He's kept me out of it completely. After I pushed the divorce through, he's never trusted me with anything about Jay. He thinks I've chosen sides, and obviously chosen wrongly."

I gritted my teeth in frustration. "Could he be at the hunting cabin? Any rental properties?" *Any new mistresses' houses?*

I wanted to say the words, but didn't. Not just because it seemed wrong to ask something like that of Ginny, but because Jay's daddy had actually been pretty faithful to my mama over the years—more faithful than to his wives. But still, even for a woman who looked fifteen years younger than she was, my mama was in her waning years. He was due to move on eventually.

I hadn't talked to my mother since the day I'd woken up in the hospital and she'd been sitting in my room, waiting for me. The scene was still so vivid in my mind.

The first words out of her mouth had been, "What did you do?"

She'd refused to believe that I hadn't goaded Jay into almost killing me. When I told her that I'd finally had the courage to ask him for a divorce, she'd raised her hand to slap me, but my face was covered by bandages.

"All you had to do was make the boy happy, Yve," she'd said. "And you couldn't even manage to do that."

"But, Mama, he—"

"I don't care what he does, you're his wife. You're screwing up the best thing that ever happened to you. And if this ruins my relationship with his daddy, I swear to the Lord above, you're dead to me."

Tears had streaked down my face, soaking the bandages. My voice had shaken when I'd ordered her to get out, because she was already dead to me.

After Jay had left me broken in our house, he'd gone out that night and picked up Valentina at a bar. I could almost picture him putting on the Southern-boy charm I knew he still possessed. She'd been on the rebound, looking for a one-night stand, and he'd pocketed his wedding band. According to her, when she'd gotten into his car, he'd gone into a rage, screaming at her and calling her my name. And then he'd driven like crazy so she thought they'd crash. When he'd finally pulled off on a long, deserted road, he'd dragged her into the backseat, raped her, then tossed her and her purse out of the car. She'd called for help and ended up in a hospital room just down the hall from me.

I hated that my actions had affected Valentina, but she'd forgiven me. That didn't mean I'd forgiven myself, though.

"Yve, are you listening to me?"

I snapped out of my trip down the memory lane from hell, and met Ginny's eyes. "What?"

Fear came off Ginny in waves. "You've got to leave town, dear. I'm afraid he's going to come after you. My offer is still good. All you need to do is pick a city. You can leave tonight. I'll arrange to have your belongings packed and shipped. He'll never find you."

I laid a hand on her shoulder. "What do you know?"

"Nothing, and it scares the living hell out of me. I don't trust him, and I don't trust my son."

I squared my shoulders and tried not to upset her with my words. "I'm not leaving. This is my home. This is *my* city just as much as it's his. I didn't let him run me out of it before, and I won't let him now." Ice coated the steel reinforcing my spine as I added, "Whatever he's gonna do, he's gonna do. I won't change my life just because I can't predict what that might be." Even as I said the words, the possibilities and risks flipped through my brain, along with the potential for this to be a downright stupid decision.

"Yve," she said. "Please. Do it for me."

"I'm sorry. I can't. I have to do this for me. This is my life. I'm done letting him rule it."

She shook her head. "You're making a mistake."

"Then so be it."

Ginny nodded, and her arthritic hand shook as it lifted to my face. "You're a good girl, Yve. I don't want anything else bad to happen to you. I just wish you'd let me protect you."

"I'll be fine. Thank you for coming to let me know, but I'm going to have to protect myself."

She pulled me in for a hug. "Be safe, my dear."

"And if you learn anything at all, please tell me."

She stepped back and released me. "You have my word. Good-bye, Yve."

I watched as she made her way back to her BMW. Once she'd driven off, I turned back to my apartment and stared up at it with dread. My keys still hung in the lock, and I really, really didn't want to go in there and see whatever might have been moved or missing.

Sometimes being self-sufficient just plain sucked. In that moment, I wished I had someone I could lean on. What would that even be like?

If I'd had a father, would this be a time that he'd come and check under the metaphorical bed for monsters? If I'd ever figured out how to date and have a normal relationship, maybe I would've had someone I could call to go in first and check things out.

But no. I just had me. And Yve counted on Yve.

Sure, I had friends. I could call Elle and she'd send

Lord. Or I could call my former employee and good friend, Charlie, and she'd send her fiancé, Simon. Even Con would come if I called him. But they all had their own lives, their own issues. They didn't need little old me pulling a Chicken Little when I didn't even know if Jay had been in my place. Was it likely? Sure as shit, yes. Who else would have done it?

My stomach cramped as I stared up at my apartment door.

I couldn't do it. I just couldn't do it.

I sat down on the bench and dropped my head into my hands. Maybe a little cry would do me good. No one would ever have to know.

Lucas

C LANDESTINE MEETINGS WITH POLITICIANS WERE
even worse than regular meetings with politicians.
Because clandestine meetings were all cloak and
dagger and required a secret password at the door of some
club that men like me—men who weren't born with the
keys to this city—didn't otherwise know existed.

The doorman shut the heavy leather padded door behind me and I stepped inside the dimly lit club. A blonde
on ice-pick stilettos nodded to me.

"Welcome, Mr. Titan. Right this way, sir."

Apparently while I hadn't known about this club, they'd
known about me. I followed her, my gaze dropping to her
ass out of habit, but not with interest. Absently I noted the
short black skirt and seam up the back of her stockings,
but nothing in me was moved by her top-notch body. No, I
seemed to have developed a fixation on a sassy, curvy woman who would rather run from me than spend a moment in

my company. All claws and teeth—and sexy as hell. It was undeniable proof that I was a masochist.

The blonde slowed in front of a closed door but didn't reach for the handle. "They're inside, sir."

Cloak and dagger, indeed.

I pulled it open and found four Louisiana state senators seated inside, puffing on cigars and looking like the Southern politicians they were.

"Gentlemen," I said in greeting.

"Titan, come in. Close the door."

I did as he asked and crossed the room to the low gathering of chairs around a poker table. There were cards and chips on the table, but no hand in play.

"I didn't realize we were planning to play."

"We're not," Hendricks said, one of the three Democrats in the room. "We just needed a reason to gather."

"Afraid of the Gestapo finding you out?"

"Not the Gestapo. Haines."

The name of the senator who had demanded the open-ended favor surprised me. "Haines?"

Shuman, the sole Republican among them, replied, "He put out the word that if you came around asking for favors, we might not find it in our best interest to entertain them."

That son of a bitch. "Is that so?"

"Damn right. For some reason he's gotten very territorial over you."

What the hell? "Why is that?"

They all looked at me like I was an idiot for even asking the question. "Because you're a good man to have a marker from. We're guessing he doesn't want anyone else to have the chance to get something from you."

And this was why I despised politics.

"So, why are you here?" I asked. "If you're not willing to go against Haines, then why even agree to meet with me?"

Winchell spoke up again. "Because we want to know what it is that would get a man like you to start asking for favors."

"Curiosity. That's why you're here?"

They all smiled.

"And yet you have no intention of helping me, regardless of what it is, because Haines put out the word that I wasn't to be helped?"

Nods went all around the table.

"Why the hell do you think I'd tell you a goddamn thing?"

Truman spoke up. "Because whatever it is, if there's a chance we can help you behind the scenes in exchange for, shall we say, *generous* campaign contributions, we might be willing to pull some strings."

Greed and curiosity. It would have been interesting if it wasn't so infuriating.

My first instinct was to tell them to fuck off. But the voice in the back of my head—telling me I'd never succeed and I was a waste of a son—that voice increased in volume.

The person I most wanted to tell to fuck off was my father, and it was his voice. A voice I'd only heard in my head for years.

I studied the four politicians, wondering if they'd be able to give me any realistic help at all. If they weren't willing to push the bill to the floor for a vote and make sure the vote went in my favor, what good were they?

But what if there was a chance?

"Okay, gentlemen," I started, using the term loosely. "This is what I need."

DEEP BREATH IN; DEEP BREATH OUT.

Scan right. Scan left.

Repeat.

I made the circuit of all of the rooms in my apartment for the ninth time, but saw nothing out of place. Nothing moved. Nothing missing.

Maybe the new locks and alarm system had done the trick. It seemed too easy, though, didn't it?

"Okay," I said to the empty room. "I guess I'll just go to bed then."

I headed into the bathroom to wash my face. My make-up had to be almost all gone, courtesy of the dunking I'd taken in Titan's pool. *Asshole.*

I stopped in front of the mirror and froze. "Oh, sweet baby Jesus," I murmured. I looked like the dried version of a drowned rat. *Lovely.* It was a miracle Ginny hadn't demanded an explanation for my appearance, which was more proof of how distressed she'd been. A shower was definitely in order, or even better, a bath.

I eyed the small tub-shower combination in my bathroom and wished for the giant claw-foot tub in the guest room of Titan's house.

Stop thinking about him, I ordered myself.

After closing the drain, I turned on the water as hot as it would go and watched for a few moments as the tub filled inch by inch. Deciding it had filled enough at three inches, I stripped and climbed in. I let the heat and steam surround me as the water continued to rise.

Leaning my head back, I tried to think peaceful thoughts, and not about the nightmares that Ginny's warnings had brought back to me. But every time I tried to push my mind to something pleasant, it landed on the black-haired, green-eyed man I wanted to forget.

But did I truly want to forget that night in the kitchen and how he'd pushed me, challenged me, and finally *taken me*? Jesus.

I'd never come so hard in my entire life. And I might never come so hard again.

Unless you have another fling with Titan, the voice in my head offered.

No. That wasn't happening again. Because he wanted an *arrangement*.

But what if I told him to shove his arrangement where the sun didn't shine and made a counteroffer of my own? I could be the one to use *him*.

I pictured Titan's mouth curling up into a smirk as I told him that I wanted to compensate him for the use of his body. Hell, screw compensation. The man was richer than

Midas, so what if I just told him that I wanted to use his body freely, whenever the whim struck me. I wanted to be able to say when and where, and for him to make it happen.

Would he be shocked?

Oh God, but the idea of Titan speechless would be worth the potential humiliation if he laughed in my face. The more I thought about the plan, the more I liked it. It was ballsy, cocky, and slightly crazy—which made it seem perfect for when dealing with Titan.

"Why the hell not?" I asked the empty bathroom. "Why not turn the tables a little?"

Determination filling me, I stood, shaking off the water as I grabbed a towel. But one glance in the direction of the steam-clouded mirror made me freeze. A scream ripped loose from my lungs.

I'm watching you.

The words were written in big block letters across the glass, and would have been completely invisible if I hadn't let the bathroom fill with steam.

Stark terror ripped through me.

He'd been here. Ginny was right. Jay was still fixated on me, and I wasn't safe.

Fight or flight kicked in harder than ever before. *Run!* all my instincts screamed. And yet here I stood in the middle of the bathroom, clutching a towel to my dripping body as I forced my brain to start working again.

He wasn't here, wasn't in my apartment. The locks had been changed, and the alarm was set. But he'd been here before; I'd felt it in my gut, and I'd been right.

With shaking hands, I wrapped the towel around me. *I will not let him win.* The choice stood before me—fight or flight—but I had nowhere to run. I could count on myself, and that was it.

So I guess fight it was.

I dried myself slowly and methodically, trying to pretend my hands weren't shaking as I told myself the feeling that had settled over me wasn't desperation, but calmness. A killing calm, if need be. I could do this. I could totally do this.

I spent the night huddled in the corner of my sitting room, one hand on the remote flipping through late-night infomercials, and the other hand within easy reach of my revolver.

It was a long, sleepless night.

28
Yve

THE NEXT MORNING, I WAS IN NO MOOD TO BE
messed with, mostly because an Yve who hadn't
slept was not an Yve who should be facing the
world without a flashing neon warning sign. Any other day,
I would have walked to work, but I didn't want to be caught
out in the open for that long. I wasn't stupid; I wasn't going
to make myself any bigger of a target than I needed to be.
But I swore I could feel eyes on me as I parked in the alley
behind the store and let myself in.

Good Lord, what I wouldn't pay to have Levi back already. His presence in the shop, while not any deterrent to
danger, would at least give me some comfort, and I'd take
what I could get right now.

My heart about leaped out of my chest when someone
banged on the front door ten minutes before opening. If it
was that skinny chick snooping around, thinking she was
going to own this place, she'd have picked the wrong damn

day to mess with this girl.

I strode to the front of the store. It was a skinny chick, but it wasn't Jennifer. At least, not *that* Jennifer.

"Hi," a perky brunette said, waving as I cracked open the door. "I'm Jennifer. Your temp."

I eyed her. "Let's see some ID."

Her forehead wrinkled. "ID?"

"Didn't the temp agency tell you that you'd need to provide it?" It was standard procedure, but usually I let people in the door first. Except today, I wasn't feeling all that trusting.

"Oh yeah, they did. Hold on." She reached into the giant bag she carried on her shoulder as a purse. It was cute, but enormous. She could carry a severed head in that thing.

Way to be completely morbid and fucked up, Yve. I cringed at the thought. Seriously, I needed to lighten up.

She pulled out her wallet to retrieve her license and handed it to me through the slice of space I'd left when I opened the door.

Jennifer Patrice Ralston. Twenty-one years old as of last month. Good enough.

I opened the door wider. "Come on in."

She stepped inside and I flipped the lock behind her. "I've always loved this store. I don't know if you remember me, but I've been here before. I bought this dress."

She executed a quick pirouette and twirl, and instead of being annoyed, I instantly decided I liked the girl. She'd bought one of my favorite dresses—red and black with a cute boat-neck collar and a wide pleated skirt—and she wore it well, especially paired with super-cute rhinestone-studded silver flats. She'd fit in just fine.

"I remember the dress, but I have to apologize, I don't remember you."

"No worries. The dress is certainly more memorable than I am."

I studied her pierced nose and shoulders tattooed with epaulets. "I think that's probably an unfair statement."

She was quick with her smile and even quicker with her giggle. The girl would be absolutely no protection, but her company was welcome.

"How about I show you around and get you acquainted with the inventory?"

She rubbed her hands together. "Let's do this."

Two hours later I had a girl crush on my new temporary employee. In fact, if she sold one more item that cost over two hundred dollars, I might just try to steal her away from the temp company completely. They'd apologized up and down for screwing up and not sending her the day they were supposed to. I wondered if that meant I could get them to void the no-poaching clause in the agreement I'd signed.

Because that's how a businesswoman thinks, I told myself. Which reminded me, I needed to decide my next course of action before I really did lose this place to the other skinny bitch Jennifer.

Part of my brain screamed that I should just go to Harriet and lay it all out, but the other part of me knew that I couldn't walk in empty-handed. Either way, I needed to set a deadline for myself. If I didn't have a plan by this time next week, I'd go to her. I might be proud, but I wasn't a fool.

The back buzzer sounded, and I checked my watch. It was time for our daily UPS delivery, which was basically like Christmas that came every day.

I headed for the door and pulled it open. "Hey, Kevin, how's things?" I asked the big black man who'd been asking me out since almost my very first day at the shop.

"Things would be better if you'd just go out with me, Ms. Yve."

He was a good man, the kind of man I should date. But that was the problem—I didn't know what to do with a good man. He wasn't the kind of guy I could invite home for one night; he was looking for a woman to warm his bed every night, the kind of man who'd take me out somewhere nice to try to impress me. The kind of man who'd wait until the third date before he tried anything serious, and then on date thirty-three, he'd probably get down on one knee and propose.

Lord knew I'd never get married again. No way in hell. There was no upside to marriage that I could see. And a good man like Kevin? I'd just break his heart.

So I said no. Again. "You know that'd just be asking for trouble."

"And yet I keep asking, beautiful."

I smiled at the compliment. "You're always smooth, I'll give you that."

"Because one day you're going to give in to me."

"I keep telling you not to get your hopes up."

When I reached out to accept the package he was holding just out of reach, he said, "What's a man got, if he doesn't have hope, Yve?" His tone was serious as his warm brown eyes bored into mine.

With a line like that, if my life weren't such a complete disaster, maybe I would consider taking him up on one date. *Maybe.*

The front door chime sounded, and I heard JP, as she'd told me she preferred to be called, chatting with whoever had entered.

"Hope can be a dangerous thing, Kev." My smile was almost certainly sad, but he didn't let it discourage him.

"I think you need someone to show you that hope is the most beautiful thing there is, except for maybe you."

"Nice line," a deep voice drawled from behind me.

I didn't have to look over my shoulder to identify the source. Titan's voice was imprinted on my memory, and probably would be for the rest of my natural life. It also seemed that my reaction to him would continue to be predictable. My entire body hummed to life as soon as it registered that he was in the vicinity.

Kevin looked over my shoulder, and lifted his chin. "Ain't no line. And you're interrupting."

"I'm interrupting the delivery guy? In what? Trying to hit on the hot shopkeeper? Tell me this isn't something that happens every day, and I'll be shocked."

My cheeks burned with embarrassment. If Titan was going to be a dick to a nice guy . . .

Kevin straightened and puffed his chest out. Built like a brick shit house, he was easily an inch or two taller than Titan, and outweighed him by at least thirty pounds.

Oh great. I was about to witness a pissing match. Just what I needed.

But Titan didn't play fair. Before I could sidestep so I could have both of them in my sight, Titan's hands came around my shoulders and a necklace dropped onto my chest.

"I think you left this at my house last night."

My palm went to my chest and I felt a pendant beneath it. An unfamiliar one.

What the hell?

I turned to look at him, my mouth opening to ask what in the world he thought he was doing, but Kevin interrupted me.

"So that's it. Figured there had to be another guy. Guess that makes me feel a little better. Hope you know what you're doing, Yve."

"Kevin—"

"I better get on. I've got a schedule to keep."

And he was gone, the back door banging shut behind him.

I whirled on Titan as I reached back to unclasp whatever necklace he'd just put around my neck. "What the hell was that?"

He shrugged. "It was out in your stock. It looked like it should belong to you."

"And you decided to *lie*?"

His eyes narrowed. "I decided to do what was expedient. The man looked at you like he was already half in love with you. You clearly wanted nothing to do with him, and I'm guessing you've been trying to extricate yourself from that awkward situation on a daily basis. You can thank me for taking care of it for you."

"I didn't ask you to—"

"Do you ever ask anyone for help, Yve?"

I paused. It wasn't the first time he'd asked me that, but how the hell did he read me so easily? The man was self-absorbed, completely selfish. He shouldn't be able to make an accurate study of my character at all.

"Does it matter?"

He took the box out of my hands and set it on the floor before backing me into the corner. With anyone else, and especially after the night I'd had, this maneuver would've had me climbing the walls—but not with Titan.

Why not?

I remembered my vow to shock him, to render him speechless. No time like the present.

"You really want a piece of me, Titan? Want a repeat performance of what happened in your kitchen?"

His green eyes flashed in the dim light of the back hallway. "You know I do."

"Then I've got an *arrangement* for *you*."

One dark, arrogant eyebrow rose. "Is that so?"

"Yes. Just sex. No strings. Whenever I want it, wherever I want it."

"And what about what I want?"

I grinned, and I hoped it looked as devious as it felt. "I don't give a damn what you want. All I want is that cock of yours and the orgasms you can give me."

His lips twitched. "I don't let anyone call the shots. Ever."

"Then you're never getting another piece of this ass." I slapped the side of my hip for emphasis.

"You tempt me, woman. You have no idea how much you tempt me."

"So give in to temptation, Titan."

He pressed both palms to the wall on either side of my head. "I don't agree to anything that puts me at a disadvantage."

"You don't want to be my booty call?" I taunted.

A growl rose from low in his throat. "When? Where?"

And I'd *won*.

I lifted my chin. "Whenever I say. Wherever I say."

The growl deepened. "Two conditions."

"I didn't ask you want you wanted, Titan."

"Two conditions, Yve."

"What?" I demanded.

He lowered his head to my ear. "You say when and where, and I say how—what position, how hard, how many times you come. You'll beg me to come every single time, do you understand me?"

I wrapped my arms around his neck. "I beg for no man."

"You'll beg for me."

"Then you better make it good."

"It'll be the best you've ever had; don't doubt it. You've gotten a taste, but that's all."

I sucked in a quick breath at his declaration. "Fine."

"And the second condition," he murmured as his lips drifted along my cheekbone and down to my mouth. "I get to kiss you anywhere I damn well please, including this sexy-as-sin mouth." He hovered over my lips, our breaths mingling further with every moment.

He waited, heartbeat after heartbeat, for an answer as my mind reeled. I'd already kissed him. What did it matter now?

I feared I was rationalizing the choice just to get me

one step closer to what I wanted—which was to have the advantage over this arrogant and powerful man.

"Whatever," I said breathlessly.

He crushed his lips to mine before the word was all the way spoken, and took control instantly, tongue diving inside, hand cupping my head to tilt me where he wanted.

Hell no. I buried both hands in his hair, wrapped one leg around his hip, and pulled him where I wanted him. His lips curved into a smile beneath mine, and I didn't care. He needed to know who was in charge.

I yanked away from the kiss. "Don't think this means I like you," I said, panting a breath.

Titan brushed a stray lock of hair out of my face. "I wouldn't dream of assuming such a thing." He laughed. "You just want my dick and the orgasms it can give you. Consider me put in my place, Yve."

"Exactly."

He leaned close again, and my heart rate kicked up in anticipation. But he didn't kiss me this time. No, he just said, "But don't think you won't beg. We'll find even ground, and it'll be when you're beneath me, taking my cock so deep you don't remember what it's like not to be filled by me."

Oh, sweet baby Jesus. My insides liquefied. I wanted that. Now.

"I guess we'll see," I said, lifting my chin. "You can leave your number on your way out."

Titan smirked and pushed off the back wall. "You're a stubborn woman. Never knew that was so goddamn sexy before. I'll be waiting for your call, Yve. Don't take too long, or I'll come looking for you."

As he turned and walked away, my gaze was glued to

his ass. All I could wonder was why I hadn't gotten two good handfuls of *that* while I'd been kissing him.

This was probably the worst idea I'd ever had. But damned if it wasn't going to be the most fun.

Unlike with Kevin, I had no qualms about feelings getting involved when it came to Titan. He had no heart, and didn't want anything from me. That made it safer. *Right?*

I reached down and picked the box up off the ground.

Time to see what Santa Claus Kevin had brought me today.

I didn't venture back into the main part of the shop until I heard the door chime three different times. Just in case. When I reached the counter, JP had just finished ringing up a sale and was handing one of our signature bags across the counter to a customer.

"I hope you enjoy that skirt. It's going to look amazing with the blouse you told me about. If you need anything else, just come back and see us."

Her smile was wide and genuine, and she looked like she fit behind the counter more than anyone had since Charlie. I mentally apologized to Elle, but there was something about a tattooed and pierced spitfire working at Dirty Dog that just seemed *right*.

She turned to me without wasting a moment. "So, who was that tall, dark, and *I'd fuck him in broad daylight and risk the indecent exposure charges* handsome guy?"

Yep. She fit right in.

"He was nobody."

168

She crossed her arms. "Well, *Nobody* left something for you."

Good boy, Titan. Way to follow orders, I cooed mentally as if he were a puppy. He'd want to strangle me for that, or bend me over and spank my ass. Which I'd probably like.

"Oh yeah?"

JP reached out and snatched a card off the counter. Handing it over, she pouted. "You're really not going to tell me who this guy is? I mean, now that I've seen his card, I can Google him, but friends tell each other this stuff, Yve."

Her words, particularly the word *friends*, struck me. "You've worked here for a day, and you've already decided we're friends?"

JP re-crossed her arms. "I don't see any other awesome help around here. Besides, I'm in the market for another friend. Last one turned out to be a bitch who stole my clothes and didn't give them back. At least if we were friends and if I keep working here, I'll know where my clothes are if you steal them, and I'll steal yours back too because they're bound to be kick-ass."

I could barely keep up with the girl. "One day at a time, girly."

I looked down at the card. Beneath his office number was another phone number written in that bold handwriting I already recognized. I assumed it was his cell phone.

Then I flipped the card over. What was written on the back surprised me.

You have a 9 a.m. appointment tomorrow at the NOLA Entrepreneur Fund.
Don't be late. Bring your business plan.

What the hell?

I remembered our encounter in the bank and the loan officer who couldn't keep his mouth shut. Titan knew I wanted Dirty Dog, knew I needed capital, so he'd just gone ahead and set up an appointment for me at the place I was considering trying to make an appointment to get a grant?

I wanted to be pissed at his high-handedness. I wanted to tear up the business card and throw it in the trash because of his ridiculous presumption. But I didn't, because I wanted Dirty Dog more. I grabbed my purse and tucked the card in my wallet. I wouldn't cut off my nose to spite my face, but that didn't mean I was going to thank him with a celebratory blow job or anything.

And with the thought of Lucas Titan's cock in my mouth, I went back to work.

Lucas

I TOSSED MY PHONE IN MY DESK DRAWER AND SLAMMED it shut. I wasn't going to stare at the damn thing and wait for it to ring. Yve would call or she wouldn't, and I wasn't the kind of punk-ass, whiny bitch of a man to wait and wonder when that would happen. It had been over twenty-four hours, and still nothing.

I'll decide when and where. That damn woman. I'd make her beg. Because this was ridiculous. *I'm Lucas Fucking Titan, and no one calls the shots but me.*

I had a state senator who wanted an open-ended favor, but I wouldn't give it to him because I refused to be put at a disadvantage—and that was in the face of the twin rewards of proving my father wrong and adding potentially billions to the bottom line of Titan Industries. And yet I'd put myself at a disadvantage to get back inside the sweetest, sassiest pussy I'd ever had.

What was it about that woman?

My office door banged open and Colson walked in.

"Come on in, why don't you?" I snapped.

His head jerked up. "What's got your panties in a wad? Need to get some? I've got this chick, she'd probably take us both on. If you're into that kind of thing." He looked at the floor. "Not saying I want to see your dick or anything, but—"

"No. And never bring that up again."

He shrugged. "Just trying to be helpful."

"Then how about you be helpful by finding me a group of senators who have backbones?"

"I'm working on it. But what you said about Hendricks and Shuman is holding true with everyone else I've contacted. Doesn't matter where their district is in the damn state, it seems that Haines put the word out to steer clear of you and the bill."

"That prick."

"He have some kind of grudge you don't realize?"

"You're the one who did the investigation on him," I snapped. "You tell me."

Colson shook his head. "No connection to you or Titan Industries on any level. Doesn't make any sense other than he wants your favor in his back pocket. He wouldn't be the first or the last. Occam's Razor, right? Simplest answer is usually the right one."

My phone buzzed in my drawer.

"Sure. Whatever. Get out."

"What?"

I pulled the drawer open and grabbed my phone. There was a text alert from an unknown number.

"I said get out." I jerked my head toward the door.

"Fine. I'll go round up more senators."

I waved him off and tapped in my code to unlock the screen. The text popped up when I clicked on the app.

Tonight. Midnight. Dirty Dog. Don't wear a suit.

I didn't take orders, hadn't for years. But this one I would make an exception for.

"What's that smirk for? Normally I recognize them all, but that one's new and different."

I glanced up, the smirk Colson had called out immediately falling away. "I told you to get out."

"And I wanted to know what the hell has you grinning like a little kid."

Scowling at him, I said, "Get the fuck out. If I want you to know something, I'll tell you."

He grabbed the door handle. "I'm watching out for you, whether you want me to or not. So deal with it." He didn't slam the door behind him like I would have, but then again, I was the boss. It shut with a decisive click.

When I looked back down at my phone, my smirk came back again. *Don't wear a suit.*

Did she think I always wore a suit?

Oh, Yve.

This was going to be fun.

I pulled up at the back door of Dirty Dog, the one the delivery guy had used, and parked. Midnight in the Quarter wasn't the safest for my car, but I was willing to take the risk. Yve Santos was a hell of an incentive. I rang the buzzer and waited.

Only moments later, the door swung open and Yve stood inside. I'd expected her in one of her retro-looking dresses since those were all I'd ever seen her wear. I was wrong.

Yve Santos might have looked gorgeous in a dress, but in cut-off shorts and a tight tank top, her hair up on her head in a sexy, messy knot, she looked . . . less polished. More real. Like a woman who was up for a night of hard fucking.

My thoughts made no sense. I liked my women perfectly coiffed and well manicured. I got the feeling that this was Yve's way of telling me she didn't give a shit what I thought about how she looked, and if we were going to do this, then I could take her however I could get her.

If she'd thought to turn me off or frustrate me, she'd made a tactical error.

"Strip," I told her as soon as I pushed inside the store.

"Fuck you."

My brows lifted and I smiled. This was going to be too much fun. "That was the plan, wasn't it, Yve?"

She turned her back on me and headed down the hallway. I caught up with her, wrapped an arm around her waist, and pulled her against my body. Hell, she was a sexy armful, even when she wiggled loose and spun on me.

"I'm calling the shots here," she said.

"No, you call the time and place, and I decide everything else. And I want you naked."

Yve's husky laugh filled the small store. "And I want you to help me move this armoire to the other side of the room so I can put together a new display tomorrow." She waved her hand from one side of the room to the other.

"What?"

"You think I'd really pick my store for a one-night stand? Come on, Titan. I'm a businesswoman, not an idiot."

I jammed a hand into my hair, wondering how I'd gotten this so wrong. "It's midnight."

She smiled. "Just wanted to see if you'd really come." She tilted her head with a mischievous smile.

"So this was . . ." I didn't even have words. I'd been played. *Lucas Titan doesn't get played.*

"A whim," she said with a wink. "Now come on and help me move this."

"You've got to be joking." I stared at the huge piece of furniture. It looked antique—and heavy.

Yve propped her hands on her hips. "What? Don't think you're strong and manly enough to do it? At least you can follow orders. By the way, you don't look too bad out of a suit. I think you look better in one, though."

I looked down at my cargo shorts and Stanford T-shirt. "You're hell on a man's ego, aren't you?"

Yve tossed her head back and laughed. "I think you've got plenty of ego to spare. Now, grab that side of it and lift. Remember—use your knees, not your back. I don't want to hear how badly a billionaire whines when he gets hurt."

With every word out of her sassy little mouth, I vowed that I'd make her beg longer to come. Keep her on the edge until she was screaming for it, willing to agree to anything. It was only fair.

I grabbed the one side and began to lift to test the weight. It *was* heavy. I stopped immediately. "There's no way you're helping me move this. I'll get someone in here in the morning to do it."

"Thanks for the concern, but you don't need to go all He-man on it. I've got a dolly. I just need help with that part."

I narrowed my eyes. "Fine. Let's do this."

WATCHING LUCAS TITAN HELP ME MOVE furniture at midnight was up there with seeing the Northern Lights in Louisiana or finding a winning million-dollar lottery ticket on the sidewalk—impossible to believe. But it was happening.

We set the armoire into place and he tugged the dolly out from beneath it.

"There."

I studied it and nodded. "Perfect."

"Now, strip."

I whirled around to face him. "Excuse me?"

"You knew what would happen when you sent that text message. You knew what I'd think showing up here. Don't tell me this was all a game, Yve."

Heat slid through me as he watched me with those predator's eyes. Green and sharp and missing nothing.

"It was a little bit of a game," I admitted. "But not the

way you think." Why was my mouth dry and the words almost sticking inside?

Titan took a step toward me. "Then tell me. And do it while you take your clothes off."

"You're so damn bossy," I sputtered.

Another step closer. He lifted his hand and pushed a curl that had escaped from my messy bun out of my face. "Because I'm the boss. Now strip. I want to see you naked. I'm not a patient man."

My hands couldn't decide whether to follow my brain—which was telling them to shoot him the middle finger, or to follow the lust flooding my system—which said to strip and then tear all the clothes off his body. It was a dilemma.

Screw it.

"There's a perfectly good counter right—"

I didn't even get the words out before Titan's hands dropped to the hem of my tank top and tore it over my head.

"No bra? Jesus. You've been prancing around here with no bra on and I didn't even realize it."

My breasts—sans bra as Titan had pointed out—were high and firm and didn't need much more support than the shelf built into my tank. And they were also covered by his hands. His big, clever hands. A low moan rose in my throat as he rolled my nipples between his fingers and tugged.

"You have the sexiest damn nipples. So responsive. You love when I play with them, don't you?"

Loath to admit I liked anything about Titan, I refused to respond. Instead, I let my hips rock toward him.

"Answer me, Yve, or I'll stop."

"Shut it, Titan. Don't ruin this."

His eyes lit with challenge. "You're going to beg me. I swear it."

"I guess we'll see about that."

"You will if you want to come," he promised as he released my breasts and gripped my waist.

I didn't even have time to open my mouth before I was seated on the counter next to the register. If I hadn't known how solid the thing was, I might have protested that I'd crack it with my weight.

Titan was unbuttoning my shorts and tugging them off before my brain had caught up with the situation. And I didn't care. I let my brain turn off, deciding that thinking was definitely overrated in this situation. I was going on age-old instinct here.

"Get on your knees," I ordered him.

"Excuse me?" Titan asked, spreading my knees and stepping between them. His fingers caught in the thin waistband of my thong and stretched it.

"I said, get on your knees. Was I not clear?" Power surged through me. "I want your face between my legs."

"Oh, Yve." Titan wrapped his fist around the waistband of my panties. "I think you're forgetting who's in charge here." He tugged and they snapped.

The heat that had already been pooling between my legs turned molten. "Just get on your knees, Titan. Maybe then we'll see if you can make me beg."

To my shock, he complied. He tossed my panties to the side, pressed his hands to the counter on either side of my hips, and lowered himself to the floor in front of me.

He was tall, and the counter put me at the perfect height. Titan knocked my flip-flops off and lifted my feet one at a time so they were pressed flat on the glass and I was spread wide—no secrets left. My balance shifted and I rocked back.

"Hold on," he said, rising up momentarily to wrap my palms around the edge of the counter by my feet. When he had me situated how he wanted me, he lowered his mouth to my center—and didn't hold back.

Lips, teeth, tongue. He tasted me, feasted on me, and within minutes I was writhing on the checkout counter of my store.

Usually I didn't come easily. With most men, I had to force myself into the moment and push away any distractions. But with Titan, I shot straight to the edge of no return every time without difficulty.

I started to moan. "I'm—"

"Going to beg," he finished as he pulled his mouth away and his tongue left my clit.

"Why are you stopping?" My words came out on harsh, panting breaths, and my frustration was impossible to miss.

"Because you're not begging yet."

"Get back down there and finish the job, damn it."

Titan's hands slid up my thighs, coasting and gripping until he spread my pussy lips and lowered his mouth again.

My body breathed a sigh of relief until he stopped an inch away.

"Beg me to eat this beautiful pussy until you come."

"Go to hell!"

He shifted, sliding a finger inside me.

Oh. God. I needed more. Right now. I was hanging on the edge and didn't want to lose my grip on this orgasm. It was huge, intense, and so, so close.

"Just—"

"Ask me nicely, Yve."

"I hate you," I swore.

"This has nothing to do with hate and everything to do with dominance. We laid out the rules of this little game, and you agreed. I came tonight at your whim, and I fulfilled my side of the bargain. I told you what you have to do. Just give me one damn word and I'll give you what you want."

"Go to—"

He thrust a second finger inside me, twisting and crooking them to hit my G-spot.

"Oh my God." I was tumbling toward the edge. He wouldn't be able to stop me, couldn't hold me back. I'd get what I needed from Titan and . . .

He pulled his fingers out and stepped away. No part of him was touching any part of me, and I wanted to scream.

"You're such an asshole," I said, releasing my grip on the counter and reaching for my clit.

"Oh no, you don't." Titan wrapped a hand around my wrist and held my fingers just above where I wanted them. "The only person making you come tonight is me. And all you have to do is say, *Please, Lucas, let me come.* That's all, Yve."

It was like staring into the face of the devil while he offered you what you most wanted in exchange for the low, low price of your self-respect.

The battle for dominance waged on as we glared at each other, and I expected my need to slip away, like water cupped in two hands. But it didn't.

Titan's burning green gaze on mine kept me on the edge. I needed to go over. I needed this.

"I hate you," I said again. This time, the words carried less heat and more frustration.

"I'd be disappointed if you didn't."

I squeezed my eyes shut and opened my mouth to speak.

"Look at me when you say it," he ordered.

My eyes snapped open, and I enunciated each word clearly, but through gritted teeth. "Please, Titan, let me come."

Triumph lit his face, but I ceased caring because he wrapped my hand around the edge of the counter and growled, "Hold on," before he lowered his mouth to my clit and thrust one finger, and then a second, inside me.

Moments.

It took only moments before my orgasm ripped through me, shattering my better judgment and my inhibitions. His name echoed off the walls of the store as I came.

I'd just started to float down off the high of my orgasm when Titan stood, gripped me again by the hips, and flipped me over onto my stomach on the counter.

"What—"

"I can't fucking look at a countertop these days, especially not in my own damn kitchen, without wanting you naked and bent over it."

I heard the tearing of a condom packet, and the heat that had just begun to fade spiked to an even higher degree. I remembered the feel of Titan pushing his thick cock into me, stretching me, *taking* me.

As much as I should have hated it, I'd *loved* it.

He was confident, commanding, and while he pushed my buttons, he didn't trigger any of my freak-outs. It made absolutely no sense, but I wasn't going to question it. Because right now, I was going to get the repeat performance I'd been fantasizing about for days.

"Speak now, or my cock is going to be inside you in less than two seconds."

"Hurry up. Two seconds is too long," I shot back.

A hot palm pressed to the small of my back, and I arched at the contact. He seated the head of his cock against my entrance, and I pushed back, wanting him inside me, but the hand on my back held me in place.

I felt his breath on my ear before I heard his words. "I decide how, Yve. How hard I take you. How many times I fuck you. How many times you come. You get me?"

"Yes, goddamn it!"

"Good girl."

His teeth closed over my earlobe as he pressed inside me. I'd expected hard and fast, but what I got was slow, delectable, and mind-blowing. Once he was buried to the hilt, Titan straightened. He wrapped one hand around each of my hips and started to move.

Every slide of his body into mine lit up all the pleasure centers in my brain. It was like Titan's cock had a magical locator system that pinpointed my G-spot and hit it repeatedly.

And this explained why I remembered his kitchen countertop so fondly and frequently—it had been some of the best sex of my life. Maybe *the* best.

"Are you going to be thinking of me fucking you right here, when you're ringing up customers tomorrow? Are you going to remember how tight your pussy was wrapped around my cock and how loud you screamed my name?"

Before his voice and his words had been a distraction from getting to the edge where I could fling myself over into oblivion, but now, Lucas Titan's voice had become a trigger all by itself. His dirty words pushed me faster and harder toward the point of no return.

"Answer me, Yve. Tell me you're going to remember this."

"Yes, damn it. Now make me come."

"You know the rules, sweetheart. You're going to ask me like a good little girl."

"I should tell you to go fuck yourself."

"But I like fucking you so much more."

"Bastard."

"Gorgeous, stubborn woman."

His words—more flattering than condescending—pushed me even closer to the breaking point.

"Hold on," he said, then shifted positions and pulled me back off the counter so he could slide a hand under and reach my clit.

"Oh my God." I moaned the instant he made contact. I wouldn't last much longer. Not between the angle of his cock dragging against my G-spot and this added mind-blowing pleasure.

"You know what you need to do," he reminded me without slowing his thrusts, and now adding the most exquisite kind of pressure.

My eyes fluttered shut and my body clamped down on him. I was *so close*. And then he stilled.

"*Please*," I cried.

"Good enough." Titan's voice was husky and rough, but he wasted no time in resuming his pace—steady and sure—

until I shattered.

This time I bit my lip so I didn't scream at all, just let the sensations wash over me, wave after wave. Titan let out a roar that would have worried me about waking the neighbors if we'd been anywhere but a couple of blocks off Bourbon Street in a city that never stopped partying.

We both stilled, our heaving breaths the only sounds inside the store. As the crazed intensity of the moment drained away, the reality of what I'd just done set in.

Really professional, Yve. You're one hell of a business-woman.

Even now I could feel the sweat dripping off my forehead onto the counter where I plied my trade—not the flesh trade. Classy, indeed.

But I'd invited him here. Part of me had known that this could happen. *Would* happen.

Titan pushed away from the counter and pulled free of my body.

Would this ever not be ridiculously awkward? With every other one-night stand or fling, I'd developed an easy camaraderie that made this no big deal, but with Titan, it was different.

I levered myself up and searched around for my shorts and tank top. Luckily both were within easy reach. I was already pulling them on when he returned from the little bathroom in the back. He'd zipped his shorts and he'd never taken off his fancy college T-shirt.

Why is this more awkward than last time? It made no sense. Because I couldn't run? Because we were on my turf?

Titan didn't seem to feel the awkwardness I did. He looked marginally disappointed at the fact that I was no longer naked.

I grabbed my torn panties off the floor and held them up. "Was this really necessary?"

He smirked, not the least bit contrite. "Seemed the most expedient choice at the time."

I shoved them in my pocket, not wanting to take the chance of having to explain them to JP in the morning if she happened to check the trash.

"Well, um, thanks for the help," I said. *Smooth, Yve. Really smooth.*

Titan's gaze landed on me and held. "Here's your hat, what's your hurry?"

"It's not like we both didn't know how this would go."

"And if I'm not done with you?"

"You don't have much choice now, do you?"

Titan's expression hardened. "And if I told you I want you to come home with me?"

I thought for a moment about that big claw-foot tub, and being astride the man in front of me while in it. Would he agree to that? Did I dare try?

No. I was keeping this simple. My terms. *I say when. I say where.* And I needed to go home, regroup, and get myself together.

"I'd say you're out of luck."

"Fine. Where's your car? I'll walk you out." His tone was curt, but the gesture was thoughtful . . . and one I wished he'd skipped.

"Car's at the shop. It's gonna be a long walk."

Titan had already turned to head to the door, and he stopped and jerked around abruptly. "The thing had a ton of work done. It should have run fine for another year at least."

"I know you lied about the bill."

"Get over it, Yve. What the hell happened?"

"I got here a few hours ago to work on inventory, and forgot I'd left my phone in my car. When I went out to get it, there was a giant puddle of oil under it. I called my cous-in—"

"Stevie with the tow truck?"

"Yeah." I was surprised he remembered. "And he took it back to the garage. I'm hoping they screwed up, and it's not something new going wrong."

"You need a new damn car. Something reliable."

I propped a hand on my hip. "I'll get right on that, Mr. Titan, as soon as I find someone to give me a loan to buy the business that basically means more to me than anything in my life, and then, you know, stumble onto a pot of gold at the end of the rainbow in the front seat of a new Ferrari."

He ignored my bitchy remarks and focused on one specific point. "How did your appointment go at the Entrepreneur Fund? Did you go? Or did you skip it just to spite me?"

I wasn't about to tell him that they'd met with me, looked at my business plan, projections, and references, then had smiled, nodded, and told me they'd be in touch soon.

Soon better be within days. I'd caught sight of the skinny bitch Jennifer again today outside the store, most likely scoping out the foot traffic. I wondered how long it would be before she made her move. I felt like an idiot waiting to talk to Harriet, but pride was a crazy, stupid thing.

Instead of sharing any of that with Titan, I glared. "I'm

not an idiot. I wouldn't skip something like that just to prove a point to you. Did you not catch when I said this place means more to mean than anything? I'd think you'd get that. Don't you feel that way about your company? Or is it just the gold in your Scrooge McDuck vault that you spend all day swimming in and counting that makes you happy?"

Titan was shaking his head as he strode toward me. "You're something else, woman. Come on." He held out his hand, and I contemplated it for a moment.

Apparently a moment too long, because he grabbed mine and dragged me along.

"Wait, my purse."

He paused and dropped my hand. "Get it and let's go."

"You're the bossiest man I know, Titan."

"How many billionaires have you met?"

"Touché." I grabbed my purse and we headed for the door.

If you'd asked me a few weeks ago how many times I'd ride in an Aston Martin in my life, I would have told you a big fat *zero*. But that number seemed to be rising fast. We neared the street corner that I'd jumped out at before, and Titan hit the locks.

I grabbed the handle experimentally and pulled the lock. It didn't budge.

"Child locks. Because someone has a tendency to bolt at inconvenient times."

"You really care where I live that much? It's not a big deal." And while I preferred he didn't know before, I guessed I was rounding the corner of *I don't really care now*.

"Which way?"

"Right. Pull into the alley. It's the green one—third house on the left. There's a little parking area."

He followed my directions and pulled up behind my building. When he flipped open the door locks, I hopped out. I didn't expect him to follow me, but Titan didn't play by the rules I set out for him in my head.

"What are you doing?" I asked.

"Making sure you get inside."

"I'm not going to get mugged on the way to my door. It's a hundred feet away."

"And yet I'm walking you up there."

We were already halfway to the stairs, so the conversation was getting ridiculous.

"Is this one of those rare times you pretend to be a gentleman?"

He didn't answer, just followed me to my door.

"What sent you running that night?" he asked once I'd slid the key into the lock.

"Nothing important," I lied.

"Something. And you wouldn't call the cops. Has it happened again?"

I punched in the alarm code as soon as I had the door open, and Titan followed me inside without invitation.

"Um, you can go now."

He eyed the security system with interest. "That's new, I bet. Are the locks new too?" His gaze dropped to me. "Whatever it was spooked you badly, and you still won't tell me a damn thing."

I dropped my purse on the tiny table beneath the mirror to the left of my door. "Look, Titan. We might be having a fling, but I don't think either of us is under the impression

189

that this is a friends-with-benefits situation."

He shut the door behind him and leaned up against it. "I have to say this is a new situation for me, where a woman wants me for nothing more than my cock."

"Don't forget your mouth and your hands. Those are important too."

"But not my money, influence, protection, or anything else I can offer."

The word *protection* rubbed me the wrong way. It was just a throwback description to keeping a woman.

"I don't need anything else from you."

"So damn stubborn." He closed the distance between us with one step. "And yet I want you more than I can remember wanting anyone else."

The words crashed into me, quite frankly scaring the hell out of me. I wanted him on my terms; I didn't want his fixation or his genuine interest.

"You shouldn't. You should only want me as much as I want you. Anything else is a mistake."

"Then so be it."

He buried a hand in my hair, tilted my head back, and crushed his lips to mine. I didn't think. I didn't move. I didn't breathe. I just let Lucas Titan kiss the hell out of me in my house and wondered when the world had gone so sideways.

He released me and stepped away. "Don't wait too long to send out the next booty call, Yve. I'm already hard."

Once he was gone, I reset the alarm and checked every room of my place. Nothing else moved or missing. I would have thought I'd imagined the other stuff—but I couldn't make up the words on the mirror.

Part of me wished I'd taken Titan up on his offer to go home with him, if for no other reason than maybe getting a decent night's sleep. But I couldn't rely on anyone but myself. That would be a mistake.

As I drifted off to sleep, I wished instead that I had a huge, scary dog to keep me company. Maybe my girl Charlie would let me borrow her pony-sized mutt, Huck . . .

31
Lucas

I STARED AT THE TEXT FROM YVE.
Eleven. Tonight. Your house.

I would have sworn she couldn't surprise me anymore. But saying she wanted to come to my place? That was unexpected.

I glanced at the time on my phone. It was after seven. I was the only one still at the office, and working my way through financial projections for my project in the event the bill didn't pass. It wasn't a good situation. Without this bill passed, we'd barely break even the first year. And for Titan Industries, that was unacceptable.

The last thing I wanted to be was one of those CEOs who indulged themselves with pet projects that wouldn't add to the bottom line. Granted, this was my company and I had no shareholders to make happy, but it still grated. I'd come this far, made billions of dollars worth of decisions, and if this project had absolutely no emotional significance and were brought to me by anyone else, I'd tell them to show me the business case and move on.

But I couldn't do that with this project. It was *mine*, and I had even more on the line here than the billions I would make if the damn politicians could pull the strings I needed.

Why? Because it was the same technology my father and I had argued about the day we'd climbed Zugspitze in Germany. Only one of us had come off that mountain breathing—and I'd come off it a killer.

He'd sworn I was wasting my time, that it would never work. But even now I was determined to prove he was wrong, that not only was my technology good, but it was marketable and valuable. *I* was valuable.

I gathered up the documents in front of me and slid them back into the file. I might as well get in a swim before Yve showed up, because I doubted I'd be able to talk her into one. I guess we'd see. It was hell on a man's ego that the last two women I'd pursued essentially wanted nothing to do with me.

My father's voice rose again in my head. *Because you're worthless. Always chasing the wrong things.*

Whatever his voice said, I did the opposite. So that meant I'd chase harder.

Yve fascinated me. She was nothing like the socialites I should be courting, but they'd simper and fawn and never tell me the truth about any damn thing. At least, not until they'd gotten a ring on their finger.

Yve didn't hold back, and for some reason her no-bullshit brand of honesty didn't push the buttons my father had found so easily. No, she kept me on my toes, and she also kept coming back, which told me she couldn't help the fact that she wanted me.

So I'd make her want me more.

Yve

THE GATE SWUNG OPEN BEFORE I TOUCHED IT.

Obviously he knew I was coming. After all, I was the one who'd set the time and place, because this was my game.

About an hour ago, he'd responded to my text with one of his own.

I'll come get you.

I'd simply replied, *No*, then hopped the streetcar to the closest stop and walked the rest of the way. Titan didn't seem like he belonged in the Garden District; he belonged in some fancy penthouse condo overlooking the Mississippi. But I couldn't disagree that I liked his digs here. I slipped inside the gate, shut it behind me, and made my way to the house.

I wondered if Jerome would be here, or if Titan would

have sent him off somewhere for the night. I hoped the latter was true, not because I didn't like the old man, but I didn't want him to overhear the screaming I hoped I'd be doing.

Why am I even here? It wasn't something I wanted to question too closely. I didn't like examining my motivations. I told myself it was simply because Titan scratched my itch in a way that no one had before. He was also the least likely person to ever want to complicate things. I gave this thing between us one more night—two, max—and then I'd never see him again. I ignored the pang of regret that followed that thought.

The front door opened, and Titan stood there wearing only athletic shorts and a white T-shirt. His hair was wet and his feet were bare.

How was that fair?

I'd purposefully dressed more casually than I normally would have, but nothing like I had when we were moving furniture. I wore a simple cotton dress, magenta with a navy blue chevron pattern. My hair was up and out of the way because I still had the claw-foot tub in mind. It seemed too intimate, though, as if it was a place people made love instead of whatever it was we were doing. But I still couldn't shake the idea. I'd just play this one by ear.

"Yve."

"Titan."

See, our greetings were even those of strangers. We *weren't* intimate. This was just sex.

"Are you going to stand there, or are you coming in?"

He held the door open wider, and I stepped inside. When he shut it behind me, I froze, my plans suddenly deserting me. How was tonight going to go? My heart thudded in my chest as nerves took center stage.

What is wrong with me?

He must have sensed that something was off, or maybe not, but he asked, "How about a drink?"

"Yeah. Sounds good. Whatever fancy Scotch you've got would probably go down smoothly."

"Then I believe you know the way."

Titan gestured ahead of him, and I nodded before heading in the direction of the conservatory. My steps slowed at the open door to the library, though. I couldn't help it; the room was amazing. I wanted to climb the ladder, glide myself around the shelves, and spend hours checking out the books.

"Feel free to wait inside. I'll get the Scotch," Titan said, and my gaze darted to his. His green eyes were lit with some kind of amusement, probably at the poor girl being in love with books. I didn't acknowledge it, though. I nodded and walked inside the library.

Even the smell was heavenly. Old books. Leather. Murphy's Oil Soap. The last scent reminded me of the parlor of Ginny's house when I used to escape there to spend time with her and get away from Jay. The smell comforted and relaxed me.

I wandered around the room, my fingertips trailing down the spines until I reached the big bay windows at the end of the room. A large, masculine desk sat in the middle of the windowed space, and it was clearly the master's desk, with a heavy leather executive chair and a sleek laptop propped open.

It seemed that Titan never stopped working. Not surprising.

I dragged my hand over the wood of the desk, wondering how expensive the antique was. And my eyes caught on the stack of files next to the laptop, specifically the one on top that had my name on it.

What the hell?

My first thought was that he'd had me investigated, had done a background check. He knew my sordid past and history.

Not possible, Yve. All those records are sealed. Jay's daddy made sure of that.

So then, what? The results of a very cursory investigation? I grabbed the file, not feeling the least bit intrusive. It was *my* damn name, after all.

I flipped it open, shocked to see my application to the NOLA Entrepreneur Fund inside. The original, not a copy, along with all of my projections, budgets, and my personal statement of why I thought I qualified for a grant. I'd poured my heart into that, had explained why the shop and the neighborhood were so important to me.

And Lucas Titan had it.

I felt like he was seeing me more than naked. That I could handle, but this was me stripped raw to the inner pieces of me that I never would have shared with him willingly. I felt violated. Spied on. Betrayed.

Why?

"You weren't supposed to see that."

I swung around to find Titan holding two glasses of Scotch, and not a hint of remorse on his face.

"I wasn't *supposed* to see that? *You* aren't supposed to have it. What the hell, Titan?" I slapped it down on the desk, and after a second thought, grabbed it back up again and clutched it to my chest. "Why do you have this? It's not yours. It's mine. My personal information. My financial information. My *life*. My *goddamn dreams*."

"I made the appointment, Yve. How do you think I got it? I'm one of the major patrons of the fund. I'm on the board. I vet a good portion of the applications myself because I want to make sure we're giving money to people who will actually make something of it instead of just pissing it away."

"You should've told me."

"Why? Why should I have told you? So you could've dug in your heels and said no way in hell would you apply?"

"So did I get extra points for fucking you?" I demanded.

His jaw clenched, the muscle ticking. "What happens between us doesn't have a goddamn thing to do with that." Titan slammed one tumbler of Scotch on the desk, grabbed the application out of my hands, and tossed it back on the pile.

"Oh, so you would've made that appointment for me regardless?"

"If I'd known that you were a half-decent businesswoman with a brain in her head who was looking to invest in the community by buying Dirty Dog? I would've at least suggested you try there."

"But you wouldn't have known except—"

"Does it really matter?"

"Be careful, Titan, or I might start thinking you're a good guy. That maybe you have some kind of do-gooder complex you hide from everyone else."

His eyes narrowed. "Don't mistake me for anything other than what you've always thought I was. I'm not a good guy. There's no way in hell I would've voted in favor of your application if I thought you weren't competent. Hell, I'm still reviewing and judging your case."

"You're the last person I want judging me, you prick."

Titan slammed down the other glass of Scotch on the desk, and the liquor lapped over the side and soaked the papers beneath it. But the papers didn't stay long, because Titan shoved them—and the laptop—over to the other end of the desk.

"You gonna bend me over and fuck me on the desk now?" I taunted him. "We know that's how you like it best."

His eyes burned into me as he reached for me. I should have been terrified, but heat pooled between my legs. I wanted him like this. It was easier to give in to lust when it was fueled by threads of anger instead of some other softer, gentler emotion. That wasn't what we did. We did this— hate fucking. And it was amazing.

Titan wrapped both hands around my waist and sat me on the desk. "No, I want you to see who's fucking you this time. I think you need to be reminded about who makes you come so hard that you forget for two goddamn seconds you despise me and everything I stand for."

I didn't wait for him to move in. I shoved my dress up my thighs, revealing that I was completely naked beneath it. "Well, at least this time you won't rip my panties."

"Jesus Christ, woman."

Nostrils flaring, he shoved his shorts to the floor, and it seemed I wasn't the only one going commando tonight. Titan's cock—thick, straight, and perfectly veined—bobbed in front of me, and my mouth watered. My thoughts from earlier this week about what it would be like to bring this man to his knees by blowing him within an inch of his life surfaced.

But he was already on me and pushing my legs farther apart to make room for his hips. The head of his cock slipped against my entrance, and he thrust inside.

"Oh my God." I moaned, unprepared for the invasion.

Tonight made every other time he'd fucked me seem tame. He pounded me into the desk, thrust after thrust, until I ached, but in the most delicious way possible.

"Beg me for it," he demanded as my body clamped down on him.

"Screw you, Titan," I said, covering my clit with my hand and giving myself the extra pressure I needed to send me rocketing over the edge with a silent scream.

He fell forward over me, the motion of his hips slowing until it stopped with his deep groan, and heat filled me.

That was when I realized it.

I slapped his broad shoulder. "You didn't use a condom, you idiot. What the hell were you thinking?"

Titan pulled away, his nostrils still flaring, but this time with rage. "Don't call me a fucking idiot." He ripped off his T-shirt and threw it at me. "You can clean up with that. And you can find your own way out." He snatched his shorts off the floor and shoved his legs into them before striding out of the room.

And there I sat, on the desk of the richest man I'd ever met, one who apparently had tried to set me on the right course to achieve my dream, and I felt like a bigger whore than my mother. My stomach twisted until I thought I'd be sick on his fancy carpet.

What the hell had just happened? What the hell had I done? Had I found a chink in Titan's impenetrable armor?

And what was I going to do now?

I cleaned myself up, thanking heaven that I was on the pill and hoping Titan hadn't been screwing around with every woman who'd tossed her panties his way. Then I slid off the desk.

As I saw it, I had two choices. I could follow him, or I could leave.

Lucas

I DOVE INTO THE POOL AND BEGAN CUTTING THROUGH the water. The rhythmic motion of my strokes could always calm my temper, but not tonight. Tonight I was on the edge. She'd better not follow me. She just needed to leave.

But, goddamn it, she has no way to get home.

I wouldn't let myself care. I wasn't a good guy. Besides, Yve was a smart woman. Both street smart and business savvy, she could take care of herself in any situation.

Except with every stroke, the almost faded scars on her body flashed through my mind. They weren't obvious, and neither she nor I had mentioned them. Hell, she hadn't even tried to cover them up—a faint slice on her arm, and starbursts on her knuckles where it looked like she'd been in a fight.

For as well as she hid it, she was vulnerable. Just, apparently, like I was.

203

I knew I should have burned that goddamn desk. I'd spent too many years being called to the carpet in front of it and told what a waste of time, money, and life I was. Idiot was a favorite endearment of my father's. Dumbass. Moron. Imbecile, if he was already cracking into the vodka. Hearing that word in the vicinity of the desk had thrown me in a way I'd never anticipated. Ever.

I should feel guilt right now for leaving her sitting there with her legs spread and my cum spilling from her body. But I didn't. I felt shame. Shame for being my father's son. Shame for being my father's killer. Shame for wanting a woman who would probably always hate me for no other reason than I was who I was. And how did I deal with that? Give her more reason to hate me by not protecting her.

God, she'd laugh in my face if I told her that it would be fine if she got pregnant. We'd handle it together. And by handle it, I didn't mean *take care of it*. A heartless bastard like me wasn't allowed to want the things that anyone else wanted, and I'd never admit that I did.

But, goddamn it, now that I had the thought in my head, I couldn't stop seeing Yve in my house, pregnant with my kid. She'd be a fiercely protective mother, standing between her child and any potential threat. She was a lioness—proud, strong, and devastating to anyone who crossed her. The boy in me, the one who'd lost his mother and faced the wrath of his father without protection, wanted that for my children.

And yet, Yve wasn't the kind of woman I *should* want. I should be picking out a former debutante, a Junior Leaguer, someone who would cement my place in society. That would be the good business move.

I kept swimming, I had no idea for how long, and part of me kept hoping to hear the click of Yve's heels on the tile floor. But it never came. So I swam until my arms, chest, and legs burned.

As I climbed out of the pool and surveyed the empty room, I decided that whatever it was we'd been doing, it was done.

Yve

34

I TOSSED AND TURNED FOR HOURS. THIS TIME IT WASN'T fear of Jay or the bogeyman that kept me up. No. It was the look on Titan's face when he'd thrown his shirt at me and told me to find my own way out.

I'd watched from the hallway while he'd gone lap after lap like a man possessed. I had more sense than to walk into a lion's den, and that was exactly what the pool room had resembled. I had one skill honed above all others—self-preservation—and every instinct had told me approaching him was not in my best interest. Whatever he was trying to swim an ocean's length to be free of, it was bigger than what had happened between us.

I didn't need that kind of baggage in my life. I didn't need someone else's problems when I could barely cope with my own. Like my long-lost ex-husband who might or might not be out to get me.

I rolled over again and stared at the clock.

Five a.m. It was a decent hour of the morning. Late enough that I could get up without having to admit that I'd been chased from my bed by bad dreams and monsters. So I did. And that was when I smelled it.

Gas.

What the hell?

Instinct borne of nothing more than that self-preservation I prized so dearly sent me into action. I threw on jeans and a shirt and shoved my feet into flip-flops, then grabbed my purse off the table and ran out the door. I dialed my cell phone as I headed toward my parking spot.

But I didn't make it to the alley on two feet. No, I made it there on my hands and knees as the force of the building behind me exploding heaved me to the ground.

"Oh my God, oh my God, oh my God," I chanted over and over again. I looked over my shoulder and brilliant orange—a color I'd never in a million years forget—blazed high into the gray sky.

Holy. Fucking. Shit.

I tried to push myself to my feet, but my arms shook too badly, so I settled for rolling over onto my ass. I wasn't the only person who lived in that building. Mrs. Jones, the elderly woman downstairs, and Astrid Thomas, a middle-aged postal worker, were also still inside.

Tears burned down my face as I pushed myself to my feet and ran toward the flames, but arms caught me before I made it two steps.

"Whoa, girl. You need to stay the hell back. Fire department is coming."

It was a man's voice in my ear, and I didn't know who he was and didn't care. I babbled incoherently about the other women, and he just held me against his chest and rocked me until sirens pierced the morning air.

It didn't dawn on me that I was homeless and owned nothing until the firemen sat me down with volunteers from the Red Cross. My brain hadn't made it that far. I was still seeing the flames and feeling the heat on my back. I was too busy being grateful that I was *alive*.

"Do you have somewhere you can go, dear?" the volunteer asked. "If you don't, that's fine. We can put you up for three nights at a motel here in town. We'll also help you get started on replacing some things by giving you a debit card with some money on it."

"I've got some money."

The kind woman, Donna, patted my hand. "I know, dear, but it's going to go much faster than you think, and this isn't much anyway. We wish it could be more, but a couple hundred dollars is all we're able to allot you because you're single."

"It's fine. I don't need it."

"Just take it."

I was too exhausted to argue with her. A sleepless night plus the physical, mental, and emotional trauma of the morning had taken its toll.

I just focused on the positive side—I wasn't dead and no one else was either. Numb, I nodded as I learned that Mrs. Jones was in Florida visiting her sister. She'd left four days ago and I hadn't noticed. Astrid had quit the postal service and taken a job working third shift at a factory.

Again, I hadn't noticed. But both those things had saved their lives. Only dumb luck and the grace of God had saved mine.

Donna and her husband—the volunteer team assigned to me—went through the whole spiel about if there was anything salvageable, there were places that specialized in items damaged by smoke, and if I had medications or glasses that had been lost in the fire, a Red Cross nurse would help me get them replaced.

But other than three nights at a motel and the debit card—both of which were more than I expected—I was basically on my own. They gave me a list of social welfare agencies in the parish that could offer assistance, but I wasn't going to be the girl living off taxpayers and the charity of others when I could find a way to provide for myself. My mama had always been so proud that our family line had never been the welfare kind. I wasn't sure when she decided being a mistress was more respectable, but it was certainly an older profession.

As I was finishing with the Red Cross, I realized I had no idea what the hell I was going to do. My car was still in the shop, I owned nothing but the contents of my purse and the clothes on my back, and all I wanted was a shower and not to cry in front of these perfect strangers. I'd been holding it in ever since the man in the alley had set me aside to answer the questions of one of the fireman. Based on my answers, it seemed that either arson or an accidental gas leak was the most likely culprit.

The thought of arson brought my mind right back to Jay and my blood ran cold.

Did he want me dead? Probably. But this wasn't his

MO.

Jay would prefer to watch the life drain out of me with his own two eyes rather than let a fire do it for him. He'd want to make me hurt. To make me suffer. I knew that much about him, and I doubted he'd found Jesus in prison.

I stepped out of the church where the volunteers had brought me—it seemed that this was standard procedure because it was too distracting to answer all of their questions while sitting in view of the remains of what used to be your home—and I looked both directions down the street. I had forty-seven dollars in my wallet, my credit cards, and the Red Cross debit card that I could use once they activated it in a few hours. It wasn't the money that scared me right now, although they were surely right. It was going to be expensive to replace everything I had. Thank the Lord for renter's insurance.

I was only a block from a CVS and a twenty-four-hour gym, where I was pretty sure I knew the manager. Either way, after hearing about my hellish morning, I couldn't believe someone would refuse to let me use a shower.

After checking out of CVS with the basics, I pulled my phone from my purse. It was off. I turned it on to find I had a dozen missed calls from Lucas Titan, ten from Jerome, another six from Elle, and four from Charlie.

I swallowed. Apparently everyone had heard about the fire. The calls that surprised me the most were those from Titan's household. Why did he bother? He'd thrown me out last night. Surely that had been a period on the end of whatever the hell we'd been doing, even if I still wasn't exactly sure what had made him react the way he had other than his general asshole tendencies. But last night it had seemed like more. I'd jabbed one of his buttons and he'd reacted.

So the question was now, who did I call first? I owed them all a call, but I was too damn exhausted to tell this story over and over again. And especially to admit that I thought maybe my newly paroled ex-husband might have just tried to kill me. Fun times.

I stared at my phone, my brain working in sluggish circles, until the screen came to life again.

Jerome. What the hell?

I picked up the call. "Hello?"

"Oh, thank God, dear, we've been worried sick about you ever since Detective Hennessy called to tell us about your house, but he couldn't tell us where you were."

Hennessy. The man seemed to pop up everywhere. Did NOLA's finest not have enough to do other than spread the word about my house burning down?

"I'm okay, Jerome. I'm fine."

"Are you sure?"

"Yes." I wasn't about to explain that I was physically, mentally and emotionally drained, and it wasn't even ten a.m. but I felt like I could sleep for a week. Except I'd probably be sleeping with one eye open because who knew what would happen to the next place I slept.

Would I ever sleep easy again? Maybe in a decade.

"Okay. Good. Very good. I need to hang up now, because I need to tell Mr. Titan that you're answering your phone. And please, if you would, answer his call."

"Wha—"

"'Bye, dear." And Jerome hung up.

Within twenty seconds, it lit up again with Titan's name

and number. Did I really want to answer it?

My brain was moving too slowly to execute sophisti-cated reasoning right now. Screw it. I answered.

"Hey."

"Where the hell are you?" Titan demanded.

"I'm about to grab a shower, not that it's any of your business." Apparently I still had some sass left in me. It hadn't been completely knocked out by the blast.

"Tell me where you are, and don't move. I'm coming to get you."

"Seriously?"

"Don't push me."

I told him where I was. I might have had sass, but I didn't have the energy to argue. Besides, his shower was nicer than the gym's. I still needed clothes, though. I had some extra stock at Dirty Dog that was in my size that I could buy, but that wouldn't hold me for long. It seemed so stupid, but now that I knew there was no loss of life, it seemed less ridiculous to mourn the loss of my stuff. Most-ly vintage, one of a kind, and irreplaceable.

I swallowed back a lump in my throat.

Well, if buying Dirty Dog didn't work out, I'd still be able to put my unique skills to work rebuilding my ward-robe. But if I didn't have Dirty Dog and I had to work at some other job, would I have to dress . . . less like me? The thought horrified me like no other. It was crazy that something so small and inconsequential could set me off, but tears spilled over my lids as a devastating sense of loss swamped me. I sat on the stoop next to CVS as I clutched my purse and let them fall.

Just a few minutes of self-pity, and I'd pick myself up

and move on.

I pressed the heels of my hands to my eyes and the tears fell faster and harder. *It's all gone. My home. My place. My stuff.*

It's just stuff, Yve. And your home didn't even feel safe anymore. My inner, more logical self tried to reason this one out, but I wasn't exactly consolable, because I wasn't ready for logic. I just wanted to cry.

The low purr of the Aston slowed by the curb much too quickly and my pity party hadn't yet concluded. I swiped the back of my hands across my cheeks, wondering how much of a mess I looked. No makeup, bed head, tear-stained face, hadn't yet showered after an explosion had destroyed my house.

Screw it. I deserved a pass today.

And I would rip his head off and feed it to him if he was a jerk. I didn't think I could handle it right now. I didn't have my walls up, and armorless was no way to go into battle with Titan.

Based on our past encounters—especially last night—I wondered if he'd just tell me to get in. But he didn't. I heard the car door open, and I looked up in time to see him crouching in front of me.

"Rough morning?"

I tried to laugh, I really did, but instead I burst into tears again.

"Shit."

He didn't say anything else, just lifted me off the stoop and into his arms before carrying me to the car. He set me inside, secured my seat belt, and closed the door.

I was swiping my tears away for what I hoped would

be the final time when he climbed into the driver's seat and shifted into gear. He still didn't speak as he drove out of the neighborhood near what used to be my house, and headed back to the other side of town. When we reached his home, he still said nothing as he helped me out of the car, into the house, and to the guest bathroom.

I sat on the edge of the tub and gripped my purse and the CVS bag. For some reason, I couldn't bring myself to meet his eyes. Too raw and vulnerable.

"You want me to start the water for you?" His words weren't harsh and they weren't soft. They were just . . . normal. As if I hadn't just bawled all over the front seat of his car.

"I'm fine."

From beneath my lids I saw him reach out. He pulled my purse and the bag from my grip and set them on the floor. A hank of my hair fell forward over my face, and he tucked it behind my ear before backing away and leaning against the door frame.

"You're not fine. But you will be." He grabbed the door's handle and pulled it closed behind him.

I hadn't known what to expect from him, but it wasn't this. Especially not after last night.

I glanced from the tub to the shower and decided that a shower was better. I didn't want to soak in the grime I'd accumulated from being flung to the ground behind my apartment.

So I turned on the shower and waited for steam to fill the enclosure before stripping off my clothes and stepping inside. I pressed both palms to the cold tile and dropped my head, allowing the hot water to pour over me.

They started as sniffles. Little hiccups and catches of my breath. And within moments, they transitioned to full-on, body-racking sobs.

I could have died.

I lowered one hand from the wall and covered my mouth. But it seemed the damage was already done. The bathroom door opened and footfalls stopped at the shower door. I didn't look up, just blinked furiously, trying to stem the flood of tears.

The glass door opened.

I stood straighter, swiping at the tears as Titan stepped inside. Naked.

"What are you doing?" I murmured, my voice rough from the sobs.

He caught one of my wrists in each hand, lowering my hands from my face.

"Holding you," he replied, and pulled me into his arms. "So you can break and not worry about falling apart. Just for today, Yve, let me hold you together."

His words pierced the shield I was desperately trying to throw up between us. How long had it been since someone shouldered my burden? How long since I'd let myself just *break*?

The sniffles started again, and the tears welled up and spilled over my lids onto Titan's solid shoulder.

Just for today.

I let myself break.

And he held me, lowering us both to the floor and pulling me into his lap, until I'd cried all my tears.

LUCAS CARRIED ME FROM THE SHOWER TO THE BED in the guest room after toweling us both dry. He said nothing as he laid me on the soft sheets. He followed me down, wrapping his big body around mine.

Cocooned in the strength and warmth of Lucas Titan, my solid walls shook and crumbled further.

Everything's gone.

I could've died.

The two thoughts played on shuffle in my brain. No more tears fell, but my body still shuddered.

Lucas's arms tightened around me. "Stop thinking about it."

I huffed out a breath. "That's impossible."

Something pressed against my hair, and if it were any-one but Lucas wrapped around me, I might have thought he'd kissed my head.

"Nothing's impossible."

"Maybe not for you," I said, sucking in a breath as warm, full lips touched my shoulder.

"For you either. Not anymore."

I snuggled back into him, pausing only a moment when I felt his erection against my ass.

That's one way to forget.

"Kiss me again," I said, turning my face toward his. "Make me forget."

Lucas wasted no time capturing my lips and taking my mouth. Flares of heat shot through me, pooling between my legs with every moment of the deep, drugging kiss.

Until he pulled away and rolled off the bed.

I reached out and grabbed his hand. "Don't go."

His eyes snapped to mine. "I wasn't leaving."

"Then what—?" I let the question trail off.

"Condom."

"Oh." I breathed out a sigh. "Yeah."

My attention followed Lucas's sculpted ass to the door between the bedrooms, the one that had been locked from my side. He unbolted it and pulled the door open. He was gone only a moment, but I barely noticed as I fixated on that open door. It was as if I'd just discovered a crack in the wall between us.

Lucas returned before I could think on it anymore. He tossed the condom to the bed before lowering himself over me and finding my mouth again.

For the first time, it wasn't pure lust charging between our bodies like lightning strikes. The passion and the hunger were there, but they were softened by something else. Something I hadn't expected to find in bed with Lucas.

My thoughts fell away as his hand skimmed up my

body to cup my breast and toy with the nipple. Heat once against pooled between my legs, and I lifted my hips to press against him.

I needed him. Inside me. Now.

I opened my mouth to say something—anything—that would get me what I craved, but Lucas was ahead of me. His lips dragged down my chest, down the slope of my breast to catch my nipple and tug before he knelt and grabbed the condom. With quick, efficient movements, he ripped open the package and rolled the condom on before lowering a knee between my legs and pressing my thighs apart.

His fingers found my center, slipped through my slickness, and plunged inside. Those clever fingers—and thumb—brought me to the edge before his other knee slid between my legs and he positioned himself above me, his cock nudging against my entrance.

Lucas's eyes met mine as he slowly, inch by delicious inch, slid inside.

He consumed me. With every thrust and retreat, he unraveled me. My mind was hazy, recognizing nothing but the pleasure ripping through my body as his fingers found my clit.

"I'm—" I couldn't even get the words out before the coils holding me together snapped and my orgasm broke free.

Lucas kept his steady rhythm, using his cock and fingers, until I couldn't take it anymore. His groan broke the silence of the room as he emptied himself inside me. Falling to his forearms above me, he breathed into my ear.

"Nothing is impossible, my gorgeous girl."

His meaning hit me, and I couldn't raise the energy

to respond. Drunk with the aftermath of my orgasm, I lay there, my mind blank for a few minutes longer.

When Lucas pulled away and headed to the bathroom to dispose of the condom, reality once again intruded. But the tears stayed away. I might be a little ragged around the edges, but I no longer felt like I was going to shatter into tiny pieces.

Had Lucas Titan just comforted me?

His words echoed in my mind. *Let me hold you together.*

Had he really meant it?

I yawned, exhaustion enveloping me. *Maybe I'll take a quick nap . . .*

My eyes slid closed as the heaviness of sleep dragged me under moments later.

Lucas

HANDS BRACED ON THE COUNTER IN MY GUEST bathroom, I stared at myself in the mirror.

What was I doing? I handled everything that came my way, but I didn't insert myself into someone's life and try to fix it. But I wanted to fix it all for Yve, even though she'd never let me.

What did I do with her now? That was the question. I'd walked out of a meeting when Jerome had called and said she'd finally answered her phone. A meeting I shouldn't have walked out of and needed to return to in order to deal with the aftermath. An empire like mine didn't run itself.

But I didn't go. Instead, I'd sent Jerome to find Yve some clothes and handle Dirty Dog. Hennessy had told us that there was nothing left of her apartment, and I'd seen it for myself when I'd sped over there immediately afterward to discover Yve was nowhere to be found. I'd known she'd be taken somewhere by the Red Cross, but no one knew

220

where. Rather than scour the neighborhood, I'd gone to the office and commenced calling her a ridiculous number of times.

Why did I do that? I wasn't sure.

Probably because she was the most stubborn woman I'd ever met, and if I were right, she wouldn't ask for help. She'd find her own way through a situation that no one should have to deal with on her own.

My phone buzzed in the pile of clothes on the floor, and I bent to fish it out. Hennessy again.

I'd gotten to know the detective when I'd been chasing after Vanessa Frost, and by *chasing after* I meant blackmailing. It had been expedient at the time, but hadn't ended the way I'd planned.

Before I answered, I glanced into the bedroom. Yve was tucked under the blanket, her eyes closed. Her chest rose and fell in a slow and even rhythm.

I could've lost her today. That was unacceptable—as was the helplessness it dredged up inside me. *No one* would take her from me.

I closed the bathroom door and answered the call. "What else do you know?"

Hennessy didn't miss a beat at my lack of greeting. "My buddy in arson says the dogs didn't pick up any traces of accelerants around the exterior, but they won't know more until the cause-and-origin guys get in there. Structure is still too hot to get inside and check it out. Still, even though the dogs didn't find anything, he says he doesn't usually see this kind of destruction from a simple gas leak. This is more along the lines of a major leak or an intentional leak. It definitely came from the downstairs unit that's been empty a few days while the lady was on vacation."

Not Yve's place.

Relief came hard and fast until Hennessy added, "But the weird thing is that the lady whose apartment it was? She says she won the ticket to go visit her sister in a radio giveaway . . . from a station that doesn't exist. No record of it. The ticket was couriered to her house the same day she won it and had to be used within forty-eight hours, which doesn't sound like any radio giveaway I've ever heard of."

"Hell no, it doesn't."

"What it sounds like is someone trying to make sure the place would be empty to potentially rig the stove and cause the explosion."

"What about the other tenant? What did she have to say? Did she have any enemies?"

"From what I've been told, she worked at the postal service until she retired a couple months ago. Got bored and decided to take a job working third shift a couple weeks back. I need more time to dig, but from what she told me, she lives a pretty quiet life. So, the question is . . . what about Yve?"

"Have you started digging?"

"You know this isn't my case, right? I'm just telling you what I've gotten from my contacts."

"Come on, Hennessy. You can't tell me you're not curious now."

"Sure I am, but I've got a ton of other shit on my desk that *is* my job that needs to get done today."

"Fine. I'll ask her myself."

"Let me know what you find out."

"Yeah, I will."

We hung up, and I wondered if Yve would tell me any more than she'd told me last time, that night in my study after I'd found her in my pool.

Now that her life could have been the price, the time for bullshit answers had passed. This all felt way too planned, and Yve's fear made her the most likely target.

I opened the door and crossed over to the bed. I'd let her sleep for a little longer, and then I would get some answers.

Even if I had to fight Yve herself, I would keep her safe. She didn't need to know it, but she'd joined the small circle of people I'd kill to protect.

Jerome still hadn't returned an hour later, and Yve hadn't woken, but my patience to figure out what the hell had happened was wearing thin. I retrieved shorts and a T-shirt from my room and went back into the guest room.

I was still six feet from the bed when Yve's eyes snapped open.

"I wonder if I'll ever be able to sleep through any noise again," she murmured, clearly talking to herself and not me. Sitting up, she pressed the heels of her palms into her eyes before dropping them to her lap and meeting my stare.

"What?" she asked.

I crossed to the bed and held out the clothes. "Here. Put these on. We need to talk."

Her expression shuttered immediately. "Can't I just keep forgetting for a while?"

"Forgetting isn't going to help us figure out who tried

to kill you."

All the ease that had remained in Yve's body drained out instantly, and for a second I regretted it—but only a second.

I needed to keep her alive. That was my first priority here. She could hate me as long as she was still alive, and I'd be happy with that. For now.

She rolled to her side and snatched the clothes from me. Sitting up, she shook out the T-shirt and held it up. She'd be swimming in it, but it was the best I could do at the moment.

"They'll work until Jerome finds you something else," I said.

She slipped the shirt over her head, covering all of her gorgeous honey-colored skin. The shorts followed next.

Standing, Yve straightened her shoulders and faced me. "Don't put Jerome to the trouble. I'll take care of that myself."

So damn stubborn.

"Do you ever let anyone help you, Yve?"

THE QUESTION HUNG IN THE AIR BETWEEN US. *Do you ever let anyone help you, Yve?*

It wasn't the first time Lucas had asked it. I'd let Elle help me the night I found out that Jay was getting paroled. Well, sort of. I hadn't wanted to be alone that night, and she'd offered a place to stay. I'd been her boss once upon a time, even though we both knew she'd only worked the job because she needed something to do and not for the money.

"I feel like you're the last person who should be judging me about this. When was the last time you accepted help? And by the way—why do you even want to help me? Again, you're you. You're not exactly the kind of guy who helps people like me."

"And if I want to help you?"

I pointed to the clothes I wore. "I consider myself helped."

"You have a plan?"

"Not yet, but I will."

The man wouldn't drop it. "Are you going to stay with your family?"

The word *family* never struck a particularly happy note in my heart. "No."

"Friends?"

I'd already considered that. Charlie and Simon had room, but they were crazy into wedding planning right now. Elle and Lord lived in Lord's little house not far from Chains, and they didn't exactly have extra room. Vanessa and Con would probably offer, but that felt weird to me given my brief past history with Con before they'd gotten together.

And that was the end of my list of friends. Six of them. Seven, if I counted Levi, who lived *here*.

"I don't know," I admitted.

Lucas gave me a brisk nod, as if something was decided. "Then you'll stay here."

"I don't do handouts," I said, uneasiness filling me. I didn't want to slide into that dynamic with Lucas—taking something for nothing. Whatever it was we'd been doing, we'd been on even ground, and that was what had made it okay in my mind.

"It's not a handout. I'm the guy you're fucking. If I want to offer you a place to stay, how is that a big deal?"

How is that a big deal? He didn't understand. He *couldn't* understand.

"Because I'm not a whore."

Lucas's head tilted to the side. "You think I treat you like a whore? How? Tell me." He paused. "Are you talking about last night? I don't react well when I'm called an idiot. A moron. Stupid. It wasn't . . . about you."

It wasn't an apology, but he was showing signs of being a mortal man.

"And yet being called an asshole doesn't bother you?"

A ghost of a smile spread over his lips. "No. Because that's true."

I had to get off this subject. I didn't want to see him as fallible, human. It made things . . . complicated. Dangerous. I remembered how he held me in the shower and carried me to bed. Yes, definitely dangerous.

Lucas needed to keep playing the asshole card for me to hold on to this delicate balance between us. This concern, it wasn't something I was used to, and it had the power to change everything.

I tried to put the conversation back on track. "I can always put a cot in the back room of Dirty Dog." Even as I said it, I knew I wouldn't feel safe there either. Not as safe as I felt . . . right here.

His lips flattened, annoyance with my stubbornness clear. "There's a bed behind you that's empty, and you have an open invite."

My resolve was crumbling. I fought to keep it solid.

"What are the strings?" I asked, because in my experience, help always came with strings.

He shook his head. "No strings, Yve. Unless you're talking about the fact that I want to fuck you, but that's no secret. This just makes it a hell of a lot more convenient."

"I don't need you to fix this for me."

"I know, but you don't need to do it all alone, Yve."

For a few moments, I let myself imagine what it would

be like to accept his offer. The lure of safety was strong. The lure of Lucas himself was even stronger.

I was wavering when his jaw tightened and he came closer. Gesturing to the bed, he said, "Sit. We need to talk. Seriously."

The sudden change in his tone sent apprehension crawling over me like a pack of spiders. "Talk about what?"

"About who the hell would want you dead. Because I just got off the phone with Hennessy, and his buddy at the fire department doesn't think this was an accident."

"But the explosion came from downstairs. It wasn't—"

He told me about how Mrs. Jones won a ticket to see her sister on a radio station that didn't exist. Apprehension turned to good old-fashioned fear.

"But still—"

Lucas—when had he become Lucas to me instead of Titan?—turned my chin to face him. "You're in denial, and you're lying to me. If there's anyone who understands what it means to have secrets, it's me. But when those secrets start putting your life in danger, it's time to come clean to someone who can help you."

My determination to be strong and deal with this all by myself suffered another foundation-shaking blow.

"Why? Why would you want to help me?"

"Because despite the fact that I'm an asshole, I'm not the kind of asshole who's going to let you face whatever the hell is going on here by yourself."

I didn't know what I'd been expecting him to say, but that wasn't it.

Wait, what had *I expected him to say?* That he cared about me?

At what point in this *not friends but we've got some benefits* thing we had going on had I started to care about *him*?

I'd watched him swim last night, wondering what the hell had made him flip so quickly, and had lain in bed thinking about it. And this morning when my house had gone up in flames, he'd been the first person I'd wanted to call, but I hadn't let myself. Because somehow . . . some way . . . Lucas Titan had become *that person* for me. The one I wanted to be around. The one I wanted to tell things to. The one who took up more space in my brain than anyone else.

No way. Impossible.

Lucas's words from earlier echoed through my brain. *Nothing's impossible.*

How had I let this happen? Another rich guy? One who wanted nothing from me but my body, which was all I was supposed to want from him.

If I wanted anything else from him, I was going to be in trouble. Because it was guaranteed I wasn't *that person* for Lucas. Men like him didn't look at women like me for anything more than what he was already getting. Right?

Could he see me as something more? A ribbon of hope curled through me . . . until my mama's voice smothered it. *He won't buy the cow if you give the milk away for free, girl.*

Well, at least Mama took her own advice. Could I take Lucas's and accept his help? Weariness settled in my bones from trying to be so strong all the time. What would it be like to let someone be strong for me?

"Yve, just tell me what the hell is going on."

I decided to relent, to let him in. As much as I could, anyway.

"I have an ex. He's not my biggest fan," I finally admitted. Mentally I acknowledged that this was the understatement of the century.

"And he's the one you're afraid of?"

My knee-jerk reaction was to say that I wasn't afraid, but I couldn't conjure the words. They were a lie. An outright lie. My muscles tensed, readying me to run every time I thought about Jay being outside the cage where he belonged. But I couldn't admit that; I didn't want to see pity on Lucas's face. That would be humiliating.

So I went for vague. "It didn't end well and he's been gone a while, and now I think he might be back. I don't know for sure where he is, but better people than me have tried to track him down, and can't." Lucas opened his mouth, but I continued quickly. "I'm not going to tell you his name, and you're not going to find him for me."

A low noise—it could easily be called a growl—rumbled from him. "Why not?" Each word was enunciated clearly.

Because I don't want to change the way you look at me, I thought. Instead, I said, "Because I want my past to stay in my past. And honestly, that explosion wasn't his style."

That scared me the most—I didn't know *who* would do something like that. Yes, Jay was the only one who made sense, and I guessed it could be possible that he'd developed a whole new brand of crazy in prison.

"What exactly was his style?" Lucas asked, sounding as if he was speaking through clenched teeth.

I looked up at him. Sure enough, that telling muscle in his jaw ticked. Knowing that his anger was on my behalf softened something in me. I swallowed, but my mouth had gone dry.

"He was more the physical type." I kept my eyes on Lucas's when I explained, "He liked to see firsthand the damage he caused."

"That first night here, when you flinched, you thought I was going to hit you. That's why, isn't it?"

"I didn't think you were going to hit me. It's a hard reaction to shake, though. It's been a long time since anyone raised a hand to me, but sometimes my body doesn't remember that."

"But he did."

I nodded.

Lucas reached down and picked up my arm, his thumb running along the faint white scar that marked it. "And what was this?"

Just the reminder brought back the memories of the gut-twisting pain. "He broke my arm because a shirt I'd ironed wasn't up to his standards. Compound fracture. The skin split way further than you would've thought."

"Jesus Christ, Yve. Why isn't he dead?" His voice was low and serious.

Because I didn't own a gun to protect myself at the time didn't seem like an awesome answer, although it was the truth.

"I don't know. Not my call."

"He deserves to be."

"Yeah, he does," I agreed, feeling no remorse for the sentiment.

"And you won't give me his name?"

I shook my head.

"And you realize I could get it with almost no effort."

I met his gaze and held it. "Please don't. Just leave it be."

"I don't think you understand what kind of man I am. Because it's not the kind who can let a piece of trash like him keep breathing while you live in fear."

"You sound like some kind of street hood who offs people who get on your bad side."

When he didn't smile, laugh, or even reply, I didn't know what to say.

A few heartbeats later, he said again, "Just give me a name."

"Please leave it be. It's over now."

"I beg to differ. You're homeless. Even if you won't admit it, you believe that explosion was meant for you."

Bile rose in my throat when he put it so plainly. I squeezed my eyes shut and forced it down. I was done thinking about this for now.

"Shit, Yve. Just let me—"

I opened my eyes and met his. "Can we just drop it for now? I . . . I don't want to talk about it anymore." I glanced at the clock on the nightstand. Dirty Dog should already have been open for an hour. I latched on to something I could control rather than this threat I wasn't able to wrap my arms around—or the shifting sands that were my feelings about Lucas Titan. "You need to get back to work, and so do I."

He shook his head. "You're not going to work. Jerome should be there by now. He'll talk to your temp and make sure the shop runs smoothly."

Just when I thought the man's overbearing nature wasn't as bad as I'd made it out to be, he proved me wrong. Dirty Dog was *my* domain.

"Not necessary. I'll be ready in five minutes. I'll find

something there to change into."

Lucas stood, and like a brick wall, he blocked my path. "No."

I raised an eyebrow. I really didn't like the word *no*, especially not when work would give me the lifeline of distraction I needed. "You can't tell me you wouldn't do the same. I'm not helpless. I've had my cry, and nothing I do now is going to change what happened. All I can do is move forward and make sure Dirty Dog continues to kick ass so I can get someone to loan me the money to buy the place."

Latching onto another subject far removed from the explosion, I stared pointedly in Lucas's direction. "And you're not going to pull any strings to help me. I don't care if you're on the board of that fund. You're going to hand my file back over and take yourself out of all the discussions. You can't be impartial, and that's not fair."

I expected him to scowl or tell me I was being ridiculous. But instead he just laughed, something he did rarely enough that I had to stop and enjoy the unique sound—a sexy-as-hell husky, deep chuckle.

When he stopped, a mocking smile played on his lips. "What makes you think anything that happens in the business world, or life for that matter, is impartial and fair? People get ahead based on who they know, not how good they are. Do you know how many applications the fund gets a month? Hundreds. You know how many grants it gives? A handful. You deserve one of them, and I'm not saying that just because I'm fucking you. I'm saying it because you're damn good at running the place. You've got the owner mentality, and now you need the capital."

"I know that," I said, inwardly glowing at his compliment. "But it doesn't mean I want any favors."

Lucas shook his head, and I decided now was an ideal time to end this conversation by walking out the door. I reached the threshold before his hand wrapped around my arm.

"You're still not going to work."

I swung around. My feelings toward him might be confusing as hell, but one thing I knew for sure—I needed him to respect me.

"You really need to stop ordering me around. I need to be busy. I'm not going to sit around here all day and relive the whole thing. I'll—" I squeezed my eyes shut, shocked when my voice started to break.

Lucas's chest pressed to mine. *Safety. Strength.* I felt both as soon as he wrapped his arms around me.

"That's why we're not going to sit around here. We're going out."

I opened my eyes and lifted my gaze to meet his. "In these clothes?"

"Don't worry about that." His thumb smoothed over the skin of my arm. "I'll make sure you're covered."

Lucas watched me silently. He and I were both so damn stubborn. I would push and he would push back. But who would give?

For the first time in a long, long time, I could admit to myself that I didn't want to make all the decisions, didn't want to have to be so strong. The fight drained out of me.

"Okay. Let's go."

Lucas nodded and slid his palm down my arm to lock his fingers with mine. "Good. You'll like this."

Five

THE SHELL DRIVE CRUNCHED UNDER THE TIRES AS Lucas guided the Aston up what seemed like a mile-long stretch of twists and turns. Huge oaks shaded it from the sun, and a sprawling plantation house, one that could have been a replica of Margaret Mitchell's Tara, sat at the end.

"What is this?"

"An investment I'm considering."

"You brought me to look at a multi-million dollar house?" I asked. I looked down at my clothes in horror. "In these?"

Lucas shook his head and drove a few hundred yards past the house before stopping in front of stables that most people would have been happy to live in. "I brought you here to ride. There are plenty of clothes inside. All different sizes, as they're used to having guests come out for riding parties."

I surveyed the stables with skepticism. "I've never been on a horse before. Ever."

He flashed a grin at me. "Then I guess you'll be so busy worrying about staying on that you won't have time to think about anything else."

His meaning was obvious. "A plan for an effective distraction."

"Of course."

"Then let's see this place," I said, pushing the door open and climbing out.

Holy. Wow. There was rich, and then there was *rich*. Lucas led me past stall after stall constructed of ornately carved dark wood—all empty.

"Horses to fill all of these come with the place?" I asked, intending the question as a joke.

Lucas squeezed my hand, which he'd taken as soon as we'd gotten out of the car. "Yes, actually. They're a big part of the reason I'm considering buying it."

My mouth barely stayed closed, saving my jaw from dragging on the floor. I did a quick count of the stalls we'd walked by. "You're not serious. That's so much work. I mean, they're amazing, but *damn*."

Lucas's laugh echoed off the stamped concrete floor and the tall, stained-wood ceilings. "And that's the beauty of having full-time grooms and stable hands. With this many animals, you really have no choice. It's in the best interest of the animals, not just the owners."

If this barn were full, that *would* be a lot of horses. "Is there a reason they have so many?"

Before he answered my question, we reached a room at the end of the aisle and a boy, probably around eighteen or so, stepped out.

"Welcome back, Mr. Titan."

Lucas shook his hand. "Good to see you, Chris. Can you tack up two mounts? Titan, and one that would be suitable for a beginner?"

The boy, Chris, looked at me as if sizing me up. He said nothing about my unconventional outfit. "Sure thing. No problem. I'll go round them up while you two change. Let me know if you need anything else."

As soon as Chris was gone, I tugged Lucas's hand. "Seriously? You're going to ride a horse named after you?"

His laugh rolled free again. "Not exactly. He's a big beast, named after the Titans, not me. Good mount. He was rehabilitated after they rescued him."

"Rescued?"

Lucas nodded. "That's the answer to your question, why there are so many. The current owner has rescued over half of them from bad situations. Some take years to rehabilitate to the point where they can be ridden again."

Lucas Titan wants to rescue horses. The revelation was . . . not what I expected.

"That's actually very cool."

His easy posture stiffened. "It's not a big deal. I'd buy it even if the barn was full of thoroughbreds and Arabians. Of which there are several. And the thoroughbreds bring home plenty of purses from the races."

He tried to hide it, but I'd caught that flash of compassion for abused animals. Still, I'd let him pretend he was all about the money if it would bring back the easiness from a few moments ago. Call me crazy, but I thought I might actually be starting to understand this man.

"The sport of kings. Seems appropriate for you."

His smile flashed again. "Obviously." Then he jerked his chin toward the room next to the one Chris had come out of. "Let's get changed."

I'd been skeptical about the clothes Lucas handed me, but surprisingly my ass looked pretty damn good in these . . . jodhpurs. The jaunty white shirt, black jacket, and velveteen riding helmet didn't look so bad either. The knee-high leather boots were amazing. So amazing that I was tempted to try walking out while wearing them.

When Lucas stepped out of the men's changing area wearing jeans and a T-shirt, I sputtered, "What the hell? Why am I the only one in this getup?"

His smile—it was coming faster and more often now—flashed again. He turned me by my shoulders toward the door, lowering his head to speak into my ear. "Because I knew your ass would look amazing in those. For the record, I was right."

I looked over my shoulder at him. "And where did your clothes come from? I didn't see jeans in there."

"I left them here last time."

His answer raised another question. "How long have you been thinking about buying this place?" It sounded as if he'd visited more than once. The kid knew him by name, although maybe that wasn't surprising. The more surprising part was that *he* knew the kid by name. But I was making judgments again. Maybe Lucas remembered everyone's names.

"A few months. I came here originally as a guest, and we've been in discussions since then. He's waiting for me to make a decision."

"What's stopping you from deciding?"

Lucas's smile faded. "I have my reasons." He jerked his head toward the stable door. "Our mounts will be ready by now. Let's go."

I tried to parse through what Lucas said and what he wasn't saying. It was clear to me that he wanted this place, but something was holding him back. I wanted to know what that something was, and I wanted to know very much.

My mind fixed on solving that mystery, we walked outside and I gasped at the giant, gorgeous beast of a horse before me. "This must be Titan."

"Yes, ma'am. He's certainly a fitting mount for Mr. Titan."

He was a glossy dark brown with a black mane. He stood, shifting on his hooves almost impatiently.

Yes, certainly a fitting mount.

"Creole Belle is yours, ma'am. We call her Belle." He stepped over to stroke the forehead of a much more petite, silvery-gray mare with a white mane. White spots speckled her hindquarters. "She's an Appaloosa. She's been here about five years and is a favorite with our guests who are less familiar with riding."

And hopefully those who aren't familiar at all.

Even though she was small compared to Titan, she looked huge compared to little old me.

The groom ran through some basic instructions and then offered me a mounting block.

Oh hell. Here we go. I stepped up on the block, my

stomach tumbling. A big hand landed on the left side of my waist.

"You're going to do great, Yve." Lucas's other hand closed around my right side. "You want me to get you up there?"

I glanced toward where the groom had been standing, wondering what he thought about Lucas's offer, but he'd already made himself scarce.

"Sure," I said, my voice wavering a little. "I can do this, right?"

I wasn't really posing the question to Lucas, but he answered anyway. "Of course you can."

He lifted me up, and with one smooth movement, I swung my leg over the other side. Belle shifted, and I grabbed the edge of the saddle in front of me.

"Where's that little handle thingy? Why don't I have one of those?"

"This is a hunt seat, not Western."

"I think I like Western better."

Lucas laughed again, and I decided I could get used to that sound. It was deep, dark, and rolling. It was almost becoming . . . comforting.

He mounted his horse and came up beside me before I could figure out what the hell my brain meant by that. Then he reached out and grabbed my reins, positioning them in my hands with his.

"Okay, so Chris gave you the basics, but we're going to take it slow for a little while with a walk. We'll work up to a trot, and you can learn to post."

"Uh, walking's good. I'd prefer to only get back on the ground when I want to, not when I fall off."

Lucas's hand closed over mine where I clutched the reins for dear life. "I won't let anything happen to you."

My eyes darted up to meet his. They were solemn and serious, at odds with the lightheartedness he'd been showing.

"I promise," he added.

They were just two words, but in that moment, coming from Lucas's lips, they felt like a vow. It seemed like he was talking about so much more than what could happen on this horse.

"I trust you." My response, while unexpected, was totally honest. I wasn't sure when it had happened, but I *did* trust Lucas.

His gaze dropped away from mine, and he released my hands. "About this, you should. About everything else, that's a bad bet." The subject was clearly closed, because he added, "Pull your reins to the right. Let's go."

Why wouldn't he want me to trust him? Why was he warning me off? It was as if he was pulling me in with one hand, but holding me off with the other. Did he have secrets to rival my own?

My curiosity demanded I find out.

As the horses walked in the direction of a trail that cut into the trees, I concentrated on letting my body rock with the movement of Belle's stride. Once I got comfortable with it, my mind wandered right back to the man beside me. I dared to take my eyes off my horse and glance at him. Lucas sat easily in the saddle, looking as if he was as comfortable there as behind a desk.

"Do you come out here a lot?" I asked.

"I've been a few times," he said, keeping his eyes ahead.

"You don't seem like the kind of man to take quite so long to make a decision."

"And what makes you think you understand what kind of man I am?"

My horse slowed as we reached a fork in the trail, and I felt like I was living a Robert Frost poem. One trail was sunny and bright while the other was darker, more shaded by the stately trees.

Two paths diverged in a yellow wood.
And sorry I could not travel both.

I'd already decided I trusted a man most considered a villain. Was I making a mistake? *I guess I'll find out.*

Lucas pulled his horse to a halt. "Which path do you want to take, Yve?"

I met his eyes. "I'm following you, Lucas. Lead the way."

My decision had been made.

We finally slowed near a big man-made lake. I had no idea how far we'd gone because I'd lost myself in the rhythm of Belle's movements and Lucas's surprisingly comfortable companionship. We hadn't talked much, just a few comments from him about my form, mostly along the lines of "heels down" and "good seat." Still, it was nice just to *be*.

Lucas dismounted and looped his horse's reins around a post that appeared to have been placed there for that purpose. He was at my side and lifting me down before I realized what was happening. When my feet hit the ground,

I stumbled, but Lucas was prepared. He kept hold of my waist as I grabbed his shoulders.

"Whoa," I said, surprised when my legs shook.

"Easy. You're not used to sitting astride for that long. Takes a little getting used to for your muscles." He lowered his head to my ear. "I've neglected putting you on top. My mistake. Then you would've had some conditioning."

I shoved his shoulder. "You're such a guy."

Lucas squeezed my waist. "One who is ready to fix that situation."

"I doubt my legs could hold me right now," I said with a laugh.

Lucas turned and pulled me into his side, his arm dropping around my shoulders. "Come on, let's walk, get you stretched out, and then you can ride me."

I jerked my head to look up at him. "You mean ride back."

Lucas's seductive grin was in place. "Do I?"

I didn't think before I said, "You know, you really can be charming as hell when you're not being a dick."

One eyebrow quirked up, and I waited for the walls to slam down into place. And waited.

"Are you complimenting me, Yve?"

I relaxed. "I'm just saying I like you this way. You're easy to be around. It's nice. My vote is for buying this place, because I think it makes you happy."

Lucas's gaze shuttered and the smile on his face faded. "What would make me happy is for you to be naked."

Apparently our conversation was over, but I was good to roll with this change of subject.

His hands slid up my jacket until he reached the but-

243

tons, then unhooked them one by one. Once he'd undone them all, Lucas tugged it off and pulled me to the bench near the lake. Laying the jacket over the top, he started on the buttons of my shirt.

I reached for the hem of his T-shirt. "I think you being naked would make me happy too."

Lucas pulled the sides of my shirt apart, and I helped drag his up and over his head. His eyes—hot and hungry this time—devoured my semi-nakedness.

"I don't say it enough, but you're fucking gorgeous. I should tell you that more often."

Something in me, I refused to pinpoint what exactly, clenched almost painfully. "Why don't you show me instead?"

Lucas pulled the shirt from my arms and laid it over his on the bench. "Gladly." He looked around. "Our options are limited, though."

"I'm not complaining." And I certainly didn't.

Lucas rolled on a condom and made use of our limited options. He held me close, both arms wrapped firmly around me as I bent over the back of the bench, and he pressed kiss after open-mouthed kiss to my shoulders, neck, and jaw. His teeth grazed the tendon along my neck as he told me how beautiful I was, how good it felt to be buried inside me, and how he couldn't let me go.

The pleasure was every bit as intense as the other times we'd been together, but there was something very different about this Lucas. He was almost . . . worshipful.

Something had shifted between us.

I moaned his name as I came, with no urging. It was the only word I could bring to my lips. And the tight grip I had on my heart began to slip.

Later, I slowed my mount with a triumphant laugh. "I trotted! And did that posting thing!"

Lucas slowed beside me.

"I didn't even fall." I pumped a fist in the air, bravely letting go of my reins with one hand for a moment. "Win!"

I still felt him between my legs. Which made this all even more impressive.

"Told you it'd be fine. You sit a horse well."

Warmth washed through me at Lucas's compliment. I hadn't been exaggerating before; I truly liked him like this. He was still every bit the arrogant man he'd always been, but now there was a certain easiness to him. I felt like someone had dug a tunnel under the walls we both kept so high, and I'd gotten a glimpse at a hidden side of him.

"Thank you."

"You do other things just as well, if not better."

I shot a sideways look at him. "You're going there again?"

His brow creased and then he smiled. "No, but it's good to know your mind is."

I rolled my eyes.

"I meant at managing Dirty Dog. I attended a ribbon-cutting ceremony yesterday afternoon for a new business started with a grant from the Entrepreneur Fund. The new proprietor was singing your praises because apparently you found her the dress she'd worn for the big day. Several of the ladies present were complimentary as well, and to be honest, they were women I never would have expected to admit to wearing anything that had had a previous owner."

I glowed at the compliment. "You'd be surprised how many society types I have as regulars. Vintage Chanel, Dior, Dolce & Gabana, YSL, Versace—I know where to get the good stuff. And it's classy to be vintage these days."

"It's a credit to you that you know what people want, how to get it, and how to make it most appealing."

"That's my job."

"And when you own the place? Are you up for the rest of the challenge?"

I glanced over at him. He didn't look as if he was questioning my abilities, but just curious.

"I wouldn't be so dead set on buying it if I weren't. Contrary to what you might think, Harriet doesn't run any of the money side. I do everything. I deliver financial statements to her on a monthly basis, and she lets me know if she has any questions. I also deliver a healthy profit margin every month, one that's increased year over year at an impressive rate." I paused. "You do know I got my business degree at UNO, right? Graduated with honors, full scholarship, and I worked full time."

He would have read it in the grant application, so it shouldn't have come as a shock.

"You're type A, goal-oriented, high-achieving. You're a hell of a woman, Yve Santos."

Before I could bask in the glow of yet another compliment, we reached the barn. Chris, the groom, met us outside. Lucas dismounted and was by my side before Chris could lead me to a mounting block. I gave Belle up reluctantly; I wasn't ready for this day to be over.

"How'd she do for you?" Chris asked.

"She was perfect. Which is kind of terrible, because now I'm going to want to do it again." And I really did. There was something incredibly relaxing about riding.

"Fitting that Creole Belle would be perfect for a beautiful woman," Chris said before ducking his head shyly.

I slid my gaze to Lucas. He was shooting a thunderous gaze at the kid, so I nudged him.

Lucas's gaze dropped to me. "How is that a problem? You wanting to do this again?"

I gestured to myself. "I was on a borrowed horse in borrowed clothes. This isn't exactly my life."

Lucas watched me contemplatively. "It could be."

What was *that* supposed to mean?

I didn't know what to say, and the silence grew heavy and awkward. I filled it with practicalities instead. "I need to go get changed."

He nodded, and the moment was gone. "I'll get my clothes and meet you at the car."

Ten minutes later we were driving home, but once again, the silence was companionable rather than awkward.

Lucas's words echoed in my head.

It could be.

I had no idea what to make of them, but my heart seemed to jump to its own conclusions, the cracks filling with hope.

A FEELING OF WEIGHTLESSNESS WOKE ME, AND I stiffened. I must have fallen asleep waiting for Lucas to finish his conference calls with Asia.

"You're fine," Lucas murmured.

"What's goin—" I mumbled.

"You fell asleep in the wrong bed. I want you in mine."

My brain was too fuzzy to argue. I was conscious of being slipped between cool sheets, but after that . . . nothing.

I woke several hours later with a big, hot body pressed against my back. I rarely slept with anyone, and I *never* cuddled.

A heavy weight over my hip and a hand held me in place, pressed to my belly just above the waistband of my panties.

Lucas spooned? No way.

I shifted, and my movements woke the sleeping giant.

"Go back to sleep, Yve."

"Why am I in your bed?" I whispered.

"Because this is where I want you."

I tried to scoot away, to put a few inches between us, but Lucas didn't release me.

"Woman, go back to sleep."

A riot of emotions crashed through me. Hope was chief among them, but I couldn't banish the strands of fear that I was getting in over my head.

Why was sleeping with someone, all curled up like this, more scary than all the sex we'd had? Because this was Lucas. And I was me.

What are we doing?

"Stop thinking so damn hard, and go back to sleep."

I shifted again, and a rush of Lucas's hot breath hit my neck before I found myself flipped onto my back and Lucas leaning on his forearms on either side of my head.

His knee slid between my thighs. "The only reason we should be awake in the middle of the night is because I'm deep inside you and you're on the edge of coming."

Heat pulsed through my lower body as I registered his erection growing against my belly.

Sex. Sex I could handle. It was everything else that confused me, scaring the hell out of me.

"Then what are you waiting for?" I lifted my hips to rock against him and twined my legs around his waist.

"Stop, Yve."

I froze. "Then let me up."

"I'm going to have to fuck you until you black out so I

can get some goddamn sleep with you in my arms, I see."

I had no time to process his growled statement, because my mind was trying to gauge what his hands were doing. In moments, my panties and the T-shirt I'd been wearing were both gone, and Lucas's mouth was on mine. He devastated and devoured before moving down to my jaw, my ear, and then sliding along my neck to my breasts.

He covered my skin with hot, open-mouthed kisses, only lifting his mouth to murmur, "So fucking soft and perfect," before sliding farther south down my body.

Somewhere along the line, Lucas had gone from being my hate-fuck to being my lover. *When did that happen?*

I didn't get a chance to answer my own question because his lips closed around my clit and once he began to tease and suck and drag me toward the edge, I forgot to care. All I wanted was Lucas.

"I'm so close—"

He pulled away, even as I gripped the smooth silk of his hair. "You're going to come with me inside you." He repositioned himself over me, the head of his cock pressing against my entrance.

"Wait, condom?"

Lucas dragged his teeth along my collarbone. "I haven't been able to stop thinking about how good it felt to be inside you without one. I'm clean. I haven't been with anyone but you since that first night."

"So am I, but—"

"You're protected."

"Yes."

His green eyes, almost black in the dim light, bore into mine. "I want you bare, and unless you have an objection, we're done with that bullshit."

I considered it for only a split second before I shook my head. "No. Just hurry."

Lucas pushed inside me—his eyes still locked with mine—with no barrier between us.

The way he took me was all consuming because Lucas Titan didn't know any other way, or at least that was the theory forming in my passion-drugged brain. But this wasn't the crazy, frenzied fucking of before. He held me close with every thrust, never letting go, never dropping my gaze.

When I finally squeezed my eyes shut, succumbing to the orgasm that dragged me to the edge, he growled one word against my ear. "Mine."

As the pleasure shimmered through my limbs, I knew everything had changed.

Five

"IF YOU WANT TO WORK AT DIRTY DOG TODAY, then Jerome is staying there to protect you. I'm not taking a chance with your safety, even if you have no problem doing it."

I faced off against Lucas in the kitchen. His arms were crossed and he was in full *lord of the manor* mode. I raised an eyebrow. "Jerome is my new bodyguard?"

Lucas dropped his arms. "Former British SAS. He might be old, but he's still lethal."

"Okay. Thank you."

It only seemed fair to concede since Lucas had arranged for Jerome to find me something to wear. A white-and-orange striped dress and a pair of purple heels—both courtesy of Dirty Dog's inventory—had been in the bathroom when I'd woken up this morning.

Woken up alone, as Lucas had already gone. Rather than spend any time freaking out over the fact that I'd wo-

252

ken up in *his* bed because he moved me there last night, I'd dressed and made my way to the kitchen—and this debate.

"But you realize he can't babysit me forever."

Lucas lifted a hand to my chin. "He can until the cops and arson investigators figure out exactly what happened and who was responsible." He paused before he added, "I'm not going to lose you to something senseless when we both know I can protect you."

It was on the tip of my tongue to say, *I don't need protection*. But the feeling of foreboding growing inside me contradicted that, along with warmth at the knowledge that Lucas *wanted* to protect me.

"For now," I said with a frown.

"Stubborn woman."

"Hey, I gave in. Don't get used to it."

"I wouldn't dare," he said, his voice low as he skimmed a finger along my jaw.

"I should go then. I'm going to be late."

"I'm not done looking at you."

Speechlessness wasn't something I experienced often, but words escaped me as he memorized my face.

"Beautiful. Smart. Determined. You should probably run while you still have the chance."

I swallowed. "And what if I don't want to run?"

His jaw tightened. "Then God help us both."

Lucas stepped away and dropped his hand to take mine. "We'll find Jerome. He'll take you to work."

I walked into Dirty Dog, my mind spinning about what to

do with Lucas. He was invading every inch of my life, and it should have made me completely claustrophobic and defensive, but I actually felt relieved. No one could argue the man wasn't capable. I'd always been the only person I could truly count on, but now I also had him. And then there was the *something more* growing at an alarming rate.

My old reactions yelled, *Dangerous, Yve. Bad idea.* But these new feelings were drowning that voice out.

"Hey, girl!" JP rushed toward me, throwing her arms around me before I had a chance to react. She squeezed me so tightly my ribs ached. "I was so worried when Jerome told me what happened! Oh my God."

"I'm fine," I said, forcing a smile to my lips as I recalled the terrifying events of the morning before, and carefully untangled myself from her grip.

"Are you sure you should be here? I mean, maybe you should take another day."

"I need a distraction," I replied with absolute honesty.

I surveyed the shop. Jerome manned the register, ringing up two ladies who'd been waiting at the door when we opened. Even though I'd only been gone a day, I examined every inch of the place, noting what had been moved or sold. *A lot of my favorites.* The fun of stocking this store with stuff I loved meant a little piece of my heart went out with each sale. And today, I supposed I was feeling a little more sentimental because . . . well, all the favorites I'd taken home before were gone.

From the looks of it, they'd had a hell of a busy day yesterday. My gaze landed on the antique dress form in the front corner near the window. It was empty. The Cinderella dress was gone.

I guess I should've nabbed it when I had the chance, I told myself, my stomach sinking with disappointment. Because now I had a legitimate reason to start refilling my closet, and in the back of my mind, I'd pictured that dress in it.

"Good day, ladies," Jerome called out, and waved as the women exited the shop.

It seemed that between JP and Jerome, I was barely needed. Which was fine with me for the moment. I was having a difficult time finding my ever-cheery shopkeeper smile.

"I'm going to dig into the inventory in the back and see if I can find a few things that will fit me." I gestured to the dress Jerome had selected. "Although you did a great job picking this one."

Jerome's forehead wrinkled, and JP piped up. "Oh, I picked it." She leaned in closer to add, "And I stopped at Trashy Diva for the underwear. Figured it'd be less weird to have me do it."

"Take your time, dear. We have this under control," Jerome added.

A few hours later, I'd selected and pressed enough clothes for a few days and finally returned to the shop floor.

"JP, you want to take your lunch?" I asked.

She paused in restacking a pile of jeans. "Sounds great. I'm going to hit the café up the street. You want me to grab you something?"

The door chimed before I could respond. Out of habit, I glanced over my shoulder with a smile and greeting. The smile fell away as soon as I saw who it was.

Jennifer. And she was wearing the dress she'd bought

the last time she was here.

I swung around to look at JP. "I'd love something. Feel free to surprise me. Jerome, if you want to go too, that's fine."

Jerome studied me and looked to the skinny blonde. For a moment I'd forgotten that Lucas had designated him as my babysitter.

"I think I'll sweep the front sidewalk."

They both headed out the front door, Jerome grabbing the broom tucked in the little hidden closet up front.

I turned to Jennifer. "Can I help you?" I asked, keeping my tone polite.

"Just stopping in. There were a few more things I wanted to pick up. I was interrupted last time."

I held my breath, waiting for her to say something about owning the place soon. But she didn't. I needed to talk to Harriet. Tomorrow.

She turned to the dress form that had held my Cinderella dress. "Did you sell that blue dress? That's the one I came back for."

In that moment, I was glad it was gone. It was childish, but I was glad she wouldn't have it either. "Sorry, it was sold."

She spun. "I can't wait until I own this place. I'll be able to keep the good stuff and never miss a thing."

I didn't know how to respond. I didn't think she understood that if she owned the shop, I would no longer be working here and the inventory would never be the same.

I dug deep and found my *don't be a bitch to the unwanted customer* attitude, one I rarely needed. "Is there something else I can interest you in?" I almost choked on the words.

She scanned the store, hands on her hips in contemplation. "I think I'll wait for you to put more out. It looks like your inventory is getting a little bare."

My urge intensified to go look through everything in the back and take the rest of the items I'd made mental notes as being *maybes* to add to my wardrobe.

"Then I guess we'll be seeing you later."

She smiled, all saccharine sweet. "Oh, you know you will. I'm hopeful next time I'll have the keys. See you soon, Yve." She strolled to the front door and shut it behind her.

Jerome slipped back inside as soon as she was gone. "I got the feeling you wanted privacy with that one. Any particular reason?"

Did I want to explain? Not really. But would I? A little.

I gave him the quick rundown on Harriet selling the store, and Jennifer's interest and her continued poking around.

"I can see how a woman like that would think she could run this like you do," he started. "But she's wrong. Dirty Dog is clearly the domain of Yve Santos, and anyone who doesn't recognize that is an idiot. I think I should talk to this Harriet woman and make sure she understands that."

His words coaxed a smile to my lips. "I'm going to talk to Harriet tomorrow. I have to. I've been putting it off because I want her to know that I'm serious. I wanted to have some idea of how I'm going to pay for it before I stated my intentions. But time seems to be running out, and I'm not going to miss this opportunity because of my own damn pride."

That was a huge revelation for me. *Dirty Dog is mine,*

and I would beg to keep it. It also raised the question: what else had my pride been holding me back from?

Jerome nodded, crossed his arms, and pressed a finger to his lips. It was officially the new pose of *thinking man*.

"Have you discussed it with Mr. Titan? He's very good at this kind of thing."

"I'm not looking for a handout."

"And he doesn't believe in giving them, so I think you're safe on that count."

JP returned, sending the chime into another cheery jingle, and two more customers followed her inside. Just the distraction I needed.

But still, tomorrow—plan or no plan—I was talking to Harriet. I'd call her before I left tonight to make sure she was free.

41
Yve

WHEN I FLIPPED THE OPEN SIGN TO CLOSED and waved JP off, I was glad the day was over. I was tired. I couldn't imagine how exhausted I would have been if I'd won my way about working yesterday. Apparently letting someone take a little care of me wasn't the end of the world. Actually, it was kind of nice.

Jerome escorted me out the back to his personal vehicle, a shiny black Audi.

"Like the *Transporter*." I eyed his spiffy black suit and bald head. "You could definitely pull off the Jason Statham look."

The older man chuckled. "Maybe his father—or grandfather. But excellent choice of movie reference regardless, my dear."

I smiled as he hung the dress bags in the back, and I climbed in.

His words got me thinking. "You're kind of like a

grandfather to Lucas, aren't you?"

Jerome's chuckle filled the car. "I like to think of myself more of a . . . favorite uncle. Admitting I'm old enough to be his grandfather is a little depressing."

Cringing, I apologized. "I didn't mean it like that. It just seems like you're close." Given that the only time I'd ever asked Lucas about his parents, he'd shot me down, I wondered if maybe Jerome could provide some insight. "You've been with him a long time, right?"

"Well over a decade."

"Was he close with his parents? He doesn't talk about them."

Jerome's glance was sharp. "Mr. Titan's relationship with his parents is something you'll have to ask him about."

So apparently I wouldn't be getting answers this way. But I wasn't done prying quite yet. "They've both passed?"

Jerome nodded. "Yes. His mother when Levi was just a toddler, and his father . . ." He cleared his throat before adding, "It was a couple years after I'd joined the household that we buried the senior Mr. Titan."

His choice of words stoked my curiosity further, but it seemed Jerome wouldn't be sharing the details. He was right—I'd have to get them from Lucas himself if I wanted to know more about the man.

A few moments later, we slowed as the gate in front of Lucas's home rolled open. Pulling in like this—with the car, the driver, the *everything*—made it seem even more surreal. As if I was playing house or something.

It's just until I figure out where I'm going to live next, I told myself, even though part of me whispered I was in no hurry to leave.

Lucas's Aston wasn't in the garage when Jerome parked, and it was on the tip of my tongue to ask when he'd return, but I didn't. It wasn't any of my business. Was it?

Jerome offered to fix me a cocktail, but I declined and headed upstairs with my clothes. I slowed in front of the guest room and eyed the door to Lucas's room beyond it.

Where did I go? Where did I belong? That was the question.

I remembered my first night in the house, how I'd thought I probably wasn't even good enough to clean the place, and yet I'd spent last night in the master's bed. I was living in a weird sort of limbo, and it seemed I belonged nowhere.

The stairs creaked behind me and I swung around. Lucas was on the top step, his expression unreadable. His gaze dropped to the dress bag in my hands.

"You can hang them in the closet with the rest."

The rest? I was still trying to figure out how to ask for an explanation when Lucas strode toward me, plucked the bag out of my arms, and pushed open the door to his room.

I followed him inside, waiting for an explanation. I didn't get one until I ventured into the closet behind him.

It was laughable to call it a closet—it was another room, and not a tiny one. One half was filled with suits, dress shirts, and slacks, all evenly spaced and neatly organized. The other half was mostly empty, except for one hanging bar that was filled with dresses, skirts, shirts, and pants. Familiar ones. Most of the missing inventory from Dirty Dog.

"What the hell?" I said, breathless.

"You thought I'd have Jerome get you one dress?" he asked.

"I-I don't know what to say." About the clothes *or* the fact that they were hanging in his closet.

I reached out and touched a shimmering blue dress— the Cinderella dress. A myriad of emotions spun through me.

"*Why?*"

Lucas stepped behind me, both hands cupping my shoulders. "As much as I might prefer you naked, you needed clothing. You obviously liked these things enough to purchase them for the store, so it made sense to have Jerome make his selections there."

Yes, it made logical sense, but it didn't make *actual* sense.

Old feelings of shame crept over me. I didn't turn, couldn't face him to get this out. The words felt wrong but I said them anyway.

"I'm not your mistress. You realize that, don't you? You realize that it is *not* your job to make sure I have clothes on my back and a roof over my head? You realize that I'm not someone you can just buy and keep in your bed because you feel like it."

Anger and dirty feelings followed the shame, even stronger than before. Because for some crazy reason, I thought things had changed. But they hadn't. He still thought he could buy me.

Lucas spun me around. "You're homeless and you own nothing. This is a helping hand, not a paycheck for fucking me. I expect you to do that for free."

His eyes were hard, serious. He released me and crossed his arms, as if waiting for me to blow up. I would not disappoint him.

I pushed back on his shoulders, putting some space between us. "Yes, goddamn it, I'm doing that for free! Because I *like* you. Maybe I shouldn't, but I do. And when you do stuff like this, it confuses the hell out of me because I don't know what we're doing here. I'm sleeping in your bed. Living in your house. Wearing clothes that you provided. *Everything* I swore I'd never do."

Lucas's jaw muscle ticked. "You swore you'd never do any of that with me?"

I shoved a hand into my hair. "Not you—anyone. Did you have me investigated? Check my background?"

His jaw relaxed only enough for him to bite out, "No, I already told you that."

I laughed humorlessly. I couldn't believe I was going to tell him this, but . . . what the hell. "If you had, then you'd know I come from a long line of very accomplished women who expect certain things when they fuck a man. Like a paycheck."

His eyes narrowed. "What do you mean?"

"Santos women—we've had that last name for over a hundred years because none of them ever marry—are excellent mistresses. It's how we're raised. I think I'm the first daughter in all that time to actually take vows—other than to the church, which is kind of ironic that out of a family of whores we've actually produced a few nuns."

Lucas tensed. "So you're telling me . . . your mother is a mistress?"

"And my grandmother, aunt, great-grandmother. Call it a family tradition."

"And you didn't . . ."

I huffed out another forced laugh. "I probably should

have. Would've been a better choice than marrying the man I did who got his pussy for free and then beat on me because he felt like it. But no, I had to be different. Had to go against the grain. I swore that I'd never get involved with another man with money again. And then you came along."

He moved closer to me, lifting a hand from my shoulder to cradle my chin in his palm. "You're finally getting with the program. Because we *are* involved."

"Out of all that, that's what you picked up on?" I asked, shock coloring my tone.

"It's what matters most to me."

Something squeezed in my chest. "I don't know what we're doing," I whispered, leaning into his touch.

"Does it matter?" Lucas asked.

"Not as much as it should."

"Good, because whatever this is, it's not anywhere close to over."

I lifted my eyes to his. "So you don't know what we're doing either?"

For some reason, the fact that he didn't have this whole thing planned out relieved me. It made it seem like we were on even ground for once.

Lucas stroked my jaw with his thumb. "For the first time in my life, I don't care what I'm doing as long as it keeps going." He stared into my eyes, and I braced for what he was going to say next. "You scared the hell out of me when you didn't answer your phone yesterday. I care about what happens to you, Yve. I care that you're safe. Happy. Smiling."

The corners of my mouth lifted. "Are you saying . . . you like me too?" It was a completely awkward, straight-out-of-junior-high question, but it seemed that both of us were on the remedial level when it came to relationships—again, even ground that steadied me.

Lucas's lips quirked. "Yeah. I am."

"Okay then." I swallowed and we both nodded. But I still felt the need to get one thing straight. I had the feeling that he was the kind of guy who'd take ten miles if you gave him an inch, rather than just one. "But don't think that means you can go buying me whatever you want, whenever you want. I'm not—"

His grip on my chin tightened, his gaze sharpening. "Listen to me. I've never thought of you like that. A whore—a mistress—would be altogether much more inclined to please me. You challenge me, rebel against me, and push me on every level. I wouldn't have it any other way."

Sweet relief, and something much more complicated, swept through me. "Okay then," I said again, unable to find any other words that would be appropriate.

"So are we good?" he asked.

I still had no clue what we were doing here, but I didn't care. I didn't want to dig in and analyze this anymore. I just wanted to live it.

"We're good," I replied.

Lucas lowered his face, and before his lips pressed to mine, he said, "Good, because I'm taking you to dinner."

Rather than argue, I reached up and wrapped my hands around his neck to pull his mouth the rest of the way to mine.

"Shut up and kiss me. We can argue about dinner later."

Lucas

RARELY DID I LOSE AN ARGUMENT, BUT OCCASIONALLY
I conceded—like tonight. Instead of the small
Cajun restaurant I'd wanted to take Yve to, we stood
before the door to one of the last places I wanted to be.

The metal plate slid open to reveal Constantine Leahy's face. His eyes widened with surprise. "No shit. Guess
I owe Lord a hundred bucks because I swore you wouldn't
be back."

"I'm sure you're good for it."

Con's eyes landed on Yve. He shook his head and repeated, "No shit."

"You letting us in or are we leaving?"

Yve squeezed my hand. It was a clear signal to *shut the
fuck up*.

"We were invited. He's letting us in," she said.

Con slid the plate shut and a moment later, the door to
the gym opened. "*You* were invited, Yve. I don't remember

266

anyone inviting him. And you're late, by the way. Elle gave up on you an hour ago."

I considered it impressive that Yve didn't blush. "Got sidetracked," was all she said as we followed him inside.

Sidetracked in the master closet. Because I couldn't keep my hands off her.

And thank fuck she couldn't keep her hands off me either. I'd never experienced *wanting* of this intensity. I wanted her all the time, and not just in my bed, in my life. I wanted to be around her. Hear her laugh. Listen to her tell me I was wrong about something.

No one challenged me like she did, and it was addictive. *She* was addictive.

That was the only explanation I had for the fact that her clothes hung in the closet we'd broken in so thoroughly, and why I would go to great lengths to keep them there. I wasn't ready to dig deeper into the motivation behind my actions just yet.

"Food should be ready in a few. Some of the boys were helping, so it got a little dicey for a bit."

The scent of basil, garlic, and tomatoes filled my nose as we moved up the hall to the kitchen. I still didn't know how Yve had talked me into this—a spaghetti dinner the night before a boxing tournament.

Con turned and headed into the kitchen, which was complete pandemonium. Elle, Vanessa, and four large boys piled spaghetti, sauce, and loaves of thick grainy bread into huge dishes on the stainless-steel table in the center of the room.

Elle spotted us first. "Well, well," she started, and I thought she'd was aiming the words at me, but I was wrong.

"Look who showed up after all of the work was done. Nice, Yve. Real nice."

This time Yve's cheeks did take on a dusky tint. "Anything left to help with?"

Vanessa turned from the sink, wiping her hands on a towel. "There are another six boys out there in charge of setting the tables, and I'm a little scared to see how it's going. Lord is supposedly supervising, so it's anyone's guess."

"Perfect. We'll handle it."

Vanessa's assessing stare landed on me. "You're still under orders to keep your knee away from Con's balls. I have plans for them later."

I choked on the visual. She was certainly no longer the society princess I'd once thought she was. "Not a problem."

Yve tugged me toward the doorway, and I followed.

Two long tables had been set up between the weight equipment and the ring and covered with white plastic tablecloths. Vanessa's concerns had some merit, because four of the boys were on the other side of the room messing around with the punching bags. Lord was with them, demonstrating something. The other two were arguing over who was actually going to set the table.

Yve snapped her fingers and they looked up. "You, plates. You, napkins and cups. We'll take flatware." They didn't move. "Now," she added, and the boys sprang into action.

"You're a general, aren't you?" I said, a smile tugging on my lips.

"I get shit done," she replied and then pointed to the pile of silverware. "You take forks, I've got spoons and knives."

"Yes, ma'am." I wasn't going to argue.

"That's right." Yve winked, her saucy grin in place. It slid away when Lord crossed the room.

"What the hell are you doing here?" He looked at Yve and jerked his head at me. "Not you, him."

"Are you going to make this a thing?" I asked. Keeping up the nice-guy act was starting to wear.

"Just didn't expect to see him back here again so soon."

"Lord—"

I placed a hand on Yve's arm. "I can fight my own battles."

She stared stubbornly back at me. "And so can I."

Lord's deep laugh boomed through the gym. "Looks like you don't need me to start shit. You two have that covered on your own."

Yve glared at him. "Do you want us to go?"

He shook his head. "No. But Con may drag him back into the ring before I let him leave. They've still got a score to settle."

I opened my mouth to retort, but Yve stepped in front of me. "Don't even think about it. We're here for the kids tonight, and nothing else matters."

A foreign feeling took up residence in my chest at Yve's defense of me—a sense of belonging. How strange that I should feel it standing in a building full of people who had their own reasons to hate me.

Lord crossed his arms. "Fair enough. But I'm going to enjoy like hell eating off a table that Lucas Titan lowered himself to help set."

I bit back a *fuck you* solely because of the boys watching us like *we* were the fight of the century. I said nothing, and instead wrapped my arm around Yve and pulled her close.

"Consider it our way of paying for our meal. I wouldn't want something for nothing, after all."

An argument broke out on the other side of the room, catching Lord's attention.

"Shit. I'll be back."

"Don't hurry," I said, not bothering to lower my voice.

Yve poked an elbow into my side. "Leave it."

I looked down at her. "I'm not exactly sure when you got the idea that I would back down from anything, but you need to reset that expectation, love." Her eyes widened, but I pulled her to the table. "Let's get this finished before Con shows up to gloat."

Yve

DINNER GOT OFF TO A ROCKY START, BUT IT finished more smoothly. Yeah, the guys threw barely concealed barbs at each other, but no blood was shed, so I considered it a win.

I was still reeling over Lucas's term of endearment. _Love_. What the hell did that mean? Was that just some weird slip? Did it mean anything at all?

As if I wasn't already confused enough, it just threw me for another loop. I thought about it for the rest of the evening, and continued mulling it over when I'd gone to bed alone because Lucas had some work to take care of. And it was still on my mind when I'd woken up once again with him wrapped around me. It sure beat worrying about whether someone—Jay, namely—might be out to get me.

And I was still thinking about it now, a week later, at Dirty Dog. I hadn't seen Lucas much over the last seven days. He was working on some crazy big project, and had meetings constantly and calls that kept him up half the night.

Occasionally I'd wake up to him climbing in bed with me, and I'd take advantage of the opportunity. One night he'd found me swimming in the pool and had talked me into skinny-dipping instead of doing laps.

We'd settled into an odd, but easy, pattern. I did my thing, he did his, and when I'd least expect it, he'd show up at the shop, lunch or coffee in hand, and spend a half hour talking business, making sexual innuendos that I'd collect on later with a dirty-text booty call, or arguing with me about letting him take care of something I wanted to handle myself, like my insurance situation. He was still Lucas Titan—bossy, arrogant, and sexy as hell—but he was becoming so much more.

The insurance company kept asking me if I'd settled on another place to live, but I'd been dodging the question. I needed to decide soon. I couldn't stay with Lucas much longer. It would be crazy, regardless of how much I was strangely enjoying him helping me out. And that grip I had on my heart? It was getting dicey.

And so was my bid to buy Dirty Dog. I hung up the phone. I'd just left Harriet another voice mail. She'd apparently left the country for a landscape painting class in France and wasn't answering her messages. I didn't have a solid plan, but I had a couple of ideas that would work if she were open to them. Lucas had given me a crash course in the business of mergers and acquisitions a few nights ago when we'd had a rare dinner together. The man's body was sexy, but his brain—even sexier.

The door chimed and I looked up, expecting another

group of the tourists who'd been a constant stream today. But it wasn't someone wearing beads with a hurricane in hand. No, it was a man in a slick suit, skinny black tie, and shoes that probably cost more than the vintage Dolce & Gabbana cocktail dress I'd just priced and put out on the dress form.

Ryder Colson. I still remembered his name, and the cheap way his long, slow examination made me feel. Lucas's number two in command.

What could he want?

"Did Lucas send you?" I asked.

Maybe it was like the times he'd sent Jerome, who'd just stepped out into the back alley to take a call from his sister. He'd continued babysitting duty on Lucas's orders, and I hadn't objected.

Lately I couldn't get over the feeling that every time I left the shop, I was being watched, and the police had no leads in what had been determined to be arson. Neither Ginny nor Valentina had any idea where Jay was, so Jerome was becoming my security blanket. Although honestly, I was getting used to him, and would miss his company when he was no longer around.

Ryder Colson's company, however, I could do without.

He wasted no time crossing the floor to stand in front of the register. "What's your angle, Yve? Looking for a new sugar daddy? Think Titan's the man for the job?"

I'd wondered how long it would take before someone made an accusation like that, but I refused to show any weakness to this guy. "Don't you think your boss can take care of himself?"

Colson's gray eyes went flinty. "My job is to have his

back, especially when someone of your . . . reputation is involved."

My *reputation*? Ooh, someone had done his homework.

"As soon as he moved you into the house, I started digging, but I honestly thought you were too smart to try that angle. And yet it's over a week later and you're still there, so I have to wonder what your plan is. If you're trying to buck the family tradition again, Titan is the wrong man to pick." Colson pressed both palms to the counter between us. "He'll never marry you."

Marry me? *Whoa. I'm still trying to figure out if I'm falling in love with the man.* The realization jarred me because I hadn't yet admitted the possibility in those words, even in my own brain.

I forced out a laugh. "Well, I'm sure not waiting for a proposal."

"Good, because he'll pick someone like Valentina Noble for that. He'll probably keep you on the side, though, if you're a good enough fuck."

Valentina's name on Ryder Colson's lips sent shock waves through me. Long ago, she and I had decided that no one needed to know of our connection because it might cause people to ask how we'd become so close.

"What are you talking about?"

A condescending smile curled up the edges of his mouth. "She's the woman Lucas has picked out to be the first Mrs. Titan, because God knows he'll probably go through more than one." He raised an eyebrow. "It's better for you to be the mistress anyway, though. If you're anything like your mother, you'll last a hell of a lot longer than a wife."

Hot shame slid through me at the mention of my mother. Colson had clearly done his digging effectively.

"What do you want?" I asked, because he had to want something.

"It's time for you to move on out of the house; you've overstayed your welcome."

"According to *you*, maybe."

Colson's mouth twisted. "Come on, Yve. Don't you think you're getting a little ambitious here? Do you even really care about him? Or are you just getting comfortable playing mistress of the manor?"

"That's not what I'm doing. And I'm sure as hell not justifying anything to you."

Colson slid a folder across the counter.

"What is that?"

"Your new place." He flipped it open and slid a glossy piece of paper toward me. It was a brochure for buildings that had been newly renovated into condos not far from the edge of the Quarter. "Convenient for Lucas to visit you from work or home."

He slid another piece of paper across the desk. It was a deed in the name of Titan Holdings LLC, and it was dated three days after my apartment had exploded.

What the hell? Something cold and slimy swam in the pit of my stomach.

"Did he buy this?"

Colson met my eyes. "Well, I sure didn't buy it for you." He leaned over the counter. "He's had a plan for you all along, Yve. Why don't you make it easier on both of you and not put up a fight? Lucas has worked too long and too hard to let a piece of ass distract him from accomplishing his goals. I'm not going to let you get in the way, especially if Valentina's father has connections we can use to get more political weight on our side to accomplish it."

I didn't know what political weight and Valentina's father had to do with anything, but I knew that Colson had overstayed *his* welcome. "Get the hell out of my store."

Colson pushed off the counter. "Ah, the store." He flipped the deed over and revealed another agreement. The heading read Asset Purchase Agreement, and a few things jumped out at me immediately—my name, Harriet's name, and Dirty Dog.

"What is this?"

"Lucas had our lawyers draft it the same day as the condo deed." His twisted smile widened. "Like I said, you must be a hell of a fuck."

It didn't make sense. None of it. Was Lucas just maneuvering me where he wanted me? All of our discussions about how I could find ways to buy Dirty Dog from Harriet—had he been playing me the whole time?

I didn't understand.

Colson slid the papers back into the folder and tucked it under his arm. "I'm sure you'll be seeing these again soon, but I wanted to make sure we were on the same page. My job is to make Lucas's life easier, and you coming to terms with this now is the smart thing."

He tapped the folder on the counter. "You're not going to make an issue out of this, are you, Yve? You're going to go along with everything because that's the only way you're going to get what you want." I lifted my eyes to his, and he continued. "Yeah, I know all about how much you love this place. I'd sure hate to see Lucas pull the plug on this deal before you get what you've been earning."

"Get out," I said, my voice low and quiet. "Get the hell out."

The back door opened, and footsteps approached. "Yve, is everything—oh, Colson, I didn't realize you had business here." Jerome sounded honestly confused by the man's presence.

"Just leaving. Good to see you, Jerome." Colson turned and strode out, the chimes jingling in his wake.

I could feel Jerome's gaze on me. "What's wrong, my dear? You look unwell. Did he say something to upset you?"

I lifted my head and studied the old man. He'd known Lucas longer than anyone, except Levi. I decided to toss my pride to the wind and ask a question I wasn't sure I wanted an answer to.

"Has Lucas set his sights on Valentina Noble?"

Jerome cleared his throat, his attention darting to the clock above my head. "Well, it's not really my place to—"

"Come on. Don't give me that excuse. Just tell me."

He shifted his weight and crossed his arms. "Before he met you, I thought it was a good chance that she was someone I'd be seeing more of. But as far as I know, he hasn't had any interaction with her since."

I hated the spike of jealousy stabbing through me. This was Valentina, someone I liked and respected; I shouldn't hate this so much. But my stomach still rebelled at the thought of Lucas and her together—the gorgeous black-haired man and the raven-haired beauty.

"What do you know about him buying a condo?"

Jerome shook his head. "Mr. Titan often buys investment properties. That wouldn't be unusual at all."

The deed had been in the name of one of Lucas's companies. Was Colson trying to twist this all around? But what was his angle? Some kind of messed-up revenge because I'd shot him down so hard?

But how did that explain the agreement about Dirty Dog? Lucas had sworn he'd stay out of it and let me decide how I wanted to handle it. Had that all been lip service? I didn't know what to believe.

The old me yelled, *Go back to the house, get your stuff, and get the hell out. You don't need someone trying to buy you.* But the new me that had seen more than one side of Lucas hesitated to jump to conclusions.

Look who's finally becoming an adult.

I decided that Lucas and I were long overdue for a chat about what the hell was going on, and I'd be sure to offer my opinion that he should fire Colson simply for being a dick.

When I wasn't in the middle of a knee-jerk reaction, I could think more clearly. I didn't believe Lucas was trying to set me up as his mistress. He'd made no bones about the fact that he expected me to fuck him for free.

This leap of faith might come back to bite me in the ass, but I was going to take it anyway.

Lucas

I STARED AT THE E-MAIL FROM MY SECRETARY. IT WAS the third of its kind relating a phone message from Judge Harold Noble, wanting to know when I was going to get off my ass and start courting his daughter. *Courting.* Was that a Southern thing?

We'd been out once, to a single society function where Valentina had proven she was charming, smart, and a perfectly pedigreed companion. She'd reminded me of Vanessa Frost—or at least the woman I'd thought Vanessa Frost was. I'd subsequently been proven wrong. Maybe I was wrong about Valentina as well.

Objectively, dating Valentina would be a good business move, and my interest had been marginally piqued—after all, she was a black-haired, gray-eyed stunner. But I had Yve in my bed, and thoughts of any other woman paled sharply in comparison.

Yve, who came from a long line of mistresses . . . It was

still hard to believe, but then again, this was New Orleans. Stranger family traditions had to exist.

She was not a good business move. Everything I'd done since I was eighteen years old had been to build my empire—and I'd been ruthless about it. Sacrifices were made, both people and relationships, all for the good of the company. There was no upside to me being with Yve except for my own goddamn personal satisfaction, which I rarely indulged.

And now it seemed I was indulging myself on both business and personal fronts. My pet project that had been slated to earn billions was morphing into a resource suck unless I gave in to Haines; without his support, no one would touch it. And then there was Yve.

I was losing my edge. I clicked on the e-mail from my secretary again. I'd never lost my edge before. And getting it back would mean both giving in to Haines and calling Valentina.

My desk phone rang, and I picked it up. "Titan."

"Hell of a greeting, Titan. I think it's time you and I had another talk."

The man had eerie timing, given my thoughts just now.

Haines continued. "You don't want to agree to an open-ended favor? Well, I've got a real specific one that I hear you might be able to help me with, at least if the gossips have it right."

"What the hell are you talking about?"

"Something that needs discussing in person. Meet me this evening. Seven o'clock." Haines rattled off an address I wasn't familiar with, but it couldn't be far. "If you don't show, I'll know you're not serious about making this happen."

"Guess we'll see then," I said, and hung up without warning.

I really, really hated politicians, and I hated ultimatums even more. Curiosity and distaste filled me in equal measure. Whatever he was going to ask for, I had a feeling it wouldn't be good.

But what wouldn't I do to prove my father wrong? I guess we'd see.

45
Yve

"H EY!" JP GREETED ME AS I RETURNED TO Dirty Dog with lunch for the two of us. Jerome had plans to meet an old military buddy, and had tried to cancel due to babysitting duties, but I hadn't let him. JP and I would be fine for a couple of hours on our own.

And we were. I'd gone up the street to our favorite café because I wasn't letting Colson put me off my appetite. I wouldn't give him that much power.

"Someone just dropped off a flyer for a super-exclusive estate sale tonight." She grabbed a neon-green piece of paper off the counter and held it out.

Excitement prickling through me, I crossed the store and plucked it from her hand. My giddiness grew as I read through the description.

Dozens of well-cared-for vintage pieces by a who's-who list of designers—jewelry, shoes, handbags, and clothes. I skimmed over the part about furniture, antique cars, guns, and the rest, then reread the top part. This had the makings of a jackpot, one I desperately needed to fill my dwindling inventory.

I didn't recognize the street name, so I pulled out my phone and Googled it. It was outside of town about twenty minutes, and the map showed an area of plantation-style homes that looked expensive. *Good sign.*

The preview for wholesale buyers was tonight from seven to nine, and i opened to the public tomorrow morning at eight.

With a smile on my face, I texted Lucas.

I won't be home until later tonight.

The act in itself seemed so damned domestic, but I was too excited about the prospect of hunting through a veritable treasure trove to dwell on it. I didn't get an instantaneous response from him, but that wasn't unusual. He was constantly in meetings, and sometimes it could be hours before he replied. It wasn't something I loved, but I understood.

But I also thought we were due for a serious discussion about what was happening next between us. I wasn't ready to consider the possibility that there wasn't a *next* for us. I was in too deep. I'd let myself slide, and I just hoped I wasn't sliding by myself.

JP and I settled in to eat our lunch at the tiny table in the back room, as I sat with one ear open for the door chime to jangle so I could step out and help any customers.

"So, you and Lucas Titan. Tell me about that," she said.

I hadn't had another woman working here since Elle, and I was seriously impressed by how quickly JP caught on and was charmed by her cheery, sweet nature. We'd settled into an easy relationship, but I was kind of caught off guard by her question. I wondered how much she'd overheard from the back room when Colson had come to visit. The steamer didn't offer much in the way of background noise, but I'd hoped she'd had her ear buds in like she normally did when taking on the monotonous chore.

"What do you mean?"

She set her fork down and lifted her soda for a sip. When she set it down, she pinned me with a curious stare. "I mean, you're living with the guy. What's it like to be dating the city's most notorious billionaire bachelor?" She paused to take another drink. "He's hot as hell, don't get me wrong, but he seems like a total prick from what I've heard."

Apparently Lucas's reputation preceded him.

"We're . . . seeing each other."

"A lot and naked?" She waggled her eyebrows.

"You could say that." I laughed. I was reluctant to share details, but part of me wanted to spill and get someone's opinion. I didn't feel right talking to Elle about him because I knew her initial reaction would be, *Why the hell are you still living in his house?* Because that was basically the daily text I got from her.

"And?"

"It's complicated?" I said, but it came out more as a question than a statement.

"I bet. But it's good?"

I nodded. "Yes. It's good."

"Then you're a lucky bitch. I was just curious, I guess.

You two seem so different that it's hard to picture—" She broke off abruptly. "I didn't mean that in a bad way."

I held up a hand. "Don't worry about it. I'm sure I'm the last person anyone would pick to be with him." I thought of Colson's words. Yeah, Valentina was a much better match.

But I'm not giving him up to her. The force behind the thought took me by surprise. I guessed I'd made my decision. Now I just had to find out what Lucas really thought about where this was going.

"Who cares what anyone thinks. If it works for you two, that's all that matters," JP said. "So, are you going to go to the preview? I'd love to come too, and see how it works, but I've got a thing tonight I can't miss."

"A thing?"

She grinned. "Yeah, an appointment to get a new tat. This hot dude at Voodoo Ink—who I've been waiting months to get in to see—finally had a cancellation. Otherwise I'd be waiting another month."

"Con?" I asked, because he was the only male tattoo artist I knew of who worked there. But he was firmly taken by Vanessa, and they'd both been spending the majority of their time at the gym, working with the kids.

She shook her head. "Nah, he's not doing much work lately, from what I've heard. It's the newer guy. Bishop. He's a sexy beast of a man. That man bun. *Seriously hot.* I've never been all about the long-haired guys, but with him, I can see the appeal. My plan is to get the tat *and* his number. I think he's single. I've been doing some digging."

"Stalking, you mean?"

JP shrugged. "Eh, let's not throw labels around, okay?"

Once again, anticipation filled me at the thought of

the estate sale. It was exactly what I needed after Lucas and Jerome had conspired to purchase a good chunk of Dirty Dog's inventory. I was still trolling my regular sources, but I needed a bulk buy. Maybe I could negotiate something tonight. The thrill of the hunt and the high of bargaining was already building in my bones. It was my fix. My addiction.

"Yeah, I'll definitely go. Hopefully it'll be a good one."

JP squealed. "Awesome!"

We finished our lunches just before the door chime rang. A little distracted, I was counting the hours before I could head out and hunt for treasures—and put my questions about my future with Lucas to rest.

I pulled up to the antebellum mansion at six forty-five. There were no other cars in the drive, which was a little crazy given the load of goods behind those doors and the fact that people like me were used to arriving early to get the best of the lot. Heck, I thought I'd really be arriving too late. I wondered how many flyers had been handed out, because I hadn't seen it advertised on any of my normal sites for estate sales.

The mansion looked like it could be the set for a show about haunted plantations. Older, not exactly run-down, but a stately lady showing her age. I parked the Blue Beast and stepped out. When Jerome had returned from his lunch, I'd shown him the flyer, and he'd immediately rained on my parade. He'd told me under no circumstances was I to come tonight, because he couldn't accompany me. I'd completely forgotten that his sister was flying in, and he'd committed to picking her up.

But I wasn't about to pass up this opportunity. So, I'd *maybe* told him a little white lie, promising I'd come with him in the morning. And I would—to pick up all of the stuff I bought that wouldn't fit in the Blue Beast.

The sound of another car coming up the road had me hurrying up the steps. Maybe I'd just been the first of the vultures to arrive.

I rang the bell and waited impatiently. Footsteps sounded from inside the house.

"What the hell are you doing here?" I demanded as the door creaked open. I opened my mouth to say something else, but the words didn't come. A sharp pain pinched my neck . . . and everything went black.

Lucas

I PULLED UP TO THE OFFICE BUILDING A FEW MINUTES before seven. I assumed I was meeting Haines at his new campaign headquarters. Part of me had wanted to decline completely, but curiosity got the better of me. Curiosity and ambition, if I were being honest.

Sure enough, the sixth-floor lobby had a big sign proclaiming Vote Haines on the door. *Never too early to start campaigning.* I let myself in, but the reception area was empty. I didn't have to wait long, however, before the man himself came out.

"Prompt. I like that in a man, Titan."

"Haines."

"Come on back. You want something to drink?"

"Not necessary." I followed him into a wood-paneled office with heavy dark furniture and leather club chairs. The scent of cigar smoke hung in the air. He crossed to a sideboard and poured himself what I assumed was bourbon.

"You sure?"

"I'm fine. Just here to find out what you've decided you want from me."

Haines replaced the top of the crystal decanter and moved toward the window. He didn't sit, and neither did I. This was a power play, and I was no stranger to winning them.

"It's come to my attention that you've got a hot little side piece."

His statement took me by surprise, but I kept my face impassive.

"I have no idea why my personal life would be remotely interesting to you," I said, my tone clearly conveying that the topic was not a discussion I would welcome.

"Well, you see, that's exactly what I'm interested in." His expression twisted into something sharp. "I've got a problem, and you're the man who can help me solve it. And since you want something from me, I thought we could make a deal."

"What the hell would Yve have anything to do with it?"

Haines's smile turned predatory. "Ah, our little Yvie's all grown up now. Haven't seen much of her in years. And yet she's once again a thorn in my side."

I stilled at his familiar tone, everything in me going cold. "You better be ready to explain yourself."

"You have no idea, do you? That I've known Yve since she was just a little thing. Six years old, maybe? Her mother is a *friend* of mine."

Yve's confession about her mother being a rich man's mistress instantly came back, and the pieces fell together.

"Her mother's your mistress, you mean. If you've got something to say, Haines, just spit it out."

He frowned, as if disappointed that his big reveal wasn't pulling more emotion from me. The man didn't realize I'd negotiated with some of the most well-respected businessmen in the world and come out the victor.

"Did you know that Yve was my daughter-in-law too? Once upon a time, instead of putting her in a nice little house of her own and fucking her on the side, my idiot of a son felt like he should marry the girl."

This reveal had the effect he desired. Disbelief. Incredulity. Rage.

All of them must have flashed across my face, and his eyes gleamed with satisfaction.

"Your son is the bastard who beat her?" My tone was quiet, deadly.

"All lies," Haines spat out, the satisfaction dying.

"I've seen the scars," I growled.

"Then she deserved it," he replied, his voice rising. "Especially because he ended up in prison because of her and that other little bitch. Some of the best years of his life— gone."

"What the hell are you talking about?" And why the hell hadn't Yve told me any of this? But then again, it wasn't like I'd told her about my deep, dark secrets either.

Haines slammed his tumbler of bourbon down on the windowsill. "Yve egged him on, told him she wanted a divorce. He was justified in being upset, and then he went looking for a good time to take his mind off it, and picked the wrong girl."

Disgust at his whole explanation, already twisting my

stomach, grew stronger. "Picked the wrong girl?"

"Bitch said he raped her, and her dad was a judge. They were on federal land when she said it happened, which was lucky for him. I got him into a minimum-security federal prison so he didn't have to be inside with all the animals in Angola."

I was speechless. Utterly goddamn speechless. And Johnson Haines was on a roll.

"My mother, without my knowledge, pushed their divorce through, and then Yve ceased to be my problem. Her mother cut ties with her, and I thought she was done causing me trouble for good. But *no*, of course not. That little bitch has to complicate everything."

"Stop right there." Any more words, and I might kill him.

But Haines didn't heed my warning and was already spewing the rest of his sordid story. "Jay, my boy, finally met a sweet little girl while he was in prison, and then he got paroled. I arranged for the two of them to move outside of town and live a quiet life, but Jay can't seem to stop fixating on Yve. His fiancée is understandably losing her patience, and afraid she's going to lose my boy. So I need Yve out of the way. Need it clear to Jay that he's never getting another shot with her. And one thing Jay has always hated was the idea of keeping a woman. That's why he married her to begin with. Didn't want to make her a whore."

Haines gave me an evil smile. "Well, guess what? That's exactly what you're going to do. Make Yve your whore. Put her up in a nice little house, let it get around town, and then find yourself a decent woman to be seen with in public. Maybe then Jay will finally see her true colors, that she's just like all the other women in her family. He's got a good thing going, and I don't trust him not to fuck up again."

A red haze clouded my vision. "You're a piece of shit, Haines. You *and* your kid. There is absolutely nothing I would do to help you, and you better understand that Yve is under my protection—not like your fucked-up mistress-keeping definition—but in the way that means I'll come after anyone who threatens her with every goddamn thing I have."

He snorted. "And you're willing to sacrifice this bill—and potentially billions—for that little whore? She's not worth it, I can promise you that."

I stepped toward him. "You say another goddamn word, and you'll have a mysterious accident involving that window and your dead body on the sidewalk."

Haines's face twisted, and he stepped away from the window. Good—he should be afraid of me. I was a scary motherfucker.

"You're making an enemy of the wrong man here, son."

"Fuck you, Haines. I'm not your son, and I'm sure as hell glad of that." I took another step closer to him and grinned when I saw his double chin tremble.

"You touch me and I'll make sure you end up in prison, Titan."

"You think you're not the kind of person someone would want as an enemy? I could buy you, sell you, and bury you so fast no one will have a chance to come to your rescue. Do you understand me? And if you ever come near Yve Santos, or do anything to cause her even a moment's loss of sleep or concern, that's exactly what I'll do. You fuck with her, you're fucking with me."

"Your bill is dead."

"Fuck the bill. I'll kill the project myself before I'd accept your help."

Haines slammed the glass down on the sideboard. "You're making a huge mistake. She isn't worth it."

"That's where you're wrong. She's worth all that and more."

I turned and strode to the door. I needed to get to Yve. Now.

I CAME TO SLOWLY. MY HEAD ACHED AND MY TONGUE stuck to the roof of my dry mouth.

What the hell happened? I tried to piece together where I was, but nothing was making sense. I opened my eyes and didn't recognize the high ceilings of what looked like a parlor in a plantation house.

The mansion. The sale.

I tried to move, but my hands and feet were bound to a chair. I looked down, but the instant I moved my head, my stomach churned with bile and fear.

Duct tape. I was duct-taped to a chair.

The old wooden floor creaked as someone entered the room, and I reinforced every bit of mental and emotional strength I had in me.

The sound of a woman humming softly preceded her entry into the room. When I saw her, the flash before everything had gone dark came back violently.

"*You.*"

"Oh, Yve. You look rather uncomfortable," Jennifer drawled, her tone mockingly devoid of any real concern. "I'm so glad you could join me, though." Her hands were folded at her waist, and I marveled at how the skinny blond bitch could jab a needle into my neck and somehow drag and duct-tape me to a chair without mussing a single hair in her perfect chignon.

But what I didn't understand was *why*.

"Who are you?" I demanded.

Her triumphant smile made no sense until she explained. "Why, I'm the next Mrs. Johnson Haines Jr."

My head spun like I'd been forced into an alternate dimension. "You can't be serious."

"Of course I am." She stepped forward and held out her hand, showing off the diamond sparkling on her finger. "He proposed the day he was granted parole."

She was crazy. There was no other explanation. "You met him in prison?"

"You don't think prisoners need someone to talk to? Someone to love them? That's not very kind of you, Yvie."

I hated that she called me by the same name Jay had— right before he'd thrown a punch or landed a kick.

"Where is he?" Strangely, I almost wanted him here instead, because at least I understood his brand of crazy. Hers was completely foreign and unpredictable, if crazy could ever truly be predictable.

"He's out, and it's not good for him to get too worked up." Her mockingly sweet tone shifted to something bitter and harsh. "Especially not about a piece of trash like you. Someone who couldn't even keep the man happy. I don't understand why he'd be still fixated on you. He just needs to *move on*."

"So he's been the one who's been—"

Jennifer shook her head and clucked her tongue. "Oh no, Yvie. Of course not. I wouldn't let him get within a hundred yards of you and your whorish ways. Sometimes men just don't know what's good for them."

"Then . . . who?"

She stepped closer, and I caught a whiff of Chanel No. 5.

"You?"

Jennifer smiled, but it was a smile of the borderline—or completely—insane person. "I still can't figure out why he's hung up on you. All he talked about for months were all the things you did wrong that he had to punish you for. You should have thanked me for moving that glass. It would've made him so angry." Her eyes hardened. "I should've left it, though. It would've shown him you hadn't changed. Not that I would've let him get inside your house. No, I keep a tight leash on my man. I'm sure you don't know a thing about that."

So she'd moved the glass. Stolen the perfume. Left the message on the mirror.

"And the explosion?"

A sickly gleeful expression stole across her face. "You-Tube is so handy. You can really learn to do anything. Except get people to stay where they're supposed to be." Her smile twisted. "Because then we wouldn't be having this discussion, now would we?"

"Why?" I demanded. "Are you crazy?"

"I prefer the term creative. Keeping tabs on you, tabs on

him trying to keep tabs on you—it got so tiring. I just want to get married and live my life. I didn't need you hanging over everything. Jay loves *me. Only me.*"

"Good. I don't want anything to do with him."

"But he just can't seem to get over his first love. So I thought I'd help." She raised her hand, and the sharp silver blade of a knife caught the light. "By cutting you out of the picture."

Lucas

I FLOORED THE ASTON AND HEADED HOME. YVE WASN'T picking up her phone, and the text she'd sent me hours ago had been completely vague. My next call was to Jerome, who answered on the third ring, thank God.

I didn't bother with a greeting. "Where the hell is she?"

"She should be home," he replied. "I'm just leaving the airport. Monica's flight was twenty minutes out and had to be rerouted to Baton Rouge due to a medical emergency. She'll be in late tonight."

"That's what Yve said. She'd be home later tonight. In a text."

Jerome was silent for a moment on the other end of the line. "She said she wouldn't go."

"Go where?" I demanded.

"A huge estate sale. Tonight. Dealers and wholesalers early preview. She wanted to go but I told her that I couldn't come. She promised she'd go tomorrow."

Yve and an estate sale. That made complete sense, but still my panic grew—panic I hadn't felt since the morning her apartment had exploded and I couldn't reach her. That morning everything had started to become really clear: Yve mattered. A whole hell of a lot. And tonight I'd chosen her over business when Haines had tossed out his ultimatum. I'd thrown it back in his face because it would have meant hurting her. Apparently I'd officially found the one line I wouldn't cross.

I wanted her in my house, in my bed, in my life, and there was no way in hell I would let anything happen to jeopardize that.

I slowed at a stoplight. "Do you have the address of the sale?" Even though the panic had subsided, a sense of foreboding washed over me. Haines's son—a convicted fucking rapist—was still out there, and according to Haines, still obsessed. And Yve was alone. I would not leave her vulnerable.

"I don't recall the address, but JP will have it. I'll get it from her and text it to you. I'll meet you there."

I almost told him it wasn't necessary, but maybe Yve would finally understand how seriously I took her safety if we both showed up. It wasn't a game, and she knew that. She knew better than anyone what her ex was capable of, and I was going to make sure she didn't take another risk like this again.

"Okay. I'll see you there."

I pulled into a parking lot to wait, but instead of texting me back, Jerome called a few minutes later.

"According to JP, she did go to the sale," he reported. "But she also mentioned something I hadn't realized. The flyer came in via a street kid today, not by mail or someone they knew."

"That doesn't sound normal."

"JP thought it seemed a little strange, especially given that it was all high-end stuff, and the sale wasn't listed on any of the normal places Yve looked."

"Give me the address."

I punched it into the GPS as he relayed it. Urgency and rage twined together in my gut.

An estate sale of high-end stuff, unusual notification, and still . . . something that Yve wouldn't be able to resist.

"GPS says twenty minutes. I'll be there in ten. I'll call you if it's nothing. But this doesn't feel right."

"Agreed. Please try to keep from killing yourself on the way there," Jerome replied.

"Done." I hung up and roared out of the parking lot.

Hennessy was my next call. Maybe it was overkill, but this one felt bad all the way to my gut.

"It's Yve's ex-husband. He's obsessed with her," I said as soon as he answered.

"Hello to you too, Titan. What the hell are you talking about?"

"Yve's ex-husband. He has to be the one who caused the apartment explosion."

"We've still got no leads, so I'll take what I can get."

I relayed the information about the estate sale and my gut reaction.

"Could be harmless," Hennessy remarked.

"I'm not taking any chances."

"Shit, man. You driving out there?"

"Right now."

"Call if you need backup."

"I'll call you if we need body bags." I hung up before he could reply.

JENNIFER CAME CLOSER TO ME WITH THE KNIFE, BUT MY fight-or-flight response was thwarted by the damn duct tape. I needed to keep her talking. I really, really needed to avoid the pain that would come with that knife. You know, or getting dead. I had too much left to live for.

Taped to a chair, facing down a crazy bitch with a knife, a lot of things became perfectly clear. I was in love with Lucas Titan.

I'd sworn I'd never fall again—especially for a rich guy—but with Lucas, it hadn't been a choice. He'd never made me feel like a possession to be owned. To the contrary, he'd made me feel like I was precious and worth protecting. I couldn't hold who he was or what he had against him, because it was all an integral part of what made him Lucas Fucking Titan. And I loved him.

I didn't know if he loved me too, but I wasn't going to die before I found out.

"Why did you pretend to want to buy the store?" I asked, both to get a conversation going and because that part still didn't make any sense.

Jennifer smiled in that crazy *I've got a whole mess of screws loose* way of hers. "Because Jay seemed so impressed that you were running it. It's just a silly little store. How hard could it really be? And it wasn't pretend. I am going to buy it and run it. Then he can be impressed with *me* running it."

I wondered if the same argument applied to taking the perfume. Because if Jay liked it on me, then he'd like it on her. She was too blond and skinny to come anywhere close to looking like me, but her style was remarkably similar, right down to the dress and pumps and hairstyle. Had she been trying to copy me in hopes that she'd somehow be more secure with Jay? Why would she even want to?

"Does he hit you?" The question was out before I could weigh whether asking it was a good idea.

She raised her chin. "Jay would never hurt me. I would never give him a reason to." Glaring, she added, "Unlike some people."

Oh, this again. The idea that I'd been abused because it was somehow my fault. Awesome. Glad we were still on that. Fuck her.

"Does he know you blew up my apartment? Does he know what you're doing right now?"

She laughed, and the sound sent ice water trickling down my spine. "Men don't need to know every little thing, silly girl. And this is for his own good. You know why? Because once he sees your name on a tomb, he'll never worry about you again."

"Aren't you afraid he'll despise you forever if he knows you hurt me?" It was a crazy assumption, but maybe if she thought he was still in love with me, then he wouldn't want her to hurt me. And I was desperate.

"He loves me. He'll thank me someday."

I tried a different tack. "I think you're miscalculating. Jay doesn't want me back. And if anything, he'd want to hurt me himself. So you're taking away something he'd prefer to do. How is that fair?"

It was the sickest and most messed-up argument I could offer, but again—desperation.

"Then maybe I'll never let him find out what happened to you."

"You think he'll just stop wondering if I go missing? You don't think that's going to make him even more likely to keep looking for me? This isn't going to work out how you planned, Jennifer. I promise."

She came closer and lowered her face into mine. "It's going to work exactly how I planned, and he'll never know any different."

The sound of gravel crunching in the driveway out front got our attention. My stomach churned again.

"Are you sure about that?"

Her head jerked up. "It's not him—" The sound of a mechanical motor droned from a distance.

The garage door. It was him.

I never thought I'd be happy to see Jay Haines again, ever, but I was hoping and praying it was him. Anything to buy me enough time to try to get away. Even if it was my worst nightmare come to life.

Jennifer dropped a hand to her hip, looking put out

and maybe the slightest bit panicked. "He's not supposed to come home for a few more hours."

"Looks like you're going to have some explaining to do."

A door opened somewhere in the house and heavy footsteps thudded on the wood floor. I braced myself for the first sight of my ex-husband in years.

My heartbeat ramped up as he crossed into the parlor. He was still tall with blond hair, but was now about fifty pounds heavier—and none of it muscle. His blue eyes landed on me, and his rounded face pinched with confusion.

"Yve?"

"Hey, Jay. How's it going? Glad you found a new friend while you were in prison." Where the lady balls came from for me to toss those words out in that joking tone, I'll never know.

His eyes snapped to Jennifer. "Jenny, what's going on? What are you doing?"

She tucked the knife behind her back, and her words came out in a tone that was nothing like the one she'd used with me. "She came after me; you have no idea how scared I was. I had to protect myself."

A bark of laughter escaped my lips. "That's your story? That I came after you? Not that you've been stalking me, breaking into my apartment, leaving threatening notes on my mirror, and oh—blowing up my apartment and then luring me here to kill me? I'm sure he's going to buy it."

Jay looked just as confused as ever. "What is she talking about, Jenny? You'd never do anything to hurt Yvie. You know that she's—"

"Your past! She's your past, and I'm your future! She's

nothing. I'm the only one that matters!"

And the train had officially pulled into Crazy Town.

Jay came closer, and it was more than ironic that at this moment, I was looking at him as if he might save me, and at a tiny little blonde like she was the biggest threat in the room. But that would be a mistake.

"How've you been, Yvie?"

The fact that Jay could start a regular conversation with me while I was duct-taped to a chair was just one more sign that he wasn't altogether there either.

I swallowed. I really didn't want to have this conversation, but I didn't want whatever the alternative was even more, because I doubted it involved me walking out the door unharmed.

He circled me before crouching near my feet. "You answer me when I ask you a question, Yvie. You can't have forgotten our rules already."

All the memories of pain and shame flooded me.

Jay's fucking rules. There were so many. Always changing, so they were impossible to keep track of or get right. Toward the end, it was a rare day when I could make it through without tripping over some unknown *rule* I was supposed to be following.

Every old scar and injury seemed to light up in ghosting pains, as if they knew what was coming. My ribs, my collarbone, my left arm, the fingers of my right hand, and countless others. I straightened, locking it all down. I was no longer a victim. I would not cower in front of him like a dog.

"I'm great, Jay. Just great. And my boyfriend is going to kick your ass when he finds out that your fiancée tied me to a chair."

It was the first time I'd ever referred to Lucas as ... anything, really. But in that moment, thinking of him gave me strength.

It was the wrong move.

"Boyfriend? You're still my goddamned wife. I don't care what the goddamned papers say. You belong to *me*." His hand swung out and caught me high on the cheekbone.

Shock—at being hit again for the first time in so long—radiated through me before the pain registered.

"What the hell?" Jennifer's screeched words pierced my ears. "I'm going to be your wife. She means *nothing*!"

Jay swung around to face her, and I couldn't help but watch. She was gesturing with the knife.

Oh hell.

"What do you think you're going to do with that, Jenny? What *did* you think you were going to do with that?"

"I'm just doing what I had to do."

Jay's lungs heaved and he lost it. He charged the skinny little blonde and ripped the knife from her hand. It clattered to the floor and skidded within inches of my feet as his hand wrapped around her neck and he lifted her off the floor.

Oh shit. I was not here to die, and I certainly wasn't here to witness a murder. Jay had caused enough damage.

I reached with the tip of my purple pump and slid the knife closer. *How the hell do I get it off the floor?* Then I slid my feet together and tried to lift, but the knife dropped to the floor again with another thump. *This shit looks so much easier in the movies.*

My ridiculous thought was interrupted by someone

banging on the door.

Jay tossed Jenny onto the couch. "Don't you dare move, Jen."

The blonde looked shell-shocked, her face pale, her hair mussed, and her tears leaving mascara-blackened trails down her cheeks.

He really hadn't hit her before. The first time was always the most shocking.

I eyed the knife on the floor again. The man was never going to hit anyone again.

Lucas

GRAVEL FLEW, PINGING OFF THE PANELS OF MY CAR, but I didn't give a fuck. I'd called and called, and Yve never answered. I'd tried to tell myself that it was a lack of reception out here, but my phone worked perfectly, so that excuse fell flat.

I roared up the driveway and pulled the car to a jerky stop, then jumped out and leaped up the front steps. I turned the door handle, but it was locked, so I hammered on the solid wood with my fist.

Footsteps thudded inside, and the door was ripped open.

A younger version of Johnson Haines stood before me. I didn't think—I didn't have to—I just swung, the moves from my boxing lesson coming into play, along with a few dirty ones of my own. Right hook to the jaw, uppercut, knee to the gut. He hit the hallway floor and instantly rolled onto his side in a protective ball.

I was on him again in seconds. Flipping him over, I dropped to my knees and wrapped my hands around his throat.

He would die.

A scream ripped my attention away from the man beneath me.

"If he dies, she dies."

I glanced to my left to see a tiny blonde holding a knife to Yve's throat where she sat taped to a chair in the middle of the parlor. Haines groaned below me, but I didn't take my eyes off Yve. She opened her mouth to speak, but the blonde pressed the blade harder until a rivulet of blood ran down Yve's neck.

I released my grip and Haines jumped up, landing a blow to my cheek before I could react. All I could see as I swung at him was the blood dripping down Yve's throat.

Rage, helplessness, and disbelief like I hadn't felt since I was on the side of that mountain at eighteen slammed into me. The rope had been fraying, and I'd had seconds to grab it, but if I did I'd likely fall to my own death.

It had been an impossible choice—risk my own life, or my father would die. The man who'd verbally abused me all my life; the man I was never good enough for. I hesitated a second too long, and when I'd lunged for the rope, it had been too late.

I'd had to live with the regret of that moment haunting me for years. If I had to live with regret over Yve, I . . . Well, it wasn't an option. I'd choose her life over mine every time.

Because I loved her.

I shoved Haines away from me and stood, holding my arms out. "I'm done. Don't hurt her."

He jumped to his feet. "You're gonna die."

Except if I was dead, I'd be leaving her at their mercy, and that would be a fate worse than death for Yve. *So, Titan, what the fuck are you going to do?* my brain taunted me.

So I did what came naturally to me—I went for the cheap shot.

Haines lunged at me, and I rammed my knee into his balls a dozen times harder than I had with Con Leahy. Fighting over the loss of Vanessa, trying to save face, was nothing compared to this.

Yve was worth more than my pride. She was worth everything.

Haines hit the ground again, and I landed a solid kick to his face. His nose crunched and his head lolled to the side.

Yve screamed.

I charged the woman, but it was too late. She'd sliced the knife across Yve's throat and lifted the blood-coated blade, as if to stab it straight into Yve's chest.

I dove at the woman, tackling her. Her head whacked the floor, and she didn't move. Scrambling to my knees, I slid in front of Yve. Her eyes were still open and tears spilled down her cheeks. Terrified at the blood seeping from the cut on her neck, I ripped my shirt off and pressed it to her throat.

Yve laughed through her tears. "I'm not gonna die. It's not deep enough. She's a pansy-ass bitch."

"Shut up, Yve."

I lowered the shirt, then gripped the tape with both hands, tearing it apart to free her. The front door flew open and Jerome slid to a halt in the foyer. Gun drawn, he spied us both.

"Oh, thank God," he said. "I heard the scream and—"

Haines—like the goddamn killer in a horror movie—surged up from the floor, wrapped both hands around Jerome's legs, and yanked his feet out from under him. Jerome went down, his skull cracking against the tile, and the gun landed between Haines and me.

We both dove for it but I was faster—because I'm Lucas Fucking Titan and this was the fight of my life.

I didn't hesitate this time. I pulled the trigger three times, aiming for Haines's heart, and he never took another breath.

"I warned you," the blonde screamed.

Fuck me. Why couldn't they just stay down?

Again she had the knife to Yve. This time, pressing it into her side.

I lifted the gun and aimed. She ducked behind Yve, using her as a human shield.

"Shoot her, goddamn it," Yve yelled.

The choice lay before me, but this time it wasn't her life or mine.

"No fucking way. I'll hit you."

A maniacal laugh bounced through the room. "She's gonna die either way."

"I'm nobody's victim," Yve said, her words a vow.

Her left elbow flew backward, and she grabbed the blonde's arm and twisted. The knife hit the floor, and the woman screamed. I was on her in less than a second, dragging both hands behind her back. She snapped her teeth like a feral dog, and Yve, gripping her side, spun.

"Where's the goddamn duct tape?"

I saw it on the coffee table. "There. Behind you."

Yve grabbed it, ripped off a piece, and slapped it over the woman's mouth. Ripping off another section, she wound it around the woman's arms, taping them together from just above the elbows and down to the wrists.

"We'll see how she likes that."

A moan from the foyer had both our heads turning.

"Jerome!"

I tossed the woman on the couch and we both ran to him. Blood pooled around his head on the floor, but he wasn't dead.

I palmed my phone from my pocket and dialed Hennessy. He could probably get an ambulance here faster than 911.

He answered on the first ring.

"I need an ambulance. Texting you the address now. Make it fast."

"No body bags?"

"Bring one of those too." I hung up and texted the address I'd memorized in the agonizingly long ten minutes it had taken me to get here.

Yve was at Jerome's side, wrapping the shirt I'd tossed at her around his head. She looked up at me, tears still spilling down her cheeks. "He's gotta be okay."

I would have told her anything to get her to stop crying. Gritting my teeth, I said, "He's going to be fine."

She blinked and nodded. "You came for me." Her voice was small and hesitant.

"Always."

Yve

MY NECK BURNED FROM THE SUPERGLUE THE ER doctor had used to close the cut Jennifer had given me, and my side twinged as the anesthetic wore off from the stitches it had taken to close the spot where she'd tried to gut me.

My instincts about her had been right. *Crazy bitch.* Hennessy had taken her into custody when he'd arrived on the heels of the ambulance—and the coroner.

Lucas and I were sprawled on an extra bed he'd requested in Jerome's private hospital room. Conscious of my injuries, he wasn't wrapped around me, but he hadn't yet let go of my hand, even in sleep. His chest rose and fell in an even rhythm that I took comfort in.

Jerome groaned from the bed next to us, and I jumped up to check on him. Lucas didn't move. I leaned over the old man, my heart aching at the sight of the bandages wrapped around his head.

"What's wrong? Do you need the nurse?"

His eyes fluttered open and the faded blues locked on me. He had a major concussion for sure, and the ER doc had requested that he stay overnight for observation. The old man was tough and had refused, but Lucas had over-ruled him.

"I'm fine. And you? You're still okay?"

I nodded. "I'm good."

His eyes shifted to Lucas. "And my boy?" It was the first time I'd heard him refer to Lucas in such a way.

"He's . . . good."

"He took a life. That never gets easier," Jerome said. "He still carries the guilt from the last time, and God knows that was an accident. Even if he believes he killed his father."

The breath caught in my lungs. "What?" I whispered.

Jerome nodded. "It's not my place to tell you the story, though."

Lucas's voice cut through the rhythmic beeping in the room. "You already started, old man. Might as well tell her the whole sordid tale, because I did kill him."

I turned to look at Lucas. "Wha—"

He swung his legs over the side of the bed, dropping his elbows to his knees and his face into his hands. "I killed him. I didn't save him, and I could have."

The story poured out of Lucas. "My father was a brilliant, crazy-as-fuck R&D director. Think Steve Jobs, but with more screws loose. He pioneered technology decades before its time. He's the one who got me interested in science and business. But he only understood the science side of the house, and not business."

Lucas looked up, revealing the torment on his face.

"Learning from him, I developed a concept that he called stupid, ridiculous, and idiotic—and he called me all the same things. But it wasn't, and I wasn't. I knew it then, and I know it now. It's what I've been working so hard to launch. I've been working on it since I was sixteen. He was a perfectionist, driven to extremes in every area of life. No one was safe from his scrutiny. He could invent beautiful technology, but with people, he only knew how to destroy."

When he paused for a moment, I sat on the bed beside him and wrapped my hand around his arm. "You don't have to tell me."

Lucas turned his gaze on me, his eyes hard, colder than I'd ever seen them. "This is the only way you'll understand when I say I'm not a good man, I'm telling you the truth."

Jerome spoke. "Maybe you should take this somewhere private, because I'm going to want to interrupt with the facts, as you clearly don't understand the truth of the matter."

Lucas shoved to his feet, and I dropped my grip on him. "The truth is that I baited him that day. I told him he couldn't climb that peak, that he was too old. He'd been livid. Backhanded me. When he'd carried gear to the car, I'd known that the day would change everything—because I was going to show him that there was something I could do that he couldn't. His competitive streak wouldn't allow him to quit." His jaw ticked as he clenched it. "Neither of us should have been up there that day. I was so far beyond my ability, it was an accident waiting to happen."

"An accident is exactly what it was, Lucas," Jerome interjected.

"No. When the rope slipped and shredded on that rock,

I had time. I could've grabbed it. I waited too long—"

"And then went over a cliff to try to save him, nearly killing yourself in the process and landing in the hospital for three weeks."

My eyes jerked to Lucas. The scars on his forearm that I'd never asked about, because I didn't like to talk about mine. The slice of a scar that ran through his eyebrow and up into his hairline. It was all coming together.

I touched the raised white line on his forearm now. "No one makes it through life without scars. It's impossible. But they're not signs of shame; they're badges of honor showing that you fought and survived. That's why I've never hidden mine, but you've never moved on."

Lucas's words came out sharp. "And you have?"

"I have now. And you're the reason why."

"I'm the worst reason." Lucas shoved to his feet and strode out of the room.

I started after him, but Jerome's voice stopped me.

"His father tore him down at every opportunity, made him believe he was unworthy—of affection, love, of anything. He's spent every minute of every day proving him wrong, and yet he still doesn't believe he's done enough. He persists in seeing himself as the villain."

"If his father were alive, I'd throw him down a mountain myself."

"He was not a good man. But his son is."

I headed for the door. "You don't have to tell me that. I already know." I reached the hallway, but there was no sign of Lucas.

I stopped at the nurses' station. "You see a big, black-haired man stomp through here?"

She smiled. "That hot one? Oh yeah. He headed for the elevator. Said he needed some air and to call if anything changed."

"Thank you." I skipped the elevator and went for the stairs. By the time I reached the bottom—four floors—I realized I'd made a mistake. *Hot. Damn.* My side and neck burned.

I pushed open the heavy door, and Lucas was walking through the exit.

"Wait, damn it!" I huffed, leaning heavily on the wall.

Lucas spun and strode toward me. "What the hell are you doing?" he growled when he reached my side.

I wheezed out a breath. "I ran down. The stairs."

He looked around. "We need to find a nurse. Make sure you didn't tear open your stitches."

I shook my head. "I'm fine."

"Stubborn."

He squatted and lifted me into his arms. My hands went around his neck as I held on.

"Take me outside. I want air too."

"You need—"

"You. I need *you*, Lucas," I interrupted. "That's all."

His arms tightened around me. "I'm not—"

I slid one hand to the side of his face and forced him to look at me. "Do you care about me?" I asked. It was time to lay it all out.

"What the hell kind of question is that? And we're taking this conversation somewhere more private." He turned and carried me through the exit and down the sidewalk to a bench. It was after midnight, and the place was deserted. He lowered me and began to pace.

"It kind of hurts my neck to keep swinging my head back and forth, so if you could just hold still, that'd be great."

Lucas froze. "Shit. I'm sorry."

"See? You do care about me," I said, forcing my tone to be lighter.

Lucas came toward the bench, towering over me in my seated position. "Of course I fucking care about you, Yve. I'm in love with you."

The words sounded strange on his tongue, as if he'd never spoken them before—and suddenly I was confident he hadn't.

"Good, because that makes it a lot less awkward for me to tell you that I'm in love with you too."

He dropped to a crouch in front of me. "That's not possible."

I reached out and skimmed my thumb along the stubble shading his jaw. "Nothing's impossible, Lucas," I said, throwing his words back at him.

He covered my hand with his, holding it to his face as he shook his head. "I had a plan. Keep you in my bed, in my house, in my life, until you couldn't remember what any other life was like."

"You were going to trick me into staying?" I asked, my eyebrows shooting up.

Lucas's frown deepened. "See, I'm not a good guy. I was going to do whatever it took to keep you, regardless of whether you wanted to be kept."

I narrowed my eyes. "So if I were miserable, you would have forced me to stay?"

His brows dropped into a deep *V*. "I would've never allowed you to be miserable."

A smile played about my lips. "But if I had been?"

He bowed his head, still not releasing my hand. "I would've let you go," he murmured.

"Like the goddamn Beast, right down to the library."

Lucas's head snapped up, confusion creasing his forehead. "What the hell does that mean?"

"You're clearly lacking in the Disney cartoon movie department. But it doesn't matter. My point is you're not the villain in this scenario, Lucas. You're the hero—and I'm not leaving your side until I make you believe it."

He reached out a hand to cup my cheek. "Then I'll never believe it."

I shook my head. "Stubborn man."

"Smart man."

"Then kiss me."

"Demanding," he said softly as he lowered his lips to mine.

"I learned from the best," I said, but the words were lost in his kiss.

For the first time, he didn't devour and conquer. Instead, Lucas kissed me softly, carefully, as if I was rare and precious—something only he had ever made me feel.

When our mouths finally broke free, Lucas pinned me with that gorgeous green stare again.

"You love me." It wasn't a question. But then again, from him, I didn't expect it to be.

"Yes."

"Thank God." And then he kissed me again. And again.

For the first time in my life, I was the girl who was going to get her happily ever after.

Lucas

THE AFTERMATH OF SHOOTING AND KILLING someone was a lot messier than the blood you spilled. There was questioning, charges, lawyers, and a hell of a lot of paperwork. Yve and I spent nearly all of the next day at the police station. Hennessy tried to smooth things over as much as he could, but even he couldn't change the facts.

I'd killed a man. It was a clear case of self-defense, but the formalities still had to be followed.

Through it all, I never let go of Yve's hand. I didn't know what exactly I'd done to make her love me, but I would figure it out so I could keep doing it for the rest of my life.

I would not lose her.

I'd Googled *beast* and *library* and *Disney* when we'd gone back inside the hospital last night, and had to be shushed by the nurse when I'd laughed so loudly that I'd nearly woken the entire unit.

Beauty and the Beast. And I was the Beast. It was fitting, I supposed. At least Yve wouldn't be surprised when I really wouldn't ever let her leave my castle. And if she tried, I'd distract her in the library.

I smiled, turning to stare at the woman beside me, and was startled when the door to the interrogation room flew open and a familiar woman stormed in, black hair swirling around her shoulders.

"Is he really dead? The bastard is really, truly dead?"

Hennessy stood to face Valentina Noble, and I struggled to make the connection of why the hell she'd be standing here.

"Ma'am, you—"

"Don't *ma'am* me, Detective Hennessy. Just answer the question."

Yve stood beside me. "He's really dead, Valentina. He's never going to hurt anyone again."

Confused, I looked from one woman to the other. I was missing something. And then Johnson Haines's rant came to mind. *The daughter of a judge.*

Valentina Noble had been victimized by Jay Haines too. The man had deserved every bullet he'd gotten, and I was glad as hell I'd crushed his nuts too.

Valentina rushed over to Yve and enveloped her in a hug. Yve winced and the other woman pulled back. "Oh my God. I'm so sorry. Did he—?" Her question hung in the air.

Yve shook her head. "His bitch of a fiancée. Don't worry about it."

"That bitch. We need champagne. We need to celebrate." Her head swiveled around. "Shit. I didn't mean to say that out loud. Can Yve and I get a moment alone?"

My fingers were still twined through Yve's, and I squeezed.

She grinned. "Lucas isn't exactly letting me out of his sight yet."

Valentina smiled. "Good for him. Smart man, and he picked a good woman. I can't tell you how glad I am that you never caved to my father's demands to ask me out. It would've just bruised your ego when I said no."

The chuckle worked its way out of my lips unexpectedly. "I have to say, I'm glad too."

"Ms. Noble, I'll be happy to escort you out," Hennessy said. "We need to get back to settling the formalities surrounding Mr. Haines's death."

Valentina released the grip she still had on Yve's other hand, and leaned in to press a kiss to her cheek. "Be well, Yve. And don't be a stranger. I think this whole bullshit can be over, about no one knowing how we're connected. It's a new day, and neither of us has anything to fear anymore."

Yve nodded in agreement, and Valentina turned and headed toward the door. Flipping her black hair over her shoulder, she stared Hennessy down. "I'll see myself out, Detective."

Hennessy's eyes never left her as she strutted out. Finally, he shook his head. "I'll be right back." Then he was out the door and after her.

Interesting.

Once we were alone, I lowered back into the incredibly uncomfortable interview chair and lifted Yve sideways onto my lap.

She looked up at me, eyebrow raised. "I don't think this is proper interview procedure."

"Like I care."

"Make your own rules wherever you go?"

"Is that even a question?"

"I guess not." She leaned into me. "I'm ready to go home now, though. Can you work that into the rules?"

"Regardless of whether we're done or not, we're leaving in fifteen minutes."

"Good. I'm tired. Hospitals suck for sleep."

Which was why Jerome was happy as hell to be out of there. His sister's flight had landed this morning, and she'd made her way to the hospital immediately. When he'd been released, she'd clucked and fussed over him relentlessly. Knowing he was in good hands, I'd agreed that we would come to the station to get everything squared away.

Hennessy came back in the room and shut the door. I raised an eyebrow, but he said nothing.

"Let's make it quick, Hennessy. Yve's had a rough couple of days, and I want to get her home."

"Well, that's convenient because I've just been informed that the DA has officially dropped all charges."

"Perfect." I stood, lifting Yve to her feet, and held out a hand to Hennessy. "You ever need anything, just ask." I had no problem making the offer to Hennessy, because he wasn't the kind of guy who'd probably ever use it. Too much pride. Like recognizing like, I guessed.

"Don't be surprised if I take you up on it."

With a nod, we left, and I took Yve home.

Did I mention I wasn't letting her leave?

"YOU CAN STOP CARRYING ME EVERYWHERE, you know that, right?"

"Eventually," Lucas replied as he hauled me into the house and carried me up to our room.

Wait, but was it? Ours? It seemed a little crazy for me to call it that. We'd said the words, but we hadn't worked out the details.

Could I just move in with Lucas? Well, *stay* moved in? Just like that? Doubts crept in, even though I knew what I wanted.

Him.

"Are you sure this is going to work?" I asked.

Lucas set me on the bed. "What?"

"You and me? Being an 'us'? Are you sure that's what you want? This is all really . . . big and sudden."

Lucas studied me. "Are you changing your mind?"

"No, not at all. I just want to make sure you're cool with

it."

He pressed a hand on the mattress on either side of my hips. "You still haven't figured it out, have you?"

"What?"

"I play for keeps. I don't let something go once it's truly mine. That's not going to change, and you—I'm keeping. You had your chance to run, but you didn't take it."

"I had my chance, did I?"

He nodded. "You didn't take it. And for some unknown reason, you love me."

"I wouldn't say it's an unknown reason."

"Good, because that means you're not going to argue with me when I tell you you're not finding another place to live, any clothes you buy are going in *our* closet, and you're getting a new car. The Blue Beast is history."

I narrowed my eyes. "If you think you're just going to lay down the law and I'm going to roll with it, we're going to have problems."

"This is the law of Lucas Titan, and if you don't like it, then fight me, Yve. Challenge me, push me, keep me on my toes. God knows you're the only woman who could—and it just makes me want you more."

"You want me to . . . what?"

"Be you. Only you. The sassy, beautiful spitfire who would never back down from me."

I smiled. "Now that, I can absolutely do. But if you touch my car, we're going to have problems."

Lucas grinned as he lowered his lips to mine. "Then I guess I'm already in trouble."

EPILOGUE *Lucas*

A FEW MONTHS LATER, I WAITED IN THE COURTYARD of Brennan's, a favorite restaurant of ours in the Quarter, wondering if she'd show. Wondering if she'd kill me once she got here. Wondering if the engagement ring and wedding band in my pocket would go unused tonight.

I crushed the thought almost as soon as it entered my brain. Yve was the best part of my life, and I needed that part to be permanent. I hadn't been lying when I told her I played for keeps.

Most people didn't do surprise weddings, especially when they weren't even engaged. But Yve was a special case. If I gave her too much time to think, I was afraid she'd see nothing but the pitfalls from her first marriage. If I were a different kind of man, I might have taken a different route. But I wasn't. And yet she still loved me.

Only a few guests were present, most notably Con, Vanessa, Elle, Lord, Simon, Charlie, Jerome, Levi, Hennessy, JP, Valentina Noble, Geneviève Haines, and Harriet.

Con wandered over from the bar and handed me a drink. If someone had told me a few months ago the man I'd once considered my enemy would be at my wedding—at my invitation—I would have told that person he was fucking crazy. I guess it was more proof that life took us on a crazy-as-hell journey, and all we could do was hold on and enjoy the ride. Although, from the way Hennessy's eyes were following Valentina around the room, it looked like he was hoping to take a whole different kind of ride tonight.

"Got you a Sazarac. Fancy enough for you?" Con asked.

I accepted it and sipped. "Not poisoned, I'm assuming."

"Nah, Yve would kill me if I killed you, and then Vanessa would be pissed. I do my best to avoid pissing her off. Have you even thought about how much you're risking pissing Yve off with this little stunt?"

From beside me, Levi chuckled and sipped his own drink. "He wouldn't listen. Trust me, I tried."

When Levi had returned from New Zealand, he'd been surprised to find Yve still staying at the house, but had given his wholehearted approval. According to my little brother, she was the only woman he'd ever met who he thought could stand up to me.

I glared at them both. "It's time, and she won't be pissed. For long," I added as an afterthought.

Con didn't look convinced, but he left it alone, moving on to another subject. "So I hear congratulations are in order on the business side too. The feds passed some regulation that makes Titan Industries' technology the be-all-end-all solution to compliance?"

I nodded. After Johnson Haines and several other Louisiana state senators had been recalled due to suspicions of accepting bribes for sponsoring legislation, the lobbyist firm I'd originally worked with had switched focus to the federal government and been successful. As a business owner, I wasn't generally in favor of more regulation, but when we were talking about something that helped more than it harmed, even I could get in line. And my technology that exponentially increased the efficiency of alternative energy used in industrial applications was certainly a good thing.

Con lifted his glass. "Then cheers. I heard about that open-source shit. That's pretty cool, and makes me think you're marginally less of a prick than I'd originally thought."

"I'm surprised you'd heard about that."

"When a billionaire decides to offer up a game-changing piece of technology for free by posting the hows and whys on the Internet, even a guy like me hears about it."

I shifted, still a little uncomfortable with this image of being some do-gooder. "I didn't give it all away, don't worry. Businesses that aren't savvy enough to implement it themselves will still come to Titan Industries for consulting and troubleshooting because we know it better than anyone." I thought even my father would have approved of that solution.

"Yeah, I'm sure. No one's going to mistake you for being a selfless bastard anytime soon."

Even without Johnson Haines and the bill I'd been trying to push through the Louisiana legislature, I'd been able to see my dream come true—but on a bigger scale. The lobbyist firm that had dropped the ball had called in favors at the federal level as a move to get Titan Industries' business back. It had been the next step in my game plan, but I'd been working on the state level first. This just accelerated everything.

But when it came down to it, my conscience couldn't allow the feds to drop a ton of regulations on small factories and plants nationwide that could run people out of business if they couldn't pay the price we'd put on it. So I'd made a decision. We'd put all of the information about the technology I'd spent over a decade developing on the Internet—for free—so anyone could create their own solutions with it. What I'd said to Con was true. We'd still make money, but not as much, and in a different way. I felt good about the decision, one Yve had helped me make.

Harriet, who I'd finally met when she'd returned from a landscape painting adventure in France—her words, not mine—bustled over, interrupting our conversation. "Lucas, my dear, please make sure you get a good full-length picture. I want to do an abstract painting of you and Yve so she can hang it in Dirty Dog. I think it'd be one more touch to make it truly hers."

When Yve had told me about the contract Colson showed her, I'd been livid. I knew he'd been on some misguided mission to protect me, but he'd almost cost me everything. I hadn't fired him, though. No, he was now leading a humanitarian project in Botswana for Titan Industries. A few years of going without might knock him back into shape.

And Yve had engineered her own solution to buy Dirty Dog when she'd met with Harriet. She'd refused to take a grant from the NOLA Entrepreneur Fund because she didn't think they could be objective now that our involvement was public knowledge. Instead, she'd worked out a deal with Harriet where Harriet financed the sale herself, and Yve paid her monthly out of the profits.

Knowing my woman, she'd try to find some way to work even harder to increase those profits and pay it off a few years early. More than anything, I wanted to pay off the loan as a wedding present, but I knew that this was important to Yve, proving that she could do this on her own. As much as it went against my nature not to interfere, I was standing back. Yve was a hell of a businesswoman, and she knew I had her back. Always.

The last loose end I could do nothing to wrap up was Haines's fiancée, Jennifer. She'd been judged to be mentally incompetent to stand trial, and had been committed to a facility for treatment. Jay hadn't been the first inmate she'd fixated on, and her family had been trying to track her down for months. They'd also been cooperative in my request to keep us updated if she was ever released.

Yve's safety was something I would never take for granted, so it made me feel a hell of a lot better that Levi had returned to work at Dirty Dog with Yve and JP. She didn't consider him her babysitter, and she didn't bitch at me too much for being an unbendable beast.

I looked down at my watch again. She was late. By two minutes.

"You thinking she's not going to show," Lord asked, joining us. He grabbed the drink from my hand and replaced it with another. "Straight whiskey. You're going to need it if you get stood up at the altar."

"Thanks," I drawled.

"Did you leave her a note or something?" he asked.

"Yes."

"What'd it say?" Con asked.

"Wear the blue dress. Brennan's at eight," Levi offered. "I read it."

I made a mental note that I needed to take his house key and find him a new place to live. ASAP.

Deep, rumbling laughter boomed through the courtyard as Con and Lord both lost their collective shit. "You're so fucked, man. She's gonna kill you—if she shows."

The maître d' pushed open the door to the courtyard and everyone went silent. Holding their collective breath, no doubt.

Yve stepped through the arched doorway, wearing what she referred to as the Cinderella dress. A smile curved her lips when she spotted me. I'd never take that smile for granted—ever.

When I'd asked her why she'd never worn the Cinderella dress before when it was clearly a favorite of hers, she'd told me she was waiting for a special occasion. I hoped that her wedding would count.

"We'll leave you to it. I can't wait to see how you spin this one." Lord, Con, and Levi each clapped me on the back, then joined the crowd on the far side of the room.

It was great to know they'd come just for the entertainment value of this moment, but all I cared about was Yve.

She walked toward me, the crystals on the dress catching the light of the chandeliers hanging from the trees in the courtyard. She looked like a goddamn fairy-tale princess come to life. Her skin contrasted beautifully with the shimmering blue of her dress, and her white heels seemed made for a wedding.

Yve's brow furrowed when she saw the gathering of people. I should have told them to all get the hell out, but I hadn't.

"What's going on?" she asked when she reached me. "Are we having a party that no one told me about?"

"Something like that."

"Lucas . . . what did you do?"

I smiled. She was right to be suspicious. I reached into my pocket, pulled out the diamond solitaire, and lifted her hand in mine and slid it on.

Her eyes widened. "Are you proposing?"

I shook my head. "We're getting married. Tonight. Here."

"What?"

"We're getting married," I repeated. "In front of your friends and family."

Yve's gaze flicked over my shoulder, and I could tell the instant she spotted her mother. "You invited my mother? And she said yes? Does she know what's happening?"

I smiled, because in that moment, I knew Yve wouldn't be saying no. "She gave me her blessing. She's got your something borrowed."

Yve's golden eyes snapped back to mine. "You're pretty sure of yourself, aren't you?"

I nodded. "I'm sure that my life wouldn't be the same without you, and I'm damned sure that I love you and you love me. I'm sure that we're better together than we are apart, and that you give me a reason to smile every day. I need you. I need this. Marry me, Yve."

She lifted her hand to her mouth, the one with the rock

flashing in the light, and nodded. "I should give you hell for pulling this, but all I want to say is yes."

I took her hand and pulled it away from her face and pressed a kiss to her palm. "Then let's do this."

As we made our way to the gathered couples in the courtyard, Yve's mother met us in the middle and pressed a folded embroidered handkerchief into her hand. "Your something borrowed."

Yve hugged her mother, and while their relationship had been rocky ever since Jay Haines's death, at least they were beginning to have one. Years of silence on both their parts had created a large divide to be crossed. But slowly, it was happening.

"I'm proud of you, Yvonne," her mother said, and Yve pressed the handkerchief to her eyes to dab away the forming tears.

"Thank you, Mama."

"So, are we having a wedding tonight?" the officiant asked as he came to stand before us.

I looked at Yve.

She'd blinked back the tears, and a smile graced her face as she nodded. "Yes, sir. I believe we are."

We locked hands and stood before him.

"Wait, your something new," Elle interrupted, hurrying toward us. She held out a silver chain with a charm.

Yve took it from her. It was a glass slipper. She looked at her former employee and tears welled again. She pulled Elle in for a hug.

"When he said you were wearing the Cinderella dress, I couldn't resist. Love you, babe."

"Love you too."

Elle stepped back, and I clasped the necklace around Yve's neck.

"Are we ready?" the officiant asked.

Yve threaded her fingers through mine and squeezed. "Yes, sir, we are," she said, staring into my eyes. "Ready for forever."

And we were—ready for a forever where our scars didn't define us, but reminded us of how far we'd come and what we'd conquered to be together.

the end

You know you don't want to miss what's coming next! Click http://www.meghanmarch.com/#!newsletter/c1uhp to sign up for my newsletter, and never miss another announcement about upcoming projects, new releases, sales, and exclusive excerpts and giveaways.

I'd love to hear what you thought about Lucas and Yve's story. If you have a few moments to leave a review, I'd be incredibly grateful. Send me a link at meghanmarchbooks@gmail.com, and I'll thank you with a personal note.

Also by Meghan March

Beneath Series
Beneath This Mask
Beneath This Ink
Beneath These Chains

Flash Bang Series
Flash Bang
Hard Charger

Connect with Meghan March

UNAPOLOGETICALLY SEXY ROMANCE

Website: www.meghanmarch.com

Facebook: www.facebook.com/MeghanMarchAuthor

Twitter: www.twitter.com/meghan_march

Instagram: www.instagram.com/meghanmarch

about the author

Meghan March has been known to wear camo face paint and tromp around in the woods wearing mud-covered boots, all while sporting a perfect manicure. She's also impulsive, easily entertained, and absolutely unapologetic about the fact that she loves to read and write smut.

Her past lives include slinging auto parts, selling lingerie, making custom jewelry, and practicing corporate law. Writing books about dirty-talking alpha males and the strong, sassy women who bring them to their knees is by far the most fabulous job she's ever had.

She loves hearing from her readers at meghanmarchbooks@gmail.com.

63255127R00207

Made in the USA
Lexington, KY
01 May 2017